P

CW01084241

Killing is in her blood

FRANCES MACKINTOSH

PIGPEN

First edition independently published in the UK in 2024
ISBN (Hardcover): 978-1-7393619-1-4
ISBN (Paperback): 978-1-7393619-2-1
Editor: Christine Beech
Cover Design: Matthew J Bird
Typesetting: Matthew J Bird

A CIP catalogue record of this book is available from the British Library.

For further information about this book, please contact the author at:
francesmackintosh.author@gmail.com

To Dan and Megan with love xx

Hunting the harmless and unsuspecting is so much fun. If you are gullible and stupid enough to trust me, then you deserve to die. I will enjoy every second of watching you take your final breath.

Agatha Taylor

Chapter One

Benjamin Stark had days left to live.

He was young, handsome and caring. His date, Agatha Taylor, planned to murder him for her gratification.

It was their third date and Benjamin was on his fourth pint. Agatha sipped her fruit juice, the downside of driving. She had no choice as you can't drag a victim along the street and not expect anyone to notice. Even on rural Northumbrian roads.

At twenty-three, Benjamin was five years older than Agatha. He pushed his floppy blonde hair out of his blue eyes and nodded in response to her question.

'I'm hungry,' said Agatha, 'so let's order a pizza. What flavour do you like?'

Agatha handed Benjamin the menu while giving him her best smile. It had been easier than she thought to reel him in and get him to like her. While Ben, as he was known, thought the BBQ Chicken pizza sounded good, Agatha was wondering if she should kill him that night or find out more about him. Either way, he would die.

She didn't want any parents or friends to come looking for him.

'I think I'll have the BBQ Chicken. What do you fancy?'

Apart from killing you, thought Agatha.

'I'll have the Chicken Kiev,' she replied.

'I'll go to the bar and order. My treat,' said Ben, as he rose from their table, kissing the top of her head as he walked past, making a mental note of their table number; thirteen.

Agatha watched his tall skinny frame as he headed towards the bar.

How much Rohypnol will I need to make you unconscious, Benjamin Stark?

It wasn't the first time she had used the powerful sedative. Two years ago, she had drugged her father before her mother, or *Maman* as she calls her, killed him.

Twenty years ago, Agatha's father, William Channing, had been nicknamed the Grey Trench Coat Man by the media. He had abducted and killed many victims with the help of his mother, Elizabeth Channing. The police only knew about three. Rebecca Bixby, Helen Boleyn and Albert Channing - his father. William had murdered Rebecca. Elizabeth had killed Helen and her husband, Albert.

William was charged with the murders of Rebecca Bixby and Helen Boleyn, and incarcerated for nearly seventeen years. He was also found guilty of false imprisonment of a 28-year-old female. He had stalked her and watched her for months before his mother had lured her to their home.

Unbeknown to the police, she was their eighteenth victim.

Continually drugged, starved and abused by William, the eighteenth victim woke from a drugged sleep and felt the chill of a lifeless body next to her. It was the naked corpse of her best friend, Rebecca Bixby. William had placed her there as an atonement after he had killed and abused her.

To escape William's capture and torment, the victim had set fire to the bedroom she had been held in for nearly fourteen days, along with the body of her best friend.

Elizabeth Channing had survived the fire and, at the age of fifty-five, was sentenced to seven years in prison. The eighteenth victim, the last person to be abducted by William and Elizabeth Channing had been a big mistake. She was no victim. Her name was Faith Taylor, Agatha's mother.

After her escape, and to avoid the media frenzy, Faith fled to France where she stayed with her parents' friends, Helena and Philip Carman, who owned a small vineyard. Five months after her capture, she discovered that she was pregnant with the predator's child.

Agatha Rebecca Taylor, named in honour of Faith's friend, was delivered by a retired midwife in the bedroom she had barely left since arriving in France. After five years, Faith registered as a French citizen and Agatha had a French birth certificate and passport, as well as British citizenship.

Despite knowing who the father was, Faith grew to love the cold and aloof child who preferred picking grapes alone rather than being with people.

When her baby was only a few months old, Faith left her with the Carmans and returned to the North East of England to give evidence at the trial, which lasted four months. Even her parents didn't know she'd become a mother. As the years passed, Faith continued to live in France, visiting her parents once a year but always leaving her child behind.

At the trial, William had confessed to killing Rebecca, and Faith testified that, in her drugged state, she didn't know her friend had been in the room. It was a blatant lie but she would have done anything to save her own life.

After the sentencing of William and Elizabeth Channing, Faith spent nearly two decades planning revenge and William's death. She needed a location where there was no one to witness her sins or to discover the body.

A rural farm.

Faith bought the disused farm and land in Northumberland online and had the farmhouse restored. She said goodbye to the Carmens, and her life in France, to return permanently to England. It was the first time the 16-year-old Agatha had left France.

Then she waited.

That had been just over two years ago.

Agatha had played a key part in her premeditated plan.

The Butterdish Café was a traditional 'fried breakfast, tea and scones' place to eat. It was an hour's drive from the farm and Faith persuaded Agatha to get a cash-in-hand job there. She happily drove her daughter there as she didn't mind the long drive. It was the café nearest to William's parole house.

She had been watching him.

The hunter had become the hunted.

Every Friday morning, William visited the Butterdish Café for a Full English breakfast and a mug of tea. It was one of those mornings when father and daughter had first met, though neither of them was aware of the connection.

Faith had confessed to Agatha who the strange man in the grey trilby hat and trench coat was and that he was a sexual predator. Agatha had been incensed that such a sinister man could be her father.

His abduction had been easy.

He had been drawn to the willowy Agatha and had started to fantasise about her. He wanted to know all about her. He wanted a nineteenth victim. He wanted to have a child with her.

He started to hatch a plan.

He couldn't take the girl to his parole house, and his mother's house had been burned to the ground. How he hated

Faith Taylor. On his release, he had made a promise to himself that, one day, he would find her and kill her, very slowly. All those years incarcerated. All those years separated from his mother. All because he hadn't killed his eighteenth victim.

William's thoughts were consumed by Agatha and he called into the café just to see her. For days, he had been watching her from across the street. He stood in the shadows and just watched, wearing his grey trilby hat and coat. They had belonged to his father, Albert, who had been a good man and the only person ever to show him kindness. But when William was only three years old, he had watched his mother stab his father to death in their kitchen.

From the kitchen door, he was captivated as he watched Elizabeth repeatedly plunge the knife in again and again. He remembered the knife slipping in her hand because there was so much blood. She had then dragged her mutilated husband out into the garden and dumped him into the large hole she had previously dug. It was covered with a garden shed, which had been a gift from Albert.

William could remember watching her from his bedroom window as she went into the garden shed during the day, just to look into the hole. It had given her great pleasure to see her husband cold and lifeless. She was always happy when she visited the hole.

Growing up, a young William was terrified that his mother would put him in the hole. The result was that he had spent all his life keeping her happy and doing anything she asked him to. Including murder and rape.

On that fateful Thursday, William had asked Agatha if she would like a coffee. She had laughed at him. She could get coffee anytime in the café. Instead, she suggested they went for a walk on her break.

He had agreed without any hesitation.

Agatha had messaged her mother who was waiting nearby in her battered Land Rover Defender, a couple of streets away, reading the latest Bernard Cornwall novel about Uhtred of Bebbanburg.

Agatha's first message simply read, 'He's here' followed shortly by another, 'It's on'.

Faith knew what to do.

So did Agatha.

She had slipped Rohypnol into his tea and waited nearly twenty minutes for it to take effect. By then, they were walking away from the Butterdish Café. William had started to slur his words and Agatha watched coldly as he steadied himself against a garden wall. Faith had pulled up behind them.

William had not seen the car or the driver but he immediately recognised the voice. Even as he fought against blacking out, he recalled her words.

'Hello, William. I've been waiting for you for a very long time.'

He had felt her touch as she shoved him roughly into the back of the car. He remembered the words she said before he had passed into a drugged sleep. The words he remembered right up to the final seconds before his solitary death.

'I see you've met your daughter,' the voice said. 'You've done well, Agatha.'

Faith had starved him to death. He had died slowly and painfully. In the end, he could no longer open his sunken eyes as they were too dry. His organs slowly shut down and fluid had seeped from him, even though liquid had barely touched his lips. As his lungs slowly ceased to work, they released a thick substance that formed in the back of his throat and gradually choked him. His final weak breath had been through cracked and painful lips. His gums had swollen and his chest barely raised.

Left to slowly perish alone in the darkness, all he had wanted was his mother.

Death had taken him days before Faith and Agatha dumped his body in the pigpen, where fifteen Large White pigs devoured his body in nine minutes. It was all done in the privacy of their farm.

Agatha was the daughter of killers.

She had enjoyed watching her father wither and die from starvation and thirst. He had deserved it.

She had missed that feeling.

'All ordered. They said it would be about twenty minutes,' said Ben, as he returned with another pint of ale and an orange juice for Agatha.

'Thank you,' Agatha smiled. 'It was my round. Here take this.'

She handed Ben a ten-pound note. She always paid cash as she liked to be untraceable. A ghost.

Very few empty tables remained as the bar started to fill with drinkers and diners. Agatha leaned towards Ben so that he could hear her. She had noticed the CCTV spotted around the bar area. Not that she cared. If Ben did go missing that night and the police tracked her down as the last person he'd been seen with, so what? She considered herself too clever to be caught.

'How's the modelling job going?' she asked.

Ben was a part-time model and worked as a barman three nights a week.

'It's good, thanks. It's for an online clothing store. I've been modelling jumpers and shirts this week. It will cover my share of this month's rent.'

Originally from Ashford in Kent, Ben had moved to the North East, after meeting Emma Beale on a night out in London. She had been on a hen night, dressed in a pink T-shirt, tight jeans, and wearing a plastic tiara. The bride-to-be had worn a flashing veil and a short white dress. There had been an instant attraction.

Three months later, Ben relocated and moved into Emma's flat. They had been so happy that first year, but then Emma had announced that it wasn't working anymore, and he needed to find somewhere else to live.

He was distraught.

Ten months later, he shared a flat with two other male models. It was cost-effective and he had someone to go drinking with.

'I have a thirty-minute drive home. Would you like a lift after we've had our pizzas?'

'If you don't mind. Thanks,' Ben said, raising his pint as a thank-you.

Agatha smiled. She could easily go to the bar and buy him another pint before they left. Slip Rohypnol into it. That should give her about twenty minutes to get him into the car before he passed out, and then drive back to the farm. She wasn't sure, or cared, what her maman would say.

Her dark thoughts were interrupted by the arrival of their pizzas. They looked and smelt good.

'Do you like going to open-air concerts?' asked Ben, before taking a huge bite.

'Who's playing?'

'There are various bands. It's a rock and indie festival. My flatmate, Peter, was meant to be going with his girlfriend but he's away on a modelling assignment. It's this Saturday.'

It sounded exciting. Agatha didn't get to experience concerts, having lived most of her life in a vineyard, and Saturday was only two days away.

'Okay, sounds fun. Thanks.'

The concert had just saved Ben's life, for now.

Agatha had made up her mind that he would die on Saturday after she'd experienced a few hours of rock and indie.

Chapter Two

I am in my pristine white kitchen. One of my favourite places. I feel relaxed and happy as I make my morning's flat white coffee.

My four-year-old Golden Labrador, Guzzle, aptly named after William's encounter with the fifteen pigs, sits at my feet waiting for his favourite doggie Gravy Bone biscuits. His patience is rewarded and he crunches two over the floor.

Yesterday, I spent the day making jam for my online business called 'From My Kitchen'. Plum and vanilla is this month's special. Fifty jars are lined up on the kitchen bench. My business has grown over the last three years and now gives me a steady income, along with the rent from my land. I still rent the pigpen to Farmer Childs for his sounder of Large White pigs, and the top field to a young farmer for his herd of Kentish sheep.

Farmer Childs is in his mid-seventies and retired from farming three years ago. Not long after his well-earned retirement, his wife died and left him feeling bereft. To fill the void, he asked to permanently rent my pigpen for his newly-acquired pigs. Over the last few months, I have taken on the role of caring for them as he suffered a mini-stroke. I don't mind, as it makes me feel powerful to think it is where William's decomposing corpse had been devoured.

Two years later, William's last moments are still vivid in my mind. I remember his emaciated body covered in dust from the cold stone floor, his cracked lips and his sunken eyes. He was a pitiful sight. His wet underwear was the only clothing that hung from his body.

Retribution.

When he and his mother held me captive and drugged me, he removed all my clothes except my underwear. That was all I was allowed to wear. William had liked to wear my dress, along with a long blonde wig which was similar to my hair. He wanted to know what it felt like to be me.

Seeing him dying from thirst and hunger on the unyielding floor of my stone outhouse, I had felt remorseful and wanted to save his life.

But Agatha stopped me. She wanted her father to die.

I would have gone against my only child and saved his life, but then he goaded me. Only days from death and barely able to speak, he revealed that he had planned to trap his nineteenth victim. Agatha.

Those words cost him his life.

I left him to die alone with only the dark for company. By the state of his body, he must have been dead for many days before I finally unlocked the heavy door and removed his cold waxen corpse.

The smell had been repellent and lingered for months after Agatha and I dragged his body into the pigpen. It became a killing pen as the pigs devoured every last piece of him.

Over the months that followed, I became attached to the Large White pigs and their pointy ears. They have their own personalities and are curious, affectionate and even trainable. The sows give birth about twice a year and often have between eight and ten piglets. Once they reach six months, Farmer Childs arranges for them to go to the slaughterhouse or to be bought by another farm.

I've named my favourite pig Macy. She's very affectionate and funny-looking with her moderately long head and broad snout. When they aren't devouring corpses, I feed them two or three times a day and Macy loves a good head rub.

Max, the boar, is my least favourite. He rules the pigpen and is always there when squabbles occur between the pigs. There is a battle going on between us. He tries to nudge me out of the way, and I have to firmly stand my ground and scold the fifty-seven-stones Max.

He had led the feeding frenzy when we left William in his enclosure.

A dead body is easy to dispose of if you have privacy and a sounder of pigs. However, apart from the smell, decaying corpses do create one big problem: maggots. I've noticed that pigs do not eat maggots. But I have discovered that chickens do.

After an hour of searching the internet, I learned that since maggots are rich in protein and other nutrients, they are a valuable food source for chickens and a great supplement to their daily diet of grain and seeds. Such information was music to my ears. Problem solved.

I already own ten white Leghorn chickens. They are known for their egg-laying and are the source of my regular breakfast of poached egg and avocado on toast. With the help of Agatha, we moved the chicken run nearer the pigpen and watched in satisfaction as they ran back and forth eating the soft plump maggots.

Living on farmland is similar to a vineyard; idyllic and peaceful. My only concern is for my daughter.

Agatha is quick to learn yet can be manipulative. At home, she is quiet and always in deep thought. What she may be planning, or even just thinking, is concerning.

I can see it in her eyes. She had enjoyed watching her father wither and die a little too much. Is my pretty Agatha about to follow in her father's footsteps?

The apple never falls far from the tree.

Chapter Three

Agatha woke up feeling excited.

As a young child, she wasn't fascinated with death but the signs of what was within her were always there. She had no empathy for others and preferred her own company, walking alone in the vineyard. She had no time or affection for anyone who cared for her. There had been no obsession to watch true crime documentaries or read about serial killers and try to understand their dark minds.

It wasn't until she had helped her mother, or 'Maman' as she called her, capture and kill her father, that she realised she had a desire to kill.

It was all she could think about.

Over the previous few weeks, Agatha's thoughts had been filled with Ben. She had fantasised and imagined different ways she could take his life. She had even written a list. In a few days, her fantasies would become reality.

She thought about her father, the Grey Trench Coat Man. She had spent the last two years reading everything she could find about him online. She knew he had stalked her maman; watching her every move until he and his mother, Elizabeth, found the perfect opportunity to strike.

She wondered how that had made him feel. Just watching and waiting. Knowing he would trick his victims into his home where they, apart from her maman, would never leave. When he was dying, William had confessed to Faith that she had been his eighteenth victim. The only one to survive. He had hidden a list in the lining of his grey trench coat. The coat the police had seized and kept while he was in custody. The coat Faith had burned when she became the hunter and captured William. Apart from his underwear, she had burned all his clothes in a large steel drum on her farm.

His confessional killing list was gone.

Agatha wanted to experience the thrill of the hunt and the power of a capture. She wanted to walk in her father's footsteps, to have her own victims to lure and keep in the same stone outhouse where her maman had imprisoned her father.

She couldn't wait to bring Ben home.

Chapter Four

It was the big day. For most people, the big day would be their wedding day. Not for Agatha. Today was Saturday, killing day.

She slept until lunchtime, as she usually did, as she was a night owl. An early night for Agatha was usually midnight and she normally liked to go to bed at about 2 am. Waking up, she smiled and then felt the surge of excitement flash through her body.

Retrieving the scrap of paper from under her pillow, she read the list she had written over a week ago. There was no need for her to look at it as she knew it by heart.

It only contained three lines. Three ways to commit murder. Three options she had created to end Ben's life. It read:

1. Recreate William's death
2. Blindfold them, have sex and then stab them repeatedly
3. Drown them

Underneath the list, she had written three words in large capital letters.

AVAILABILITY VULNERABILITY DESIRABILITY

These were the selection criteria for her victim.

She had been thinking about her father's confession before he had slowly withered. He had wanted her as his nineteenth victim. The death count had increased after his release when he had butchered two prison officers.

How could he have abducted and killed so many people without detection?

Her thoughts resulted in her three firm criteria.

Number one was availability. They had to be easily available to her. Perhaps someone who had a routine, either drank in the same bar, worked in a shop or went running in a rural space.

Number two was vulnerability. She wanted someone weak, harmless and especially unsuspecting. She didn't want anyone who might fight back once she had drugged them.

Lastly, she wanted desirability. Her victims had to be attractive to her. She wanted them good-looking, young and of slim build. Too large and she wouldn't be able to move the body.

Ben fit all three criteria.

Lucky Ben.

Leaping from her double bed, she hurried over to the dressing table, picked up a notepad and tore out a page.

How will you die tonight?

Tearing the piece of paper into three, she added a number to each one. 1, 2 and 3. Each number represented the way Ben's life would end that night from her killing list.

Folding the pieces of paper carefully, she placed them into a discarded blue sock on her bedroom floor. Then she shook it. Pausing for a moment to absorb the feeling of anticipation, she judiciously picked one.

Carefully and very slowly, she unfolded it and read the number. Folding it up again, she placed it in her back pocket before throwing the sock onto the floor.

She quivered with excitement.

She now knew how Ben's life would end.

Chapter Five

Benjamin Stark, or Ben to his friends, placed the three pints down on the bar.

'That's £14.97, thanks.'

The customer placed his Mastercard against the card reader. Ben nodded his head in acknowledgement when 'Approved' and a large tick appeared on the small screen.

It should have been his day off. Instead, he was covering for Amy who was off with Covid. The Swan was a typical country pub and he enjoyed working there part-time. He saw the same faces, often sitting in the same seats, ordering their regular ale. The large open fire was a popular spot in winter and the locals liked to pull the tables closer and play dominos for small amounts of cash. Often, one or two dogs were lying asleep near their owners, raising their heads slightly if another dog came in.

Ben liked the close-knit community feel of the place.

It was just after noon and his shift was due to finish at 5 pm. That would give him just enough time for a shower before meeting Agatha at 6.30 pm. They would have an hour before the concert started. He hoped she would like the music.

He'd never met a girl like her before. She was quiet, yet assertive, and loved to have a good time when they went out but she never spoke about, or met up with, any of her friends. Ben wondered if she had any. He was drawn to her, yet felt slightly cautious, as there was an air of danger which excited him.

He had been on several unsuccessful dates since he broke up with his ex-girlfriend Emma Beale. He still missed her. It was her idea to live together in the North East. He had wanted the same thing and left his friends and family behind in Kent without any reservation. He thought they were happy and hadn't seen the breakup coming. There had been no closure or explanation as to why she ended things. As soon as he moved out of her flat, she had blocked him on her social media platform and changed her mobile number.

None of his many dates, even Agatha, matched up to Emma.

His afternoon in The Swan had, so far, been pleasant. He had engaged in the usual banter with some of the regulars and given away a packet of beef-flavoured crisps to Maximus, a black Labrador owned by Tony Archer. Tony spent two hours a day, every day, sitting at the end of the bar, enjoying a few pints of Landlord.

Only fifteen minutes left of Ben's shift, and his life was about to change.

He hadn't seen them come in as the bar was fairly busy, and he had just taken payment for two pints, but he recognised the voice immediately.

'Two large glasses of Pinot Grigio, please.'

He stared into her familiar brown eyes. Her shoulder-length raven hair was pulled back into a ponytail and her plump pretty face had a cautious smile.

'Coming up,' replied Ben, as he pulled his eyes away and opened the small fridge door to retrieve the wine.

'That's £14, please.'

He placed the wine on the bar and his heart hammered in his chest.

'Thank you, Ben,' she said, as she paid by credit card.

'You're welcome,' he muttered.

'I've missed you.'

'I've missed you too, Emma.'

*

At 5 pm, Ben headed over to Emma's table and sat in the empty chair. 'I'm Ben,' he said and extended his hand to the unknown female sitting next to Emma. She shook it briskly.

'Dawn, nice to meet you. I've heard an awful lot about you.' She winked at him before pushing her large-rimmed glasses slightly back up her face. 'I've got something better to do, which is code for I'm leaving you two alone to catch up. I'll be back in half an hour.'

She blew a kiss at them both before pushing her chair away and sweeping up her large tote bag from under the table before striding to the exit.

'She seems nice. Where did you meet?'

'At a yoga class. She's quite loud at times and doesn't fit in with the group. We started talking and then, having a coffee after class became a regular thing.'

The unspoken words between them hung heavily in the air. They sat in silence. Emma sipped her wine and, fidgeting in his seat, Ben checked his watch. It was 5.15 pm and he was going to be late to meet Agatha.

But he was not in a hurry to leave Emma.

'Why, Emma? Why did you push me away?'

She slowly picked up her wine and took a mouthful. She had rehearsed the words over the last couple of months. Now the moment had come, they had deserted her.

Ben waited for a response, searching her face for a hint of what she was about to reveal. Her eyes remained fixed on her glass.

'I was pregnant.'

He was stunned. He was only twenty-three years old and Emma was twenty-two. He wasn't sure how he felt about her declaration.

For a moment, their eyes locked.

'I felt it was too soon for us. We had only been seeing each other for about a year when I found out. I didn't want you to know or feel trapped.'

'It wasn't your decision to make. You should have told me.'

Ben felt angry. The heartache he felt, when she had pushed him away, once more consumed him.

'Did you keep the baby?' he asked.

He held his breath, waiting for the answer. In the next second, he might find out that he was a father.

'After you left, I went to a clinic. I didn't think I was ready to become a mother.'

Ben lowered his head. He felt sad.

Why is she doing this to me?

'I didn't go in. I couldn't. It didn't feel right. Instead, I went to a café and looked at baby clothes online.'

'You've had our baby? I'm a father?'

Ben said the words a little too loudly and other drinkers turned around.

Retrieving her mobile phone from her bag, Emma pressed her thumbprint onto the screen. It fired up and, looking at the screensaver for a second, she turned her phone to share an image with Ben.

A smiling baby lay on an explosion of pink. Ava's favourite blanket. The baby had her mother's dark hair and eyes. Speechless, he gazed at the image, taking in the life-changing moment.

The time on Emma's mobile phone read 5.28 pm. He needed to leave.

As she watched him gaze at the photo of their daughter, Emma felt a mixture of guilt and remorse. When she had forced him out of her life, she had convinced herself that it was the right decision but, as their baby grew, so did her shame of denying her child a father.

She had kept a close eye on him, following him secretly on social media with a fake profile. He had posted pictures of nights out, the scenic rural views of Northumberland and pictures of him working at 'The Swan'. There were no photos of him with girls.

Ben handed back the phone. The baby was dressed in white on a pink blanket but he still wasn't sure if he had a son or daughter.

'What's the baby's name?'

Emma smiled. 'It is Ava Benedetta Beale. She's four months old. Her middle name is after you.'

Ben smiled. He had a daughter called Ava. He liked the gentle-sounding name. He kept his thoughts to himself regarding Benedetta.

'I'm so sorry for not telling you, Ben. I was confused. Scared.'

'I know that now and I want to be part of her life.'

'That's great!' squealed Emma, attracting further glances from the regulars.

'I have to go. Can we talk tomorrow and arrange a time when I can see her?'

'I was hoping you'd move back in,' grinned Emma.

Chapter Six

Agatha was incensed.

Only ten short minutes ago, she had been in a great mood, having spent the hour before getting ready. Her long blonde hair was straight, her makeup subtle and she was wearing her favourite denim jeans and green sweatshirt. A thick padded jacket lay on the backseat; perfect for an outdoor concert.

Having preselected the number which would foretell Ben's death, she had come prepared. Rohypnol was in the side of her car door; the drug her father had chosen for his victims.

By 6.30 pm, she had parked in the lay-by and was waiting.

It was 6.40 pm.

No one kept Agatha waiting.

Her hands squeezed the steering wheel hard and her knuckles turned white as she imagined it was Ben's throat.

How dare he keep me waiting after I said I'd drive.

There was still time. It was only half an hour's drive to the outdoor indie concert. But that wasn't the point. From her point of view, everything was on her terms or not at all.

She couldn't think straight as anger pulsated in every pore of her body. She couldn't decide whether to wait a bit longer or drive away. Picking up her mobile phone, she checked her messages.

Nothing.

Her anger exploded and she threw the phone onto the backseat.

*

Ben hadn't responded to Emma's suggestion for him to move back in. His mind was in a whirl. He'd gained a daughter and the opportunity to get back with the girl he loved.

There had been no time to go home and shower. Running fifteen minutes late, there was no other option but to wear the same black jeans and black T-shirt he'd worn for work.

Something told him that Agatha wouldn't be pleased.

They had arranged to meet in a lay-by about a forty-minute bus ride from The Swan, followed by a ten-minute walk. It was nearly 6.50 pm and, now only five minutes away, he quickened his pace. He wondered if he should have kept their date and if Agatha would still be waiting.

Ben had told Emma about Agatha. He explained it was very casual between them and they were going to an indie concert that evening. Emma hadn't looked convinced that it was only casual. They agreed that he would text her when he got home and they would meet to talk the next day, after his shift at The Swan.

As he hurried down the abandoned lane towards Agatha, he made up his mind. He wouldn't see her again after that night. Instead, he would focus on rebuilding a relationship with Emma and being in Ava's life. He felt excited.

Part of him wished that Agatha was not waiting for him.

*

Agatha was angrily pacing up and down beside her 18th birthday present from her maman, a 10-year-old Land Rover Discovery 4. She loved it and it was great to drive around the country tracks. Although she didn't own a driving licence, she had learnt to drive from the age of fourteen, illegally, in France.

She didn't officially exist in the UK. She was a ghost.

Glancing at her watch, she decided to give Ben three more minutes and then she would leave.

How dare he keep me waiting!

Picking up a large stone, she threw it in the direction of a murder of crows which were pecking at something in the nearby field. They scattered. Turning swiftly away, she climbed back into her Land Rover. Staring straight ahead, she didn't move as her hand rested on the keys in the ignition.

Running up the empty country lane, only moments away from her, was Ben. Anger bubbled within her.

How should I play this? Tell him to turn back? No one keeps me waiting.

Slowly, she moved her free hand around to feel the back pocket of her jeans. She could feel her killing list.

I'm not going to show you any mercy, Benjamin Stark.

He opened the driver's door and they were face-to-face.

'I'm so sorry, Agatha. I covered for Amy at work as she has Covid.' He was still gasping from running the last ten minutes.

She allowed no emotion to show on her face. If she unleashed the boiling anger, he would probably call their date off and walk away.

'I was just about to drive off, but you're here now. What's the best way to head for the festival?'

Ben leaned into the car and kissed her on the cheek. He was relieved. He had expected her to be annoyed with him. Giving her his best smile, he closed the door and walked around to the passenger side. Climbing in beside her, he apologised again.

'I am really sorry for being late.'

She responded with a shrug of her shoulders.

'I'm not too sure of the best way to go,' he continued. 'I'll see if I can get Google Maps up.'

Whilst Northumberland is a very beautiful part of the country, the vast fields and trees aren't always the best for a phone signal. He pulled his phone from his jacket pocket and stuck his thumb on the sensor. It fired up, along with a phone signal. Agatha followed his directions and, thirty minutes later, they arrived at a huge field where the festival was being held.

It was crammed with people and cars. Attendants in hi-vis jackets directed revellers to parking spaces and gave directions to the festival. Having parked up, Agatha and Ben made their way past the many food and drink concessions.

Something didn't feel right. Agatha had noticed that Ben hadn't taken hold of her hand. He seemed distracted. It was time to ramp up the artificial charm.

'Are you going to get a drink or something to eat?' she smiled.

'I fancy a burger and a pint. Are you getting anything?' Ben had to raise his voice to be heard as there were thousands of people at the event and a DJ was warming up the large crowd.

'I'll take a look.'

Together they headed towards a burger stall which also sold cans of various beers, lagers, ciders and soft drinks. They joined the queue and the conversation between them was strained. When it was their turn, Ben ordered a chicken burger, two lagers and a bottle of water for Agatha. He didn't want to keep queueing, so he thought that doubling up on his drinks was a good idea. So did Agatha as she wanted him drunk, as it would be easier to drug him.

*

Agatha had enjoyed her first outdoor concert. She had enjoyed watching the bands, none of whom she was familiar with. She had especially liked Primal Scream who were headlining the event. '(I'm Gonna) Cry Myself Blind' had the crowd swaying, with their arms above their heads. After ten pints, Ben was feeling more relaxed and embraced the concert's vibe, bouncing around and singing at the top of his voice, even though the band had left the stage.

The concert was over and his life was about to change for a second time that day.

'Come on, it's time to drop you off.'

Agatha took hold of his arm as they made the ten-minute walk back to the car. She'd had enough of being surrounded by people and was grateful not to suffer from enochlophobia. There was no escape from the large crowd, as hundreds of chanting people were heading in the same direction. The consumption of lager was now evident in Ben's lack of ability to walk without swaying. As Agatha tightened her grip, her anger started to fizz. She was going to enjoy every moment of Ben's death as she had found him infuriating throughout the date.

Unlocking the car, she helped him into the passenger seat. He toppled in and rested his head against the seat.

'I feel sick,' he muttered.

Rolling her eyes out loud, Agatha climbed into the driver's seat.

Slipping her hand into the car door, she carefully removed the Rohypnol and a bottle of water. It was less than a third full. Ben sat motionless and his eyes were closed.

This is going to be so easy. I can feel the excitement curse through me.

Unscrewing the top of the bottle, Agatha gently added the powerful sedative.

A loud ringtone filled the car. Ben opened his eyes and pulled his phone from his pocket. He looked at the caller ID and then at Agatha, before hitting the decline button.

Too late.

'Who is Emma?' hissed Agatha.

Ben let out a big sigh. He was tired, drunk and he wasn't going to see Agatha anymore.

'She's my ex-girlfriend.'

'Why is she calling you? It's nearly 11 pm.'

'She called into The Swan today.'

'What, wait! You've been with your ex today when you are seeing me!'

'Calm down, Agatha. There's nothing between us.'

'What did she want, Ben? Is that why you were late? You left me waiting because you were with her?'

Agatha's anger swept through her body.

How dare he! How dare he see anyone else! He has broken my trust.

Ben didn't look too good. His hand rapidly felt for the door handle. He found it with just enough time to throw it open before vomiting onto the grass. Agatha just watched. When finished, he wiped his mouth on his jacket sleeve and sat back.

Agatha loved the disadvantages of others.

It was time to strike.

'Here, let's not argue. It's okay. Have some water.' She gave him her sweetest, darkest smile.

'Thank you.'

Ben drank the water laced with Rohypnol. Agatha watched, fascinated. The last person she had drugged was her father.

She felt powerful.

'I'm a dad.'

Agatha was surprised. 'What did you say?'

'Today, Emma came to the pub to tell me I'm a dad. That's why she ended things. She was confused. Now she wants to get back together. To be a family.'

Agatha wanted to kill him, there and then. Looking around, she decided to wait as there were too many people and cars. She felt for her special piece of paper.

Ben was starting to lose consciousness and his words were garbled. 'I need to go home.'

His last revelation had unleashed the fire of fury within her. She was in hunter mode. Locking the car doors, she turned to face him. He was moments from prolonged unconsciousness.

This is fun!

'You are not going home, Ben. Ever.'

Laughing to herself, she started the engine. Then she leant over Ben and seized his mobile phone. Lifting his thumb, she pressed it against the screen and then hit 'shut down.' She didn't want anyone else trying to track or contact him. Ever. She couldn't wait to take him home.

Chapter Seven

Emma felt crushing disappointment when Ben didn't answer his phone. She had been counting down the minutes until the concert finished and he should be home. He had said he wasn't going to stay out late but she could not ignore the uneasy feeling she had that he was on a date with another girl.

It was her own doing. She shouldn't have pushed him away. Picking up her phone she sent him a message. 'Message me when you read this. Can't wait to catch up tomorrow. I hope your night went well. xx'

That was a lie as she hoped he'd had a lousy time.

One tick appeared beneath the message instead of two which indicated he hadn't yet received it. Sighing, she placed her phone down, thinking that he mustn't have a signal.

She hadn't been entirely truthful with Ben regarding how she knew he would be at The Swan. When they had lived together, she had downloaded an app to both their mobile phones to allow her to track where he was. She knew it was wrong, but it made her feel secure in their relationship.

She had tested him on more than one occasion when they had been together. Once he said he was going to the gym, which the tracking app confirmed. However, an hour later, she saw that he had left and gone to the pub. Her trust issues had surfaced and she called to ask when he was coming home. He had answered on the third ring. He'd be home in an hour as he had bumped into an old school friend in the gym and they were catching up over a pint. The app was her comfort blanket and her reassurance.

Scrolling through her phone, she opened the Mspy app. She decided that Ben must either have no signal or he had turned his phone off, as his location was not shown.

Why would he turn his phone off? Unless he knows that I had been tracking his movements all this time.

She felt restless. Climbing out of bed, she pulled a sweatshirt over her vest top and pyjama bottoms before heading to the kitchen to make herself a cup of tea.

She was stopped in her tracks by Ava waking up. A high-pitched cry signalled that she was hungry. Picking her up, she offered the cranky baby words of comfort and they headed to the kitchen, where there was already a bottle of milk made up in the fridge. It just needed warming.

Maybe once Ben moves back in, he'll feed Ava sometimes.

The thought made her smile.

She didn't know Ben would never be coming home.

Chapter Eight

Usually, the drive home on the remote Northumberland roads was an incredibly scenic experience. Agatha loved winding her way through the rugged landscape, surrounded by the stunning views of rolling hills, lush forests and expansive moorlands with birds of prey soaring overhead.

All she could see and feel was darkness. There were no streetlights on the narrow winding roads. She had navigated them carefully and skilfully so many times before but now, only the moon and her full-beam headlights partially lit her way. Pressing her foot on the accelerator, to take the blind bends at speed, just increased her excitement. Ben was still unconscious and she wanted to get him home.

The Land Rover Discovery held the road as she hit all the crooks and turns for mile after mile. Turning up the radio, 'Paint It, Black' by The Rolling Stones filled the car. She loved the old songs. Not long now before playtime was less than fifteen minutes and she would be home.

Ben's fate lay in Agatha's back pocket on a neatly folded piece of paper which Agatha would carefully put back into the sock. She liked the 'lucky dip' approach to killing.

*

Agatha turned down the volume of the radio as she approached her home. She turned into the entrance where the faded white sign displayed the words 'Crow Springs Farm'. She didn't know why it was called that. Maybe it was because they had crows regularly pecking at the fields and nesting high up in the trees.

Dipping the headlights as she made her way up the long drive, she didn't want to disturb her maman and have to explain why she had a drugged man in the passenger seat. Continuing past the white farmhouse, she pulled over near the pigpen. She could hear the chickens clucking and scratching nearby. She hated chickens. She disliked most animals.

Switching off the engine, she turned and spoke to an unconscious Ben.

'I'm so excited. I've created a killing list. It means that you will die one of three ways depending on the number I'm about to show you. Your number is in my back pocket. I thought I'd bring it on our date. Before I do, I'll tell you what the options are.'

Ben remained motionless. Agatha shrugged her shoulders and giggled.

'Number 1 means I will recreate William's death. He was my father but I helped Maman to capture and kill him. He died just over there in that stone outhouse. He starved to death, eventually. Then I will feed your corpse to the pigs. They will devour you in about nine minutes.

If number 2 is on the paper, I will blindfold and cable-tie you to my bed before seducing you. It will end with me repeatedly stabbing you, slowly. Then, guess what, Ben? I will feed you to the pigs.

If it is number 3, you will be drugged and drowned in a very large watering trough. I am interested to know how long it takes a person to drown. Then I will feed you to the pigs. Either way, Ben. You are going in the pigpen.'

Leaning over, she kissed him on the mouth. He was unresponsive. Slowly, she removed the small piece of paper from her back pocket and flicked the interior light on.

'Just so you know that I'm not cheating, Ben, and reading out another number.'

Ben remained slumped and motionless.

'Here we go,' she said, proudly. 'Drum roll, please!' Smiling, she slowly unfolded the paper before revealing it to an unseeing Ben. 'What do you think? Are you happy?'

She folded the paper and returned it to her back pocket until she could return it to the sock. It had a large number '1' on it. Agatha was about to recreate the Grey Trench Coat Man's death.

Humming to herself, she stepped down from the Land Rover and headed to the stone outhouse. There were no windows or light. Just a stone building that contained a heavy door. She unlocked it and pulled the door wide open.

Walking back to her vehicle and Ben, she unclicked his seat belt and pulled him sideways onto the cold earth. Grabbing his ankles, she dragged him into the cold dark tomb. He started to groan.

Agatha quickened her steps.

Once inside the doorway, she removed all his clothes except his underwear, before drawing him further into the darkness. Gathering all his belongings, she threw them onto the backseat of the Land Rover before returning to close, bolt and lock the outhouse door.

Ben had no way out and no one to hear him.

Agatha was looking forward to a good night's sleep in her new T-shirt. It was hers now. Ben would never need it again.

Chapter Nine

I can't sleep.

An internal feeling is putting me on edge. I know its cause. Agatha.

She has been in a very happy mood these last few days. Yet the smile on her face has been more a smirk than a happy smile. It was the same look her father had.

Even though I know every part of him has vanished from this earth, I still think of him regularly. I still allow him to have power over my thoughts.

I fear he lives on in my only child.

She has gone out tonight to an outdoor concert with a friend whom I don't know, and she wouldn't say. I didn't think Agatha had any friends. She's too much of a loner and has very little tolerance for others.

Hearing her car, I am relieved she is home.

Stretching over the bedside table, I switch on the white bedside lamp. I need to see her.

Pulling back the large white goose-down duvet, my bare feet sink into the soft deep pile of the white carpet beneath my feet. Retrieving my dressing gown and slippers, I head to the landing to wait.

*

Agatha parked the Land Rover next to the large white farmhouse. A windscreen of mature trees grew on the north side to protect the property against the bitter winter winds.

Climbing into the backseat, she recovered Ben's clothes. Scooping them into a large pile, she raised them to her face and inhaled deeply. They smelt of the outdoors and an aftershave she wasn't familiar with. Placing them on her knee, she went through the pockets of his jeans. There was one handkerchief, a few coins, keys and a wallet.

Stuffing the keys and wallet into her jacket pocket, she folded the jeans before dropping them onto the floor along with his trainers, socks and jacket, after checking those pockets too. They were empty.

Picking up his phone, she headed towards the house carrying his T-shirt. It was her trophy, her keepsake.

As quietly as she could, she opened the front door. Stepping into the darkness she crept along the passage where she passed the kitchen and glanced in to see if Guzzle was sleeping there. Sometimes the dog would bark if you snuck in during the night. At other times, you were greeted with a slightly raised sleepy head before his eyes closed and he went back to sleep. There was no sign of him. She continued past the lounge and up the stairs.

It was only when she looked up that she saw her maman watching her.

'How was your night?'

Agatha forced a smile before answering, 'It was fine. The music was very different to the 80's stuff you listen to.'

She had continued moving up the stairs as she spoke and they were now only a touching distance apart. She wanted to get to her room to slip on the T-shirt and relive the last few hours in her mind.

She was proud of herself. Her first victim.

Faith stood, still blocking Agatha's path. There was something about her child's demeanour that was making her very uncomfortable. She continued the questioning.

'Did your friend enjoy it too? What was their name again?'

Agatha looked her mother straight in the eyes. There it was again. The same look her psychotic father had.

'I never told you their name, Maman. Now, I'm going to bed.'

Faith didn't move. She matched her daughter's stare as they stood in partial darkness. The only light was seeping from Faith's bedroom. Slowly she moved forward and took hold of the T-shirt in Agatha's hand. Agatha held on tight and pulled her arm back, trying to free it. Faith didn't let go. They stood eye-to-eye, each holding a part of Ben's T-shirt.

'What's this?'

Agatha paused before answering. She didn't want this to escalate or for her maman to become suspicious.

'It's a T-shirt. I found it on the ground at the concert. Thought I could wear it around the farm.'

Faith let go and moved aside to let her pass.

Agatha was an exceptional liar. She had said the words with such conviction that, for a second, she had believed it herself.

Faith didn't believe her. She watched her daughter make her way to her bedroom and close the door without a second glance or even a goodnight.

Heading back to her own room and the warmth of her bed, Faith decided to keep a very close eye on her daughter over the next few days.

Chapter Ten

Back in the privacy of her bedroom, Agatha locked the door and brushed off the irritation she felt towards her maman.

Walking over to her bed in the dark, she switched on her bedside lamp. The room was spacious and minimal. There was no clutter as she didn't own many things. She never asked or needed very much. Just her thoughts and being outside.

Throwing off her jacket and top, she pulled on Ben's black T-shirt. The white logo read 'The Swan'. She now knew why he hadn't had time to get changed for their date. He had been with his ex-girlfriend, Emma. And now he was a dad!

Well, not for much longer.

Pulling off her jeans before climbing into bed, she went through Ben's small brown wallet. It held a £20 note, a debit card, a gym membership, a student card and a loyalty discount card for a supermarket.

And one small passport-sized photograph showing two people hugging.

It was Ben, looking very happy, with his head leaning against a girl with raven hair, dark eyes and a pretty round face. Agatha crushed the photo in her hand. Her breathing had turned heavy, and anger swelled within her. Releasing her hand, the photo fell to the floor.

I should be the only girl Ben wants. How dare he bring that photo on our date!

She thought about the pleasure she would feel once thirst and starvation took hold of him. Ben's handsome face and perfect body would start to break down and his organs would fail him.

I might take a photo of him then, to remember him.

In the meantime, she needed some sleep and a plan to keep her maman away from the stone outhouse. She would have to feed the pigs and the chickens. The thought did not please her as she liked animals as much as she liked people. Very little.

Chapter Eleven

I love early Sunday mornings.

The 'From My Kitchen' online business has taken over one hundred orders since yesterday, so I have a busy day ahead. The plum and vanilla jam is still my bestseller, followed by raspberry and gin, then rose and elderflower. I have enough stock to get the orders out as the jam is made in large batches weeks ahead. However, I am going to have to spend next weekend making jam to cope with the demand.

First, I will take Guzzle for his morning walk, feed the pigs and chickens, and then spend the rest of the day packaging orders.

Heading to the kitchen sink to wash my coffee cup, I get a surprise.

Agatha has walked in. She is dressed in a black T-shirt and leggings and is wearing a jacket. It is 6.30 am. She is never up this early.

'Is everything alright?' I can't keep the surprise out of my voice.

'It is. I know you are busy with your business and I thought it was time I gave you a hand. Do you want me to feed the animals?'

I don't trust her. The last time she fed the pigs was with her father's corpse. What is she up to?

'That would be great, thanks. Can I make you some breakfast?'

'No, thanks. I'm not hungry yet.'

Walking over to the sink, she picks up a glass from the draining board before wandering over to the water dispenser at the fridge. Filling her glass, she takes a long slow drink.

'I think today is going to be thirsty work,' she laughs.

Smiling, she turns to head back out of the kitchen.

'I'm off to feed the pigs and chickens,' she says, over her shoulder.

'Thank you. Bye for now.'

I muster a smile back at her. My only child and I don't trust her. I decide to give her twenty minutes, then I will take Guzzle out on his morning walk, calling by the pigpen to see what she is up to. It will give me a chance to check on my favourite pig, Macy. She loves me to rub her head whenever I pass. I can also check that Agatha has collected the chickens' eggs.

*

Hurrying from the kitchen, Agatha felt excited. She was now indispensable to Ben. His life, and how quickly it ended, was completely in her hands.

It was usually about a five-minute walk from the kitchen across the land to the stone outhouse. With adrenaline streaming through her body, she made it in three. Pausing at the large metal door, she knew her maman wouldn't be too far behind. She had seen it in her face. The distrust. It made her smile to herself.

For now, there was no one around; only crows pecking at the earth.

'Can you hear me, Ben?' Agatha's voice was neutral. She wanted him to like her.

Silence.

'Ben, it's me.'

She was about to unlock the door to check that she hadn't already killed him by giving him too much sedative when she heard movement. Moving her ear closer to the door and checking that her maman wasn't coming across the field, she spoke loudly.

'Ben, can you hear me?'

'Agatha! What's happening? Where am I? Let me out.'

'Calm down. You are where you deserve to be. Making me wait for you when all the time you were with your ex-girlfriend.'

'I'm sorry, let me out. I'm dying of thirst. Please, Agatha!'

Ben started to bang on the door.

'Bang as loud as you like. No one can hear you. You are miles from anywhere.'

He continued to bang and shout for help. It was true that they were miles from the next farm but she had the feeling that her mamam might be only minutes away.

'Ben, stop yelling. I have something to tell you. Ben! Shut up!'

Ben paused for a moment. Mainly because his head hurt and he felt exhausted and nauseous.

'That's better,' said Agatha. 'Now feel to the left of the door near the ground. Last night, I left you a bottle of water.'

She could hear movement behind the door. She knew she didn't have much time as her maman would be walking Guzzle very soon.

'Ben, have you found it?'

'Yes, I've drunk it. Now, can you let me out? I'm freezing. Where are my clothes?'

'I'm not going to let you out yet, Ben, but I'll be back later. I have to feed the animals now. Bye!'

'Agatha! Agatha!' Ben continued to yell as she walked away, smiling.

He'll quieten down soon. Anyone would after drinking water laced with a large dose of Rohypnol. Won't the silly boy ever learn?

I can't have Maman finding him.

Chapter Twelve

'Come on Guzzle. Let's go for a walk and see what Agatha is up to.'

I love my Golden Labrador. The word 'walk' always gets a reaction. His wagging tail hits my leg numerous times.

Heading to the front door, I lock it behind me. I don't know why; maybe out of habit. There is no one for miles around. You can't get to the cottage without being seen coming up the driveway.

Guzzle dashes off in front of me. He pauses for a second to see which way I'll head. He knows the way in either direction.

'This way, Guzzle. Let's see Macy.' I point in the direction of the pigpen.

Guzzle takes off. It is only a five-minute walk and he'll wait on the way for me to catch up. Some dogs don't get along with pigs. Guzzle is indifferent to them. At times he's curious but mostly keeps his distance. His presence seems to bother the pigs more.

It's a nice day today. There's a chill in the air which should clear as the afternoon approaches.

I can see the pigpen ahead. It's near the stone outhouse. I rarely go in there as I feel that William has seeped into the concrete. His soul is trapped in the darkness. Yet I don't want to knock the building down. I suppose it's similar to having a comfort blanket.

There is no sign of Agatha as I approach. Maybe she has been and gone. Maybe she hasn't been at all. The last one is more likely to be the case. I make my way to the small barn where we keep the feed for the pigs and chickens.

'Hi, Maman. Are you checking up on me?' asks Agatha, overly cheerful. She has been in the barn and is now carrying two old blue buckets filled with swine feed. Apparently, pigs have around 20,000 taste buds, so the smell and taste of their feed are important to them.

They thoroughly enjoyed eating William.

I smile back. 'Absolutely! I feel I need to keep an eye on you.'

She locks eyes with me for only a second before forcing another smile.

'No need, Maman. I'm good. Today, I feel really happy.'

'That's good to hear, Agatha. What do you feel happy about?'

She continues to head towards the pigpen and tips the buckets into the large trough. The noise level goes up as the pigs jostle for prime position. Agatha heads back in the direction of the barn to collect more feed. I follow, waiting for her to answer my question.

'I've met someone I like.'

This wasn't what I was expecting her to say. Usually, she just about tolerates the human race.

'That's great. What's their name and where did you meet?'

Agatha has her back to me. She stops suddenly and turns to face me. There's excitement on her face. The last time I saw that look was when she saw her father's corpse lying in the stone outhouse.

'He's called Ben and we've had a few dates. He likes me. I met him in a bar.'

I'm slightly thrown by her news. I didn't know she had any friends to go to bars with.

'That's great if you are happy. Can I meet him?'

Agatha smirks. This is making me very uncomfortable. She has her father's smirk.

'Maybe. I need to know I can trust you.'

She's playing me but I don't yet know what the game is.

'Agatha, of course, you can trust me. What on earth do you mean?' I try to sound light-hearted. 'Aren't all parents meant to embarrass their child when they bring a boy home?'

In the barn, I scoop up the small pellets. I'll feed the chickens while Agatha finishes off the pigs.

'When are you seeing him next?'

'Sometime today.'

'Does he live on a farm too?' Something isn't right. There's something she isn't telling me.

'He's on a farm. Now, no more questions, Maman. I'll decide if you can meet him. You head back with Guzzle, and I'll finish off here and bring the eggs back too.'

Agatha is never helpful. She wants me out of the way. I scan the land to see if I can see anything different. Nothing. Just crows, sheep, trees, fields, and a kestrel overhead.

'Okay. Thank you. I need to go into the village later to pick up more supplies. We could grab a drink or something to eat in The Swan.'

Her expression has changed. Something I've said has annoyed her. This is the Agatha I know. Impulsive and hot-headed.

'I don't want to go to the village. There are too many smiley people.'

'Okay, no problem. Can I get you anything?'

'Cable ties.'

'Can I ask why?'

'I'm going to start looking after the tomato plants in the greenhouse. I need them to tie the plants to the bamboo sticks.'

We have a small greenhouse. It is a hobby of mine as I like seeing things grow from tiny seeds. Usually, I secure the tomato plants with brown string. At the moment, they are about 6" high. There are also lettuces, cabbage, beetroot, spinach, chilli, chives and thyme starting to grow.

I do not believe that she needs cable ties for the greenhouse, but I'll get them.

'Yes, sure,' I say.

Agatha has her back to me again and pours more feed into the troughs.

'Come on, Guzzle. Let's go. See you in a bit, Agatha.'

'I'll be about an hour. I'm going to go for a walk.'

I nod my head as I turn back to the cottage. It was then that I see Agatha looking at something. It is only for a split second, but I see it.

She is looking at the stone outhouse.

Chapter Thirteen

Agatha watched her maman walk back across the fields. Guzzle left her mistress's side to chase the crows which were silently stabbing at the earth. At times, Agatha wished they were still living in France, working in the vineyards and stopping before the day got too hot, to enjoy a chunk of homemade bread and local cheese. But not today.

Excitement swirled around her.

She wouldn't have met or lured Benjamin Stark into the stone outhouse if they were still living in France. The thought of opening the door thrilled her.

She was, after all, her father's daughter.

She remembered the day he had lain there, dying on the same cold hard stone floor where Benjamin now lay. He had admitted to killing seventeen young women and had kept a list hidden within the lining of his grey trench coat. Unaware, Maman had burned it when she disposed of his clothes. Her maman would have been the Grey Trench Coat Man's eighteenth victim, had she not escaped. She would have been just a name on his killing list. As would Agatha.

He had confessed that he was coming for her too. She would have been another victim, even though he had known in the end that she was his daughter. She had taken pleasure in playing a part in his murder. She hadn't done it for revenge for what he had done to her maman. It was for another reason.

She liked it.

Picking up her discarded jacket from the ground, she removed Ben's black Samsung phone from her pocket. Holding the side button down, the phone fired into life. The screen asked for a fingerprint or PIN code.

'No problem,' she laughed aloud.

Glancing over the fields, she couldn't see anyone around; only sheep and birds overhead. She let her jacket fall from over her arm as she meandered towards the stone outhouse, humming a tune. She knew he would be fast asleep. Rohypnol takes about twenty minutes to work and the sedation lasts roughly between four and six hours. It also causes partial amnesia so, if he did stir, he was unlikely to remember anything. Whilst the drug dissolves without colour or taste, it adds a blue tinge to water. Agatha found out that the manufacturer had altered this to stop it being used as a date rape drug.

An easy way around that is to keep your victim confined in darkness.

Placing Ben's phone momentarily on the ground, she pulled back the large bolt and undid the padlock. The key was kept in the feeding shed.

Peering into the dark, it took a moment for her eyes to adjust. She could smell and feel the cold. Anyone else would have thought that the cold stone tomb was empty. She felt powerful as she scanned the floor, looking for her victim.

She found him.

Leaving the door wide open, she allowed the light inside as it was still dusk. Ben was lying on his left side in the foetal position, still wearing his Emporio Armani black and tan boxer shorts. Agatha pushed him with her foot and he rolled onto his back without a sound or response. For a moment, she stood and watched.

She enjoyed watching him.

Kneeling, she smelt his underwear. It smelt of urine. That pleased her as she had caused him to wet himself. He was vulnerable and powerless. She watched him for a moment longer before taking her hand and moving it over his chest. It was baby-smooth. He had shaved his chest.

'That might be itchy in a few days, Ben,' whispered Agatha, in his ear. 'You won't be shaving your chest in here.'

She kissed the side of his face and then his mouth. Nothing. He was unresponsive.

'I came in here for a specific reason, Ben,' continued Agatha, as she tenderly picked up his right hand. 'I need you to do something for me.'

Taking his hand, she placed his thumb on the sensor on his phone. It unlocked immediately.

'I'll be back later, Ben. You'll get used to living here with me. I'll let you know all about how your body will break down with no food or water. After you slowly die, I'll dump you in the pigpen, or killing pen as I like to call it, and I'll watch as the pigs devour you in about ten minutes. Don't worry though, you've got a few weeks to live yet.'

Agatha didn't look back as she stepped into the daylight, briefly setting down the phone as she locked and bolted the heavy door. Checking that it was securely locked, she went back to scrolling through Ben's WhatsApp messages. She was going to enjoy the next hour getting to know him a little bit better.

Ten miles away, Emma Beale was relieved and puzzled. Ben had finally turned his phone on so she could now track him. She wasn't familiar with his location; Crow Springs Farm, Stannersburn, Northumberland.

She knew her friend, Dawn, wasn't available to babysit as she had gone to visit her parents in Manchester for the day.

That's okay. I will just have to take Ava with me.

It was time to find Ben.

Chapter Fourteen

Agatha wandered back to the farmhouse, with her eyes fixed on Ben's phone. The WhatsApp messages were mainly to his friends. She had learned that his parents were still alive, and he had one sister. She had read the messages on the family's WhatsApp group.

Opening the front door, she kicked off her boots and headed to her room. Her maman's Land Rover wasn't outside as she had gone into town. Guzzle was lying on the kitchen floor. The large Golden Labrador lifted his head at the sound of the door and then went back to sleep.

Once up the pristine white stairs, Agatha entered her bedroom and closed the door behind her. The 'number sock' that had sealed Ben's fate still lay discarded on the floor. She was pleased that she had picked out number 1. It was fun recreating her father's demise.

She switched from WhatsApp and started to scroll through Ben's gallery. Already, an hour had passed. There were thousands of photos. He was quite a nice-looking guy if blonde floppy hair, blue eyes and skinny was your thing. There were lots of photos of him on a night out with two guys. Agatha presumed they were his flatmates. So far, none of him with any girls.

He must have gone home to Kent last Christmas. There were photos of him around a table with a girl, who looked about sixteen and had the same eye and hair colour, and others whom Agatha thought were his parents. They both looked in

60

their mid-fifties, were attractive and even wore paper hats. There were two elderly ladies, possibly his grandmothers. They all looked so happy. A different upbringing to Agatha. Her maman did her best but her mind always seemed to be elsewhere. And it had been. She had been planning Agatha's father's murder for nearly two decades.

Scrolling further down, she stopped. Annoyance, mixed with anger, triggered within her. There was a photo of Ben with a girl of similar age. Raven hair, brown eyes and a plump kind face. They looked as though they were in love. Agatha had never been in love. She didn't know if she really loved her maman. She felt incapable of loving another person.

Scrolling on, there were hundreds of photos of them together. Some looked like they had been taken on holiday, maybe to Spain or Greece, and others on nights out. Some were of the two of them kissing or cuddling. In one, the girl was dressed up; maybe at a hen do. It was the first photo of them together on his phone.

Agatha immediately started to highlight all the photos with the girl in them and pressed 'delete'. Ben was hers now.

After she was satisfied that she had deleted all inappropriate photos and messages on the phone, she switched it off. She didn't want anyone to track it, so she would never switch it on again. Leaning over, she placed it safely in her bedside drawer.

She would create a special box to keep tokens from the men she murdered. Her maman had the perfect-sized box in the kitchen, which she used to send out larger orders of her jams to small businesses.

Rolling off the bed, Agatha started to make her way downstairs. Excited, she wanted to start the box off by putting

Ben's phone in it. She was still wearing his black T-shirt with 'The Swan' logo named after the pub where he worked.

Or used to work in.

Guzzle was still lying in the same position, so she walked around him to access the cupboard where her maman kept the flat-packed boxes. The kitchen, as always, was pristine and all-white. Maman didn't do untidiness and germs. It was a reflection of her days captured by William and his mother. Agatha had read about it online. It seemed that her father and grandmother had lived in squalor.

Taking out a box, she started to happily fold and assemble it. She sang the love song 'La Vie En Rose' in French to herself. Agatha was bilingual and, sometimes, she and her maman spoke French to each other as they were both fluent.

'What do you think, Guzzle? Is that the perfect size? Not too wide, not too tall and it will slide perfectly under my bed. My father had a list of his victims. I'm going to have keepsakes.'

She jumped as Guzzle started to bark.

She recognised that bark. Someone the dog didn't recognise was approaching the farmhouse.

'Guzzle, stop! You made me jump. It's okay.'

She stood at the side of the kitchen window to watch whoever it was. She could tell by their car that they weren't local. It was a white Volkswagen Up city car. No good in winter to get over the fields or hold the winding roads.

She watched as the driver pulled up near her old Land Rover. She couldn't make out the face at this distance. She checked her watch. Only an hour had passed since she had seen Ben. He would be in a drugged state for a few more hours.

The driver got out of the car and walked to the rear passenger seat. Opening the door, they leaned in before emerging with a small bundle in their arms.

A baby.

Agatha recognised the raven hair and plump face.

'Guzzle, this is going to be fun,' said Agatha, coldly. 'The game has just got some new players.'

Leaving the box on the kitchen table, she headed to open the front door with a smile falsely planted on her face. When the stranger approached, the door was already open to welcome her.

Emma Beale did not even have to ring the bell.

Chapter Fifteen

I can't get Agatha out of my head.

I know she is up to something that I don't need in our lives or won't like. I can sense it.

Instead of shopping locally, I have driven for forty miles. I need to think, and I need time away from Agatha. I park up in the centre of Northumberland, in a beautiful part of the North East named Alnwick. You can have broomstick lessons in nearby Alnwick Castle, which is now famous as the location for the Harry Potter movies. It is also the home to the Duke and Duchess of Northumberland.

I rarely come here as I prefer to remain local and unseen. When I do, I visit Alnwick Garden. It is spectacular and I especially love the mysterious Poison Garden which is full of over one hundred deadly plants. I have the brochure at home and I feel it will come in useful sometime soon.

Things you wouldn't expect to be poisonous can grow in the common family garden. All parts of the Laburnum plant are poisonous and Atropa Belladonna, which can be found in Asia and parts of Europe, is better known as Deadly Nightshade and its dark berries can be lethal. The farm has Convallaria Majalis growing wild, which is also known as the Lily of the Valley and is toxic if eaten. Always good to know.

Today, Alnwick will be quiet. It usually is on a Sunday. Most of the smaller shops will be closed. The last Friday of the month is a beneficial day to make the hour's drive to the farmers' market where I stock up on local bread, meats and fish. There is also a good selection of restaurants.

Today, I am going to take my time. The place is unusually busy, probably with tourists or there might be something on at 'The Playhouse'.

I head in that direction and turn right into the main town. It isn't a long walk. I browse the shops that are open, for about ten minutes, including picking up cable ties for Agatha from the nearby 'we sell everything' shop, before heading to one of my favourite restaurants, 'The Plough', which also does accommodation.

Climbing a few steps, I pull open the heavy door and head to the bar. A young dark-haired boy looks up and smiles.

'Do you have a table booked?'

'No, sorry. Do you have any free for one?'

I'm used to eating alone. I used to sit in cafés and watch William before I abducted him. The thought still feels good.

'Yes, sure. Follow me, please.'

I follow him past the ladies toilets and up some stairs. The dining area is only about a third-full and a bored-looking couple glance at us as we pass. Half-eaten food is discarded on their plates and they are each doing something on their mobile phone, with a bottle of red wine standing between them.

'Will this table do?'

'Yes, thank you.'

It is near the window where I can people-watch. There is a lone man seated at the next table. He locks eyes with me and doesn't look away.

'I'll just get you some menus.'

The waiter returns within a moment and hands me the menus.

'Someone will take your order shortly.'

I nod and offer him a smile as he hurries back to the bar.

I can feel the man's stare. I look at the menu, but I can't take it in. Something is appealing about the stranger.

'I can recommend the Plough's Ultimate Burger.' His voice is smooth. He's not from the North East; maybe from the South East.

'Sounds good. Not the Sunday roast?' I reply.

You look good. This is going to be an interesting lunch.

He ignores my question and, instead, asks another. 'Are you meeting a friend?' His stare is intense, his question loaded.

'No, just me.' I return his stare.

'Join me then. I was just going to order more wine.'

I knew you were going to ask. This is exciting. I know you can feel the chemistry too.

I move to the attractive stranger's table as the waitress approaches to take my order.

'The lady will have the Plough's Ultimate Burger and a large glass of Malbec.'

I notice that he doesn't say thank you. I nod my thanks to the waitress. I have never had a man order for me before. I have to be in control.

'What's your name?'

'Faith. It's Faith Taylor.'

'Nice to meet you, Faith. I'm Tom Quick.'

'Nice to meet you, Tom.'

We are smiling at each other. Flirting with our eyes. I haven't felt chemistry like this before.

He looks in his mid-fifties. Even seated, he looks very tall, with salt and pepper wavy hair, slight stubble, chocolate-brown eyes, perfect veneers and a strong jawline. He's dressed in an open-neck light blue shirt and black jeans. He has an expensive look about him.

I wish I looked how I did years ago, instead of slightly overweight with mousy hair.

'Do you live in Alnwick?' he asks.

'No, about an hour's drive away. What about you?'

'About thirty minutes, but I had a meeting nearby. Can we exchange numbers?'

Straight to the point. I like that, Tom Quick. How do I explain that I have a mobile but I rarely switch it on? I have a fear of being tracked. It's in the car and I don't even know the number. It's an old 'pay as you go' Samsung.

'I don't usually give my number to someone I've just met,' I laugh.

Only the Carmens in France and Agatha have the number. My business is run online via email.

'Give me your number and I'll message you.'

'When?' he asks with a smile.

I watch him for a moment before answering.

He's very charming. I'm attracted to him, but I don't trust him. I think he uses charm to lure people in. He might be dangerous. The thought is arousing, I want to find out more. If it goes wrong, there is always the pigpen.

'Very soon,' I smile, matching his charm.

We make small talk, neither of us giving much away.

The waitress approaches our table and places a very large burger in front of me accompanied by fries and salad. I am not sure how I am meant to eat this and keep up the chemistry between us!

'Can I get it to go, please? Change of plan.'

'Yes, no problem.'

We both watch as she takes the plate away. On the table, his mobile phone rings. He doesn't answer. Instead, he silences the ringtone.

'What would you like to do now? This place does accommodation.' He slowly runs his hand through his hair. I see that there is no wedding ring as he pulls the cuff of his shirt down. He's preening himself, intently staring at me while he awaits my reply.

'As soon as you give me your number.' I smile and lean closer to him across the table, playing the game. 'I'm going to leave with my lunch and head back home. Alone.'

He doesn't like my response. The smile remains fixed but the eyes are angry.

This man is used to being in control and getting what he wants. I'm going to enjoy playing you, Tom Quick. I'm going to enjoy peeling back the layers to expose who you really are.

'That's a shame,' he says. 'I was hoping we could get to know each other more. Enjoy a leisurely Sunday afternoon in bed.'

His tone of voice has slowed down. He's trying to process what is going on between us. The waitress returns with my lunch in a large polystyrene box. It smells delicious and I'm going to devour it as soon as I'm back in the car.

'Would you like to pay by cash or card?' she asks.

'Card,' replies Tom and, before I can object, he takes his wallet from his back pocket and removes a credit card. The waitress smiles and holds out the machine.

'It's gone through.' She smiles at us before leaving us alone.

'That was very kind. Thank you.'

'Not at all, Faith. You now owe me lunch.'

You are crafty, Tom Quick.

I pick up my shopping and place my lunch carefully in one of the bags. Tom remains seated, drinking his wine, just watching me.

'Nice to meet you. Would you like to give me your number?' I ask.

He removes a small white card from his wallet. 'Call me soon.' The insincere smile is back.

'I will and thanks again for lunch.' I take the card before turning to head out of the restaurant.

Tom remains seated.

Outside, I stride back to my car. I look a little out of place. Alnwick has a friendly mellow feel to it where people don't stride; they walk, slowly. I can feel Tom's card pressing into my hand.

I'm pleased to be back at the busy car park, where I find my car keys and press the button. Opening the driver's door, I climb in and place my shopping and lunch on the passenger seat. I can see a driver, who is looking for a space, stop and indicate; waiting for me to pull out.

They can wait. I am going to eat my lunch first. I ignore them and turn over the small card, still in my hand.

Tom Quick

Chief Executive

Northshireland County Council

On the back of the card is a work address and a mobile number.

I remember reading that about 21% of corporate executives are psychopathic, which is the same percentage, according to one study, as prison inmates.

Tom Quick, let the game begin.

Chapter Sixteen

Lil Hunt was frustrated. Yet again, her partner of five years had not answered any of her calls in the last hour. His mother, Ruth, wanted to know if he could take her to a doctor's appointment on Wednesday. Ruth always phoned Lil with her issues, as she knew Lil would pick up.

There have always been two different sides to him. The charming, humorous and charismatic public side and the manipulative, deceptive and exploitive private side. Tom Quick was a narcissistic sociopath. Lil has wanted to leave the relationship for the last three years.

But Tom wouldn't allow it.

They lived in a picturesque, four-bedroom detached property in Felton with green views of ancient trees and lands. She used to have her own career as a local journalist which Tom insisted, she gave up. He told her that she didn't need to work and that he wanted her at home during the day, even though he was rarely there. If he was at home, he would disappear to play golf. Or so he said.

The start of their relationship had been idyllic. He had been so charming and attentive, making sure that Lil never detected who the real Tom was, until they started living together and she had no income of her own. He took care of all the household bills and she had to ask for money and explain why she needed it. If she met a friend for coffee, she had to ask Tom for £20. He then decided if she could have it or if she had to earn it.

He had a sadistic side that took pleasure from her suffering or pain. He loved humiliating or embarrassing her. She had been reminded, often with bruises, that she was lucky to have him. He liked to brag about the other women who were interested in him.

Last year, they had gone on holiday to the Caribbean. Complete luxury. Lil had loved looking out over the crystal-blue waters from the beach. She had wandered over to the pool bar to get them both a drink and the bartender had poured them two Malibu cocktails. He had joked with her that she was very pretty. Lil was 50 years old, four years younger than Tom, and very attractive. Not that she believed it as being with a narcissistic sociopath had worn down her self-esteem.

Once back in their hotel room, Tom had turned angry. He wanted to know why she had humiliated him by flirting with a bartender. She never saw the punch coming. She just felt it as it connected furiously with her stomach. He left her, doubled over on the floor, and didn't return until the early hours.

At 6' 3", Tom Quick was easy to spot in a bar. He was a handsome man, and he knew it. That afternoon, he went back to the beach and got chatting with 40-year-old Harriet Hatman. She was a solicitor, on holiday with her best friend, celebrating her special birthday. Tom turned up the charm and took them both out for lunch, followed by evening drinks and then sex with a very drunken Harriet on the beach.

When he finally returned to Lil, he told her gleefully about his lovely afternoon and great sex. He emphasised that it was her fault for her throwing herself at the barman. She hadn't. Tom went into detail about how Harriet had been better-looking than her and had a great body. Lil knew then that she would never be good enough for the deluded Tom who was obsessed with power, status and control.

As tears rolled down her face, he laughed. He often told her that she was too sensitive. He enjoyed seeing her upset and was incapable of showing any guilt or shame for his infidelity.

She knew he had also had an affair at work since the holiday. He hadn't tried to hide it. The other woman had worked in the Human Resources Department before it came to an end, and he sacked her. He would come home from the office after 9 pm, smelling of sweat and The Body Shop's White Musk Flora, with orange foundation and scarlet red lipstick smeared over his collar.

He had blocked all avenues for Lil to seek support. She no longer worked, never saw her friends and he would get angry if she phoned her mother. The only person she spoke to was his mother, Ruth, who was as abusive as her son. Lil was worn down and tired. There were no good times in her life. No matter what time Tom came home, Lil was expected to be there. That was not negotiable.

When it came to their sex life, she was expected to be submissive. It was very different to the early days, when Tom had been gentle and considerate in the bedroom, two or three times a week. Now it happened, thankfully, only once a month. Tom would tie her hands and place a plastic bag over her head. He liked to watch her struggle for breath before tearing it off. Not because she could suffocate but because seeing her lips turn blue excited him. It aroused him watching her fight for breath.

He didn't care if she died. She was easily replaceable.

*

Tom Quick left the restaurant and headed home. He had left the house that morning at 7.30 am for an informal meeting with some land developers. It was boring and he was glad when it was over. He had then gone straight to a personal meeting at 9 am.

Jillian Flowers used to work for Northshireland County Council in the Regeneration Department, which was when she had first met Tom. It was not love or lust at first sight. She couldn't stand him.

Tom saw the aloof Jillian as a bedroom challenge. Very different to his usual type, she dressed in sensible clothes and flat shoes, with her hair cut unflatteringly short and her face carrying minimal makeup. Plain and uninteresting was how Tom had seen her. On the other hand, he saw himself as charismatic and powerful and, in his mind, no woman could resist a powerful man.

On that occasion, he was right.

Three months later, after her promotion to Senior Regeneration Officer, they started an affair. That was eighteen months ago. Whenever he was in Alnwick, Jillian would make sure she worked from home that day and they would spend an hour in the bedroom. Sometimes the sex bored Tom as Jillian played the submissive role a little too well. She never complained, even when the cable ties cut into her wrists.

He needed a new challenge.

That morning's sex was okay but Jillian had gained weight and become upset when Tom unkindly said she looked fat and unattractive. He had left without saying goodbye, after using side cutters to release one of her hands from the cable ties. He had left the small pliers in reach for her to release the other.

As the day drew to evening, his mind was on Faith. There was something dark about her that he found dangerous. He remembered how angry he had felt when she hadn't stayed longer in his company, opting instead to take her lunch with her.

She needs to be taught that you don't walk away from Tom Quick. Ever.

Chapter Seventeen

Emma felt nervous as she approached the white door to the white farmhouse. Large flowerpots stood on either side with an explosion of colour. Holding her baby tightly to her chest, she went to ring the doorbell before noticing that the door was ajar. She could see a figure dressed in black behind it.

'Hello,' called Emma, 'I'm looking for Benjamin Stark.'

The door swung open, and the two young women stood face-to-face. Agatha took in the pretty plump female who stood before her, holding a sleeping baby dressed in pink, with a bag slung over her shoulder.

Ben has a daughter, thought Agatha, before doing what she was so skilled at. Switching on the artificial charm. Controlling the desire to kill mother and baby on the spot.

'What makes you think he's here?'

'He was meant to call me last night, but he didn't. Then, this morning, I tracked his phone to this address.'

Merde! Never again will I check a victim's phone when I'm at home!

'Are you Agatha?'

What the …? I don't like this! Ben has said too much. Now the game has changed. I have just trebled my victim count.

'Sorry, I know this is awkward,' stated Emma.

I must remain calm and controlled.

'Is it? Why?' feigned Agatha.

'Ben said that you two were going on a date last night. Are you Agatha? I'm Emma Beale.'

Ben needs to learn not to gossip.

'I am Agatha. He's been doing work on the farm but we didn't go on a date. I don't know why he would say that.' She followed the blatant lie with a shrug of the shoulders. 'Please, come in,' she continued, 'and I'll get him for you.' Lying came naturally to Agatha.

'Thank you. I'm confused why he would say you were dating.'

'I can explain,' said Agatha, as she led the young mother and baby into the kitchen. Guzzle followed, before lying back down, quietly watching the two women. 'He wanted a relationship, but I wasn't interested. Instead, we agreed to be friends and he would help with some of the work on the farm.'

'He's very caring,' replied Emma.

He's going to be very dead, quicker than I had planned.

'Can I see him?' smiled Emma. There was something about the pretty willowy girl that unnerved her. She wanted to see Ben and leave as soon as possible.

'You will see him. He's about five minutes' walk from here. Near the pigpen. But first, I'll get us a cold drink and you can tell me more about him.'

Emma didn't object. She could do with a drink and the kitchen looked beautiful. Everything was clean, welcoming and pristine white.

'Is it okay with you if I breastfeed her?'

'Sure, go ahead. I'm just nipping to the bathroom, then I'll get us those drinks.'

Why would anyone want a baby? They are so loud and restrictive!

Leaving the kitchen, Agatha closed the door and ran upstairs to her bedroom. The game had begun and she needed to make the next move. She felt energised. Opening the bottom drawer of her bedside cabinet, she retrieved the powerful liquid sedative. It was the second time that day that she had used Rohypnol.

Emma would be her first female victim.

Entering the kitchen, she headed to the cabinet where the drinking glasses were kept. She had to act quickly as she wasn't sure when her maman was due back. Emma was singing to the baby while feeding her. Agatha felt no remorse or guilt for what was about to happen.

With her back to mother and baby, she added a large dose of the sedative to Emma's glass and then topped it up with blueberry juice to hide the blue tinge of the drug.

'There you are. Enjoy,' said Agatha, as she placed the glass on the table in front of Emma. 'It's organic blueberry juice. Apparently, it is very good for you.' She smiled.

'Thank you. Ava has gone back to sleep. She's such a good baby.'

Agatha watched as Emma cuddled the sleeping Ava with one arm and picked up the deadly drink with the other.

This is so easy. I'm actually enjoying myself.

Emma gulped down half the glass.

'You just have to grab food and drink when you can with a baby. I eat a meal as if someone is going to whisk it away!' she laughed.

That's your fault for having a baby!

'Where did you meet Ben?' asked Agatha.

'I was on a hen do, down south. I think it was love at first sight for us both,' beamed Emma.

There's no such thing as love at first sight. Just two lonely people deceiving themselves.

'Then Ben moved to the North East to be with you?'

'Yes, he's from Kent. His parents and sister still live there.'

It was them in the photos.

Emma picked up her glass and drained it.

Good girl. Not long now.

'I have to get Ava home soon. Can I see Ben now?'

'Sure, let's go.'

Agatha watched coldly as Emma stood up from the table, still holding Ava tightly in her arms, with her bag over her shoulder.

'This way. Come on, Guzzle.'

I'm luring you into a false sense of security by bringing the dog.

Agatha led the way across the field and pointed.

'He's working over there, near the chickens and pigpen. The pigpen is my favourite part of the farm,' she grinned.

Emma peered into the distance, trying to catch a glimpse of Ben. No sign. Agatha quickened their pace knowing what was about to happen.

Emma stopped, clutching her head. She bent her knees and lowered herself and the baby to the ground.

'I don't feel good,' she murmured.

'I don't care.'

You and your baby are going to die.

Emma tried to hold her baby close, knowing that she was going to blackout. It was too late. Ava rolled onto the grass from her mother's chest where, uninjured but shocked, she started to cry.

Agatha ignored her. Picking up Emma's legs, she pulled her roughly across the field before dumping her outside the stone outhouse. Putting her ear to the door, she shouted to Ben, 'I have someone here to see you!'

Silence.

'I've also met your daughter.'

Still silence.

Walking back across the field, Agatha picked up a crying Ava. Guzzle had been nuzzling the child, trying to offer comfort.

'Shut up!'

Agatha carried the baby under her arm and strode back to the outhouse. Placing the screaming baby on the grass, she removed Emma's clothes, leaving only her underwear. The same item of clothing her father left his victims in, and the same clothing they had left him in to perish.

Leaving the baby clothed, she wrapped her in the pink blanket that Emma had wrapped her in when she had lovingly lifted her from the car. Unlocking the large door, she could see that Ben was still unconscious and lying in the same position she had left him in earlier. Lying on his back.

Grabbing Emma's legs, she heaved her into the cold stone tomb next to Ben. She had kept her word. Emma could now see Ben, even if they were both drugged.

Next, she picked up a wailing Ava. She placed the baby in between its parents. Hopefully, that might shut it up. The baby was a concern. Her maman might hear it if she came to feed the chickens or pigs.

Should I kill the baby now or let the family die together?

She looked at the pigpen. The pigs would take only minutes to dispose of a baby.

Guzzle barked and started to run towards the farmhouse. Her maman was coming back.

Merde! Emma's car is parked out the front. How will I explain that?

Quickly, she gathered Emma's clothes and bag and moved them out of sight. She'd hide them under her bed later.

She would have to think more about Ava. For now, she closed and locked the heavy door and headed back to see her maman. She had to make sure that Faith didn't go near the stone outhouse.

Otherwise, I might have to kill her too.

Chapter Eighteen

The burger and fries are delicious. It's not my usual food of pasta, chicken and fish dishes, with lots of homemade bread.

Tom Quick governs my thoughts. There is something dangerous and exciting behind those brown eyes. I won't message him tomorrow. He is a man who is used to getting what he wants. I'll make him wait.

The drive back is so peaceful. The winding rural roads are quiet, and sheep with their lambs are a common sight in field after field. It's about three months since lambing season and I can see the lambs are now a good size. Some of the sheep have blue or red dots sprayed on their backs. Blue means they were carrying a single lamb and red means twins or triplets. It's a colourful sight.

Since I was young, I used to daydream about what it would be like to murder someone.

My birth mother murdered her boyfriend and, as he lay dying, she poured bleach down his throat. That was the reason I was adopted by Martha and James Taylor. They were great parents. I inherited their home and money when they passed. Most of it went on buying and renovating Crow Springs Farm.

Yet I never felt I belonged with my adopted parents. They were too kind.

I've always liked my environment clean and very tidy; some might describe it as sterile. William Channing had kept me in a filthy dark and damp room. After my escape, my need for cleanliness was magnified. Now, my home is cleaned daily and most of the décor and furnishing is pure white.

I know it is a compulsion which started in my childhood. I would tidy my bedroom, then tidy it again, to alleviate the bad thoughts. Intrusive thoughts about killing.

When William lay dying, I was going to save him. I would never have let him leave the stone outhouse but I would have let him live longer. Looking back, it wasn't my guilt that wanted to save him; it was wanting to show Agatha what empathy looked like. I could sense that she was enjoying her father's suffering. I felt the same.

Watching his body liquefy as he starved to death didn't leave me feeling fulfilled. I want to take someone's life with my own hands. To see the fear in their eyes and to feel life spill from their body. I find the thoughts arousing.

I want to watch Tom Quick as the last breath leaves his body. Living at Crow Springs Farm is so peaceful and private, and it is the perfect location to dispose of a body.

A hawk flies overhead before suddenly dropping to the earth. In the rearview mirror, I watch it pause momentarily before soaring off with what looks like a mouse in its claws. I admire how it takes its prey by surprise. I will remember that.

Pulling into my drive, I can see the front of my farmhouse and something is wrong. There is a white Volkswagen Up parked outside. We never get visitors. Whoever that vehicle belongs to is not local. That's a city car.

Pulling up behind, I take a closer look. Leaving my shopping in the car, I walk towards the unfamiliar vehicle. There's a baby seat in the back. Why do I think this has something to do with Agatha?

Guzzle greets me at the front door, bounding around from the back of the house. Just behind him is Agatha.

'Hi, Maman. Did you have a good trip?'

I ignore the question.

'Do we have guests?' I gesture towards the car.

'No, someone broke down just at the end of our road and we pushed the car to safety here.'

She's smiling. She knows I know she is lying as the car is perfectly parked. That is Agatha. She blatantly lies and doesn't care if you catch her out.

I continue to head towards the kitchen. There is something out of place. A glass with a blue liquid in it and another on the side near the sink.

'Tell me more about the breakdown. Whose car is it?'

I can see the annoyance on her face.

'It was some young girl. She broke down and her dad came and picked her up. They are coming back for the car in a few days when they can get a mechanic out.'

'Was she on her own?' I'm staring into her eyes and she isn't blinking. Another sign that what she is about to say isn't true.

'Why so many questions, Maman?' Agatha shakes her head. 'No, just her.'

'And you invited her in?'

Agatha pauses before answering. Her eyes move to the glass on the table.

'Yes, it's a warm day. I made her a blueberry drink. Did you get the cable ties?'

She's trying to change the subject.

'That was very kind of you. You've never invited anyone in before.'

Not invited, Maman. Kidnapped, yes. I hope you don't meet Ben and his little family.

'Cable ties. Did you get any?' Agatha is making it clear that the conversation regarding the car is over.

'I did. Would you like me to help you in the greenhouse? There are quite a few tomato plants.'

I know the answer before it comes. Neither do I believe that the cable ties are for the plants.

'No, thank you, Maman. I'm going to go to my room now.'

Agatha kisses me on both cheeks and leaves the room. She rarely kisses me.

I watch her leave the room before picking up the glass on the table. It has a faint pink lipstick mark on it. I sniff the glass and it smells of blueberries. Placing it in the sink along with the other glass, I run hot soapy water and will leave them to soak. Turning, I head back out of the kitchen and out through the front door.

I want to check the mystery car to make sure that there isn't a body in the boot.

Chapter Nineteen

Tom pulled his black BMW X5 onto his drive and killed the engine. It was only 4 pm but his boss, George Shakespeare, the Leader of Northshireland County Council, was on leave for another five days to celebrate his 60th birthday. In Tom's world, that meant he wasn't accountable to anyone, even on a Sunday, if the Leader or one of his directors rang him. He could do, and would do, what he wanted. He cared little about what the residents of his borough thought.

Walking into his luxury home, he headed straight for the front room and dropped his keys on the coffee table. It was a beautiful room, with olive settees against the pale grey walls. Lil had chosen the colour scheme. It was one of the few things he had allowed her to decide.

'Lil?'

Silence.

Annoyed, he tried the kitchen. It was a huge space with traditional white country-kitchen units, black granite worktops and a white granite island. The kitchen led into a vast orangery which had three large sofas, a television, glass side tables and large palms in terracotta pots. Lil was asleep on the middle sofa.

Tom stood for a moment, watching the sleeping woman and picturing Faith's face. He felt aroused for the second time that day.

Marching over, he grabbed Lil by the hair. 'Get up!'

Lil jumped, disorientated. 'Sorry, Tom. What time is it?'

Tom didn't answer. He hauled her to her feet and started to lead her quickly out of the room and through the kitchen.

'Tom! You are hurting me. Stop!'

He increased the grip on her hair. They were at the bottom of the stairs before he spoke and let go of her. 'Bedroom. Now.'

Roughly, he pushed her towards the bottom step of the stairs. Lil's heart sank. She knew what was coming. She also knew that, to survive the humiliation, she had to go to that place in her head where no one could hurt her, and she was safe.

She had learned over the years to switch off. She'd think about when she was young and the days they had spent at the beach, with her dad playing with her in the sea and her mam wiping sand from her hands before she ate her chips.

Slowly, she lifted her foot and started to climb the stairs. Tom was behind her, calling her names and belittling her. 'Come on, you fat bitch. Hurry up. You are lucky to have me. Don't you forget it.'

Remaining silent, Lil headed into the bedroom. It was always over quicker then.

'Strip!'

She started to fantasise that it was a warm day and her mam was gently rubbing suntan lotion into her pale skin. Removing her jeans, she mindlessly stepped out of them. Next, she slowly unbuttoned her white shirt and dropped it to the floor.

Tom watched her every move. Smiling, he could see that she was uncomfortable.

'Look at me!'

She moved her eyes to Tom's.

'Now, take your underwear off, slowly.'

She could do this. Her mind allowed the sun on her back and the warm sand beneath her feet. Unbuttoning her white bra, she let it fall from her body before removing her matching knickers. She stood naked.

'Get on the bed, bitch. Splay your legs and arms.'

She complied.

Tom went to the bottom drawer of his bedside cabinet. He removed four lengths of rope. Taking his time, he secured her arms and legs to the bedposts, tightly.

He stood back, picturing Faith's face instead of Lil's.

'You will not enjoy what is about to happen. First, I am going to take photos of you. These will be shared if you ever cheat or try to leave me. Then I am going to do my favourite thing to you.'

Without further explanation, he walked to the side of the bedroom and picked up his backpack, tipping his gym kit onto the floor. Walking over to Lil, he placed the bag over her head and zipped it as far as it would go. He loved that part. He would take her roughly and only release her head when her lips turned blue. He loved watching her gasp for breath.

Lil's body remained motionless as her mind enjoyed running in the cold sea with her father.

Chapter Twenty

Ben woke, cold and confused. He was so tired.

Am I still asleep? Did the crying wake me?

He could hear the cries of a baby. Opening his eyes, panic surged through him. It was still dark.

Am I blind?

Pushing himself up to sitting, he felt the cold hard surface beneath his hand and felt the same coldness on his legs. He wasn't blind. He was surrounded by a thick darkness apart from a chink of light coming from under, what must be, the door.

Agatha.

His mind was slowly focusing. He remembered being in her car and hearing her voice as he blacked out.

The noise is so loud.

Feeling around him, he felt something soft. It was the source of the noise. Tentatively, he felt for the head and moved his hands a little further down. Gently, he picked it up.

'There, there.' His words were slurred.

The noise didn't stop.

Feeling the soft skin, he tried to mollify the baby by stroking its head and the side of its face. The baby moved its head and started to hungrily suck on Ben's finger.

What is going on? Why am I in the darkness with a baby? Is this real?

He felt so tired and disorientated.

Ava!

Within the sluggishness of his mind, he remembered that he was a father.

Is this my baby? If so, where is Emma?

Keeping the crying infant tightly to his chest with one arm, he felt around the stone floor with the other. Nothing to his right side. To his left, he felt cold flesh. He recognised the feel of her hair and the plumpness of her face.

Is she naked?

Anxiety gripped him. Feeling along the cool skin, he felt that she was wearing her bra. It was damp and her breasts were lactating.

'Emma, Emma!'

Gently, he shook her shoulder. No response.

Feeling for her chest, he removed one of her breasts and gently placed Ava on her. Silence filled the darkness and all he could hear was the gentle sound of the baby suckling.

His body ached. He couldn't move as he held a protective hand on Ava's back, making sure his daughter didn't roll. The movement was draining his energy and his arms and legs were hard to control. The muscles relaxed.

He wasn't sure how big the cold hard enclosure was or why his baby and ex-partner were there. He was so thirsty. He needed to sleep.

No, I can't sleep. I need to protect my baby.

Ben's arm gently fell from the feeding Ava and slid to the floor as sleep overpowered him.

*

Agatha was restless. She wanted to go over to the stone outhouse and see if you could hear a crying baby. Yet she knew that would raise Maman's suspicions and she didn't want her interfering in her fun.

They were both in the front room where everything, including the décor, was white and pristine. Faith was on her laptop.

'Are you working, Maman?'

Faith paused, lost in thought.

'Er, yes.'

Her screen didn't show orders for her homemade jams or inspiration for a new flavour. Instead, it had a photo of an extremely toxic plant which, in severe cases when eaten, can cause heart problems and kidney failure. It looked a little like wild garlic with small bell-shaped flowers. Convallaria Majalis, known as 'Lily of the Valley', was common in the UK and grew on her farm.

Perfect.

Faith loved experimenting.

'Do you have lots of orders? I'm happy to take care of the pigpen and chickens again tomorrow.'

'Thank you, Agatha. That would be helpful.'

Faith watched her only child, stretched out on the sofa and reading a psychological novel she had bought her for her birthday, last year. 'Trois Jours et Une Vie' by Pierre Lemaitre was about a child who killed his friend by mistake.

Agatha liked to speak and read French. She had a slight French accent, mixed with the northern accent, which revealed that she had not lived her childhood in the UK.

She rarely helps me out. Suddenly she is offering support for two days running. I know I should start watching her more closely but I won't. My focus has moved to Tom Quick and, tomorrow, I'm going to carefully pick some Lily of the Valley and place them in a vase. I've just read that water will absorb the toxins.

I can't wait to see the side effects.

Chapter Twenty-One

I wake, feeling happy for a Monday.

Switching on my mobile phone, I type in a message. 'Good morning. I have a couple of hours free today. Coffee in Alnwick?'

I deliberately don't add my name and send it to the number on his business card. Saving his number to my contacts as May Bells, another name for Lily of the Valley.

It is 8 am. I doubt a man of power and control will sleep in late. He will be working.

No reply.

Leaving the phone on my bedside cabinet, I head for the shower. There's someone downstairs. I follow the noise and shout down. 'Agatha is that you?'

Guzzle bounds up the stairs with his tail wagging.

'Get down!'

He knows he isn't allowed upstairs. Instead, he turns on the stairs and runs happily up and down a few times, making me laugh. Agatha appears at the bottom of the stairs.

'Morning, Maman. Do you have plans today?'

'Morning. I was thinking about driving into Alnwick again. I had a lovely lunch there yesterday.'

Agatha smiles as she calculates that Faith will be gone for at least three hours.

'Nice to see you going out, Maman. I'm just off to feed the pigs and chickens. Then shall we have some breakfast together?'

We never eat breakfast together.

'That would be nice. Shall I make omelettes?' I ask.

'Yes, please. I'll be about half an hour,' she replies.

'Okay, I'll just jump in the shower first.'

'See you soon. Come on, Guzzle.'

Agatha smiles and tries to hide her excitement as, finally, she will be able to check out how her guests are enjoying the stone outhouse. No breakfast for them. The accommodation doesn't come with any food or amenities. No breakfast for the pigs either. She needs them to be hungry for their large meal later today.

I watch my daughter walk across the field from the upstairs window. Guzzle is running around doing his own thing. I can't quite see the pigpen from here. At least she is finally helping me out. That will give me time to myself.

Turning away from the rural view, which I never tire of, I head to the shower. Like most of my home, the bathroom is white. Turning on the shower, I hang my robe on the back of the door and step in.

The water is warm and rejuvenating. Reaching for my razor, I shave my legs. Ready for when Tom messages me back. I know he will.

I can sense it.

*

Tom Quick had been up since 5 am. He did a morning workout in his home gym and was just getting showered and dressed for the day when Faith messaged. There was no work that day as he was on annual leave. It was a special day. He was meant to be going to his mother's 80th birthday lunch, and then the party with Lil. Not that he could take her. Not the way she looked.

Last night, after he had removed the sports bag from her head and untied her hands and feet, she had lashed out at him for the first time.

That was not how he expected her to behave. It was unacceptable conduct. Tom had thoroughly enjoyed himself, fantasising that she was Faith. It had been the best sex they had ever had.

He had dealt with Lil's insolence by pulling one of the ropes tightly around her neck until she had lost consciousness, followed by repeated punches to her head, face and stomach. Now his hands hurt because of her. She couldn't go looking like that, with her injured face. She was still in bed.

Lazy bitch.

At 9 am, he responded to the message.

An hour is enough time to make someone wait for a reply.

'See you at The Plough at noon. I'm paying.'

He would call to see his mother, miss the party, and spend the afternoon in bed with Faith.

*

I hear my phone ping just after 9 am and immediately read the message. I reply, 'Can't wait.'

The drive will take me 45-60 minutes, depending on the traffic and tourists. That gives me two hours before I need to leave.

There are a couple of things I need to do in that time. Firstly, I'm going to pack an overnight bag and, secondly, I'm going to go into my front garden and pick the Lily of the Valley and place them in a vase with only a small amount of water. Then, just before I leave, I will pour the water into a bottle and take it with me.

But first; I need to make omelettes and have breakfast with Agatha.

Chapter Twenty-Two

Ben woke to a crying Ava.

He felt so groggy at first that he didn't respond. Then he remembered that he was no longer alone. Placing his hand out to feel for the baby he had left on Emma's chest, he could only feel the chill of her bare skin. No Ava.

Ignoring his thirst, he pulled himself onto all fours and felt around in the darkness. The cries intensified.

'It's okay, Ava. Daddy is coming.'

His hands swept the cold hard floor but all he could feel was space and Emma.

'Emma! Wake up, Emma!' Ben shook her shoulder as hard as he could.

Reaching over her body in the pitch dark, he searched the floor. His hand hit, what he presumed was, the distressed baby's blanket. Gently, he felt around and picked up the infant. The baby had rolled across her mother's body and had been lying facedown.

'Shush, it's okay.'

Ben held his baby tightly to his chest. He could feel something sticky on her forehead. Congealed blood. The baby had a head injury.

Emma began to stir. Ben had hoped the sound of her hungry baby would have woken her sooner. He had no idea what Agatha had given her.

'Why can't I see?' Emma struggled to get the words out. Ben sensed that she was also trying to stand up.

'Emma, we are in a dark building or something. Stay calm. I'm here.'

She sat back down and stretched out a hand. Ben found it and they embraced, with Ava between them. Her crying was ear-piercing.

'Do you think you can feed her?'

Emma nodded in response and then remembered that Ben couldn't see her.

'Yes, pass her to me.'

Ava was handed to her mother and soon latched on. The silence was more deafening than the crying, seconds before.

'Why are we here, Ben? I don't feel too good. I'm so thirsty.'

'I don't know why. I can't remember how I got here. I just know I went to the outdoor concert with Agatha and wanted to phone you as soon as I could. We got into her Land Rover and she was going to drop me off. Then I woke up in here, in only my underwear. I've spoken to her through the door. She told me to drink the water she'd left. Don't drink it, it's drugged. How did you get here?'

'You didn't call or message, so I tracked your phone to the farmhouse.'

'We are at a farm?'

'Yes, this is where Agatha lives. She let me in and offered me a drink. She said she was going to take me to see you. We walked across a field and I remember seeing a pigpen, a chicken run and a stone building.'

'I thought I could hear a weird noise sometimes. It must be the pigs.'

'She also said you wanted a relationship, and she didn't. That you were doing some work here,' continued Emma.

'What! No. We weren't even going out. Just a few dates. That's all.'

'I'm sorry I pushed you away and kept Ava a secret.' Tears rolled from Emma's tired eyes.

'We'll get through this, Emma. We can start now. Let's be a family. I've missed you so much.'

They tightened their embrace but were careful not to crush Ava, who was starting to fall asleep.

'She needs changing,' said Emma.

'We'll wait until Agatha comes back and try and reason with her. There's two of us and only one of her,' Ben replied.

What they didn't know was that Agatha had been outside the heavy door for most of their conversation. She couldn't make out their words but it didn't matter. She knew that they were awake and conversing.

Just like old times for the two of you. Don't get comfortable, as one of you is going to die in the next few hours.

She turned away and started to head back to the farmhouse, with Guzzle running ahead.

She had an omelette to eat.

Chapter Twenty-Three

Lil Hunt pretended to be asleep.

She could hear Tom showering in their ensuite. Normally, she was never still in bed after 9 am on a Monday. Instead, she would normally be heading back home after her Yin Yoga class. Today was different. Today, Tom Quick had gone too far.

It hurt to breathe. Her stomach ached and, when she first woke, her face was stuck to the pillow with congealed blood. She knew it was his mother's 80th birthday lunch followed by a party today. Hopefully, he would be gone in the next hour. She was then going to pack a bag and leave him.

Her plan was to get in the car and head off to Wales. It was a place she had never visited but had heard that parts of it were rural and beautiful. She'd find a B&B. She had never asked why people paid Tom in cash but he kept a lot of it in the bottom drawer of his desk. She was going to take about £2,000.

'Get up, you lazy bitch,' scorned Tom.

Lil's heart rate increased. He was standing next to the bed. Abruptly, the covers were pulled back, exposing her battered naked body.

'Get up,' he commanded.

Slowly, she swung her legs over the side of the bed using her hands to come to a sitting position. Pain shot into her abdomen and ribs.

'Stand up and face me,' scorned Tom. He loved humiliating her. It gave him such a buzz.

Lil stood with her gaze lowered to the floor.

'Stand up straight. Pull your shoulders back,' he shouted.

Lil did as she was ordered. Her face showed the pain she was in. Tom stared at his battered partner and smiled. He could see the bruising on her torso and face.

'Look at the state of you. You did that to yourself. That will teach you to raise your hands to me. Now, apologise for being a bitch.'

'Sorry,' mumbled Lil.

'Like you mean it,' said Tom.

'I'm sorry, Tom.'

'You are too ugly to be seen with me, so you will stay in. I'm going out for the day and probably won't be back tonight as I have a date. I plan on having sex with them and will tell you all about it when I decide to come back home. Don't even think about leaving this house as I'm locking the doors and taking your phone, house and car keys with me.'

Lil's heart sank.

'Now, tidy up this bedroom and clean the ensuite.'

Lil slowly moved towards her robe which was hanging on the back of their bedroom door.

'What are you doing?' bellowed Tom.

'Getting my robe,' whispered Lil.

'Did I say you could wear your robe? Did I?'

Lil shook her head.

Grabbing her by the hair, he dragged her into the ensuite and pushed her onto the floor.

'You will clean the floor as you are.'

Lil stayed still and pictured the beach. Her dad was there! A 6-year-old Lil ran over to him as he handed her a large ice cream with a chocolate flake in it. Then they walked hand-in-hand over to her mam and he handed her an ice cream too.

Tom watched as Lil remained motionless. He thought about handing out more pain and humiliation, but his hands were still sore from the punches he had subjected her to. Besides, he didn't want to be late for Faith. He wanted her to meet the charming, humorous and charismatic Tom Quick.

Lashing out with a kick, which connected with his partner's side, he turned and left the room.

Lil remained in her own mind, eating creamy ice cream which was running down her little hand and arm. Her fantasy ended when she heard the front door and then, moments later, Tom's car as it drove over the pebbled drive.

Pulling herself off the floor, she headed back to bed. She was in too much pain to move, and she knew he would have locked her in. There was no escape. When the time was right, she knew what to do.

Kill him.

Chapter Twenty-Four

I'm eager to see what the day will bring. I have packed an overnight bag, for the first time!

I've also styled my mousy brown hair and put a little makeup on. Too much and Agatha will be asking questions. I'm wearing blue jeans, a white shirt and flat strappy sandals. Slightly overweight but not too bad for nearly 48 years of age.

Setting the table, I am waiting for Agatha. For breakfast, I have prepared a mushroom omelette with spinach and avocado on the side. A bunch of sweet-scented Lily of the Valley stands in the centre. Such a delicate beautiful flower, yet deadly.

Guzzle bounds into the kitchen. He knows I've made him a plain omelette. I always do.

'Smells good, Maman,' says Agatha.

'Take a seat. I hope you have washed your hands.'

'Maman! I'm not five years old. Yes, I've washed them!'

I smile and place her food in front of her. The coffee is already on the table.

'Santé!' says Agatha, raising her coffee cup.

'Cheers!' I respond in English.

'What are your plans while I'm in Alnwick?' I ask.

'I need to clean the pigpen and collect the eggs from the chickens. Do you need me to do anything else?'

'Can you water the greenhouse please and feed Guzzle later?'

'Sure. When are you back?'

'I'm not too sure. I was thinking about maybe staying over.'

Agatha's head snaps up. Her fork is poised motionless in front of her open mouth.

'Maman, you never stay out. Who is he?' she shrieks.

I keep my cool.

'There's no one. I just fancy a change of scenery.'

'Okay. If you say so.'

'Finish your breakfast, please. I want to tidy everything before I leave.'

Agatha says nothing and she looks deep in thought. Whatever she is up to, she'll have free reign today. The thought is slightly unsettling but the lure of Tom Quick is too strong to ignore.

Agatha places her knife and fork together.

'Thank you, Maman. Can I go to my room, please?'

'Sure.'

Leaving a third of my breakfast, I'm too excited to eat so I clear the plates away. Guzzle is grateful for my leftover omelette. I load our plates and cups into the dishwasher and wipe the kitchen bench down. Pristine again.

Taking a metal water bottle from the cupboard, I pour in the water from the vase. I then squeeze in six berries from the plant. This is going to be a fun day.

Carefully placing the water bottle in my large tote bag, I head out of the kitchen. Standing at the bottom of the stairs, I shout up to Agatha. 'I'm off now. Not sure when I'll be back but don't worry, I'll be fine. I have my phone.'

Agatha appears at the top of the stairs. 'Have fun.' She smiles.

'Thank you. Enjoy your day.'

'I plan on having a great day,' she replies.

'Don't do anything I wouldn't do,' I joke.

'Absolutely.'

'Bye, then.'

'Bye, Maman.'

I feel uneasy leaving her. She will be nineteen on her next birthday and it is time she fends for herself and helps me more around the farm. But being helpful or kind doesn't come naturally to her.

Cruel and impulsive. Yes.

I turn up the radio in the car. 'Absolute 80s' is my favourite station. Frankie Goes to Hollywood and their huge hit 'Relax' is playing. That is exactly what I intend to do as I head towards the alluring Tom Quick.

Chapter Twenty-Five

With a sneer on her face, Agatha watched her maman pull away. She was thrilled that she could have a killing day without being interrupted.

It was all planned in her mind. It was over two years since she had helped dispose of her father's corpse. That was a long time to carry a longing to harm and murder another person.

She started to pull her killing kit together.

The discarded sock still lay on the bedroom floor. She liked to keep it there. Looking inside, the small numbered pieces of paper were still there. She knew off by heart what they stood for.

1. Recreate William's death
2. Blindfold them, have sex and then stab them repeatedly
3. Drown them

Opening her bedside cabinet, she removed her stash of Rohypnol, cable ties and another small piece of paper. She wrote a number on it and, after carefully folding it, placed it into the sock.

'I need to add to my list,' said Agatha out loud to herself.

It was number 4.

4. Slash their throat (females only)

'This is so much fun,' she shrieked to herself.

Looking at her watch, she noted it was after 11.30 am. Time to feed those pigs.

*

Ben and Emma had fallen asleep with Ava snuggled gently between them. Earlier, they had complained of headaches and their heart rates had slowed.

The hard cold ground bit into their hips and backs. Their bodies were covered in dust, their stomachs rumbled with hunger and their throats were dry from dehydration.

They were also covered in urine and excrement. Ava's nappy needed changing but she had no protection and her waste matter had to flow freely. Her blanket still kept her top half warm.

Emma started to stir. 'Ben, are you awake?'

No reply.

She raised her voice. 'Ben!'

'I'm awake.' He sounded groggy.

'Ben, we need to escape. I'm so thirsty and cold. My fear is that if I don't eat or drink soon, I won't be able to produce milk for Ava. She has just peed on me again.'

'Okay. When Agatha comes back, I'll ask her to let you and Ava go.'

'No, Ben! We go together. Can't the two of us overpower her?'

'I don't know, Emma. My legs and arms feel weak.'

The sound of the bolt stopped their conversation. Agatha had arrived. She had only opened the door a fraction. She had placed a large rock behind it in case they tried to overpower her.

'It smells worse than the pigpen in here,' she laughed. 'Don't try anything stupid. I have a gun.' She didn't. But she did have her killing kit and a very large sharp kitchen knife.

'Do you both know why you are here?'

She didn't give them a chance to answer before continuing, 'Ben and I could have had something special, until you turned up in The Swan, Emma, making him late for our date.'

'I'm sorry. I just wanted to tell him about his daughter.'

'Shut up!' yelled Agatha. She could feel an angry outburst building within her.

This is all your fault, Emma Beale. You have less than ten minutes to live.

Agatha took a step back and pulled off her backpack. She needed her special sock. Now. She found it and drove her hand in, looking for a number. Grabbing a piece of paper, she pulled it out and immediately opened it.

Number 1.

'No. I've already done that,' she said to herself.

Putting her hand in again, she pulled two more out.

Number 2.

'No, I'm not sleeping with a girl.'

Ben and Emma remained silent. They were confused about what was happening but they could sense Agatha's anger.

'Yes!' she yelled.

It was Number 4.

Her anger dipped slightly and she felt in control again.

'I have decided that one of you may leave. You can decide between you. The baby doesn't count.'

She knew this was part of the game as there was no way that Ben wouldn't let Emma go.

'You have to go, Emma. Take Ava with you,' Ben said.

'No, Ben! I don't trust her. Let's stay together. Let's see if we can push the door open and then make a run for it. She can't catch us both at once,' whispered Emma.

'What about the gun?'

'Do you believe her?'

'I don't know. She's crazy.'

'I'm getting bored,' called Agatha. 'If one of you doesn't leave in the next ten seconds, I'm closing this door and not opening it for a month. In that time, your bodies will have broken down and you will die slowly and painfully from starvation. Trust me. You won't be my first victim.'

'I love you, Emma. You go,' said Ben, hugging her tightly.

'I'm not leaving you. We will go together. Walk with me to the door and, when I say, let's push it open and run. I'll take Ava.'

'Okay,' whispered Ben.

Together they walked from the darkness towards a psychopath with a killing kit.

'Which one of you is leaving?' asked Agatha, even though she was sure of the answer.

'Please let Emma and Ava go,' Ben replied, shielding his eyes from the daylight behind the slightly open door.

'No! I said just one of you. The baby stays.' There was a dangerous anger in her voice.

Emma and Ben exchanged a look.

'Okay, Emma will go. Do you promise to at least provide baby milk for Ava?' asked Ben, hopefully.

Agatha laughed aloud. 'Don't be stupid!' she said.

Leaning slightly forward, she grabbed Emma by the arm and pulled her through the gap in the door. Ava nearly fell to the ground, while her mother struggled to hold her firmly with one arm. She had no intention of leaving her daughter behind.

'Ben, now!' yelled Emma.

Pushing Agatha with her shoulder, Emma moved away from the door to allow Ben to come through. But she wasn't quick enough.

Agatha sensed what was about to happen and, without hesitation, pushed the rock with her foot closer to the door. The gap was too narrow and Ben couldn't make it out.

Emma started to run.

Enraged, Agatha tried to slam the door shut. Ben let out an animalistic cry. His arm had been in the way. Withdrawing it quickly, he fell to the ground just as Agatha closed and bolted the door shut.

Turning around, she could see the plump Emma trying to run for her life with a 4-month-old infant in her arms.

You silly girl. You have really pissed me off.

Agatha's willowy frame bolted after her, but not before she had snatched up the killing kit.

'I'm going to kill you,' yelled Agatha.

Terrified, Emma ran as fast as she could with the effects of Rohypnol still in her system. Ava, startled by the sudden movement, bawled.

'I'm coming for you,' roared Agatha, well aware that they were the same words her father, a psychotic serial killer, had said to her not long before he perished.

And she did.

Emma made it easy for her. Losing her footing, she crashed down and landed on her side as she tried to protect her baby. Agatha was on her within seconds. A fierce predator bringing down its prey.

Emma curled into the foetal position, clinging tightly to Ava. She was ready to give her life to protect her baby.

And she did.

Agatha straddled Emma before pulling the large kitchen knife from her killing kit. Grabbing her by the hair, she pulled her head back to expose her throat.

Emma screamed.

'Number 4, slash their throat (females only),' raged Agatha. She drew the knife deeply across the terrified mother's throat. Blood gushed from the gaping wound and the only sound from Emma was her choking.

Agatha stood over her and watched her take her last breaths.

'You should have let me have Ben,' she said, coldly. 'I want you to know that I'm going to kill Ben and your baby.'

Emma held her bloody hand out, trying to pull Ava closer and away from the monster standing over her. She was too late. She died with her arm outstretched, inches from her child.

Agatha looked around. As expected, there was no one in sight. They lived miles away from the next farm or people.

Ignoring the screaming Ava, she grabbed Emma by the legs and started to drag her towards the pigpen. She hoped her maman wouldn't notice all the blood spilt on the grass.

It was time to feed the pigs.

Chapter Twenty-Six

The drive to Alnwick is picturesque and peaceful. With twenty minutes to spare, I stay in the car to check my makeup and then check it again. Putting the necessary Northumberland parking disc on display, I decide to take a slow walk from the long-stay car park and arrive early. I'm going to order the wine and wait for him at the table he has booked. I want to see his reaction.

My overnight bag, for now, will stay in the car even though I have no intention of going home tonight. I can sense how this will go.

Climbing the familiar steps to The Plough, I head to the end of the bar and am greeted by a young dark-haired man.

'Hello,' he smiles. 'Do you have a table booked?'

'Yes, the name is Quick.'

'You are upstairs. Let me show you to your table.'

He leads the way and I follow him up the stairs in silence. I feel nervous, mixed with excitement.

Entering the upstairs dining area, I pause momentarily. Tom Quick is already seated at a table in the window. He looks up and smiles slowly at me. We are in matching outfits. He's wearing a white shirt with the top two buttons open, and dark blue jeans.

There is a bottle of red wine on the table and two glasses. He remains seated and watches me as I move towards him.

'Thank you,' I say, dismissing the young man who has shown me to the table. Tom stands up and walks around the small table, towards me.

'Faith, you look lovely.' He hugs me tightly. I can feel his strength and he smells great.

'Thank you. You do too. I see we got the same memo about what to wear!' I joke.

'Yes, we seem to be naturally in sync with each other.' He picks up the bottle of Malbec and pours me a glass, maintaining eye contact. I notice that the back of his knuckles on both hands look sore.

'Thank you,' I say, picking up the large glass and taking a sip. It tastes great. He watches me for a moment before picking up the menu.

'Let's eat,' he says.

I have noticed that he talks in commands.

I'm not hungry as it has only been a couple of hours since I had breakfast with Agatha. Ignoring the main meals, I look for the light bites section which most menus have. They do paninis, along with fries, salad and coleslaw.

'I'll have the chicken, pesto, tomato and mozzarella panini, please.'

'Are you eating it here or taking it with you?' He isn't smiling. His eyes flash with anger. It is a threat that I am not to leave this time.

He is threatening the wrong woman.

I don't like your tone, Tom Quick. Are you a danger to women? Is that what I'm sensing here?

'You are about to find out,' I say, smiling at him and deliberately shrugging my shoulders. I'm wondering how I can get some of the toxic water into his drink, if necessary.

You won't be as intimidating then, Tom Quick. When you are vomiting with severe stomach pains.

A young blonde waitress appears at our table. 'Are you ready to order?' she asks.

'Yes, please. I'll have the chicken and mozzarella panini, please.'

I smile at Tom. I purposely ordered first. He is watching, stone-faced.

You need to learn, Tom Quick, that I have a voice.

'It comes with pesto and tomato too. Is that okay?'

'Yes, lovely. Thank you. And for you, Tom?'

The waitress scribbles down my order. I'm trying not to smile. Tom looks confused as to what has just happened. This is a man who obviously controls and dominates.

I'm going to enjoy breaking you down, Tom Quick.

'I'll have the BBQ pulled pork and cheddar panini.' He makes no eye contact with the waitress or even says please.

'It won't be too long. Can I get you any more drinks?'

'Not yet,' comes his reply. There is silence between us as she leaves. I have no intention of filling it and I wait to hear what he has to say.

'When we go out next time, Faith, wait for me to order for us both. That is how it is. That is my way.'

'What if I don't want you to do that? You might order something I don't like.'

'I won't. I'm never wrong.'

You are wrong if you think you can intimidate and control me. Eventually, it will cost you your existence.

I decide to stir him up just a little. 'Your hands look sore. Did things get heated at work? Is that how you sort out differences? Fisty cuffs in the car park?' I laugh because I think it's a funny image.

He looks at the back of one hand and then the other. 'I hit someone repeatedly who deserved it.'

'Who?' I ask.

He starts to laugh.

'Your face,' he says. 'You look so shocked. I was doing the gardening yesterday and I caught my hands a few times laying flagstones.'

I don't believe him.

'Poor you.' I'm flirting now. 'I'll rub them better later for you.'

Tom isn't the only one at this table who can use artificial charm.

'I look forward to it. I've booked us a room.'

It was what I had expected yet, hearing it out loud, it slightly unnerves me.

'Does that come with wine too?' I smile.

'No. I've ordered champagne for the room.'

The paninis arrive. They look good and my appetite has now increased.

'Bon Appetit,' I say.

'Enjoy,' he replies.

I take a small bite. It is hot and appetising.

'Don't eat too much. We will be going to our room soon. Check-in is usually 3 pm but they know who I am so the rule doesn't apply to me,' he says conceitedly.

'Can't wait,' I say, although that is a lie.

*

Agatha's arms were fatigued and her lower back ached.

'You are one heavy bitch. Did you know that?' she puffed to Emma's corpse.

She had dragged the bloodied body across the field by its ankles towards the pigpen. A scarlet trail marked the way they had come.

Emma's peach sports bra and pants were covered in blood, grass and dirt. Her head bobbed from side to side and her throat gaped open. Agatha had sliced through her windpipe.

They were near the stone outhouse when Agatha stopped and let Emma's ankles thud to the ground. She could hear shouting. It wasn't Ava although she was still faintly crying in the distance, lying where she had fallen from her dying mother's arms.

Walking to the heavy door, Agatha stood and listened.

'Help! Help!' bellowed Ben.

'Help! Help!' mimicked Agatha.

'Agatha! Let me out. You've gone too far,' he shouted.

'You will come out of there when you are dead. So shut up and save your energy,' she scolded.

'Where's Emma?'

'Emma is here, Ben. She doesn't look great though. In fact, she looks like shit. Do you think that is because I've slit her throat?' She was enjoying herself.

Ben let out another animalistic sound and started to cry.

'That's the game, Ben. She got number 4. Slash their throat (females only). You have to apply some pressure though.'

He didn't respond. Agatha could hear the distraught sounds through the thick door.

'Bye, Ben. I'm off to feed the pigs. They haven't eaten today,' said a cheery Agatha.

'Wait! What about Ava?'

'She's alive. Do you want her, Ben?'

'Yes! Agatha, please don't harm her,' begged Ben.

Agatha paused while she processed what to do with the baby. 'Okay, let me dump Emma into the pigpen and I'll get the screaming baby for you.'

'You can't feed Emma to the pigs. Agatha, no!'

'Ben, you have one choice. You can have Emma in there with you or that baby. Which one?' She was enjoying the psychological cruelty of the situation. Ben's tears intensified.

'Ben, hurry up and decide. I have to have a shower and move Emma's car.'

'Ava.'

Agatha just about heard his murmured response the first time. 'What was that? You need to speak up as this door is pretty thick.'

This is fun.

'Ava,' came his louder response.

'Okay, Ben. You've decided that we feed Emma to the pigs. I'll do that and then I'll go and find your screaming baby. Back soon.'

Agatha moved from the door and Ben slid down it on the other side. He had never felt emotional pain like it. Sobs racked his body.

Picking up Emma's cold legs, she dragged her through the dirt and over to the pigpen. Max, the dominant boar, moved towards the trough, sensing it was feeding time.

'Hi, Max. I've got something special for you today.'

Agatha bent down, removed the deceased girl's underwear and stuffed it into the back pocket of her jeans. The pigs wouldn't eat it and she didn't want her maman discovering it.

Opening the gate to the enclosure, she dragged the naked corpse into the centre of the sounder of squealing Large White Pigs. Max was the first to bite and pull the flesh away from the bone.

Agatha knew that, in about ten minutes, most of Emma, including her bones, would be devoured. Maybe not her teeth. Last time, when she and her maman fed her father to the pigs, some of his teeth were left behind.

She would find the baby and then check back on the pigs.

Closing the pigpen enclosure securely, she headed back the way she came. The journey was much easier, without a body to drag.

Following the dark stain of Emma's blood, she walked along her own special track. She kept her head down, watching her feet take step after step along the bloodshed. Humming to herself, she was content with her day's achievement.

She stopped at a large dark stain absorbed in the earth. It was the killing site but there was no baby.

She had been so engrossed in following the blood path that she had failed to notice that the baby was no longer in the distance. Confused, she scanned the horizon.

'Merde!' she muttered to herself. Then she saw the baby.

In the distance, Ava was being dragged across the field by a fox. She stood watching the scene while she decided what to do. She was used to seeing foxes around the farm. They often tried to get into the chicken run but they seemed to prefer the eggs rather than the chickens.

It was the baby's fault for crying excessively.

What she witnessed was indeed a problem, as she had told Ben he could have his baby back. That had been the deal. His baby or its mother.

Breaking into a light jog, she ran in the direction of the fox. There was a fence and thick undergrowth at the edge of the field. If the fox dragged the baby through there, she wouldn't be able to follow on foot. She'd have to get her car and drive around.

The land was uneven so she took her time. She didn't want any sprains.

She had already passed the child's discarded favourite pink blanket and had picked it up. There was blood on it and it was hard to tell if it was from Ava or her mother. Listening carefully, Agatha could no longer hear the baby's cries, only the pigs in the distance and the caws of the crows.

Then she saw her.

Ava lay motionless, not far from the brambles, and there was no sign of the fox. Striding over to the infant, Agatha nudged her with her foot.

No response.

There were scratches on her small delicate face, an injury to her forehead and a large bite mark on her leg. It was only when Agatha picked her up roughly under her arms that she saw the blood on the back of her head. She had sustained a nasty head injury. Probably by being dragged along by the fox as there were a lot of large stones in the earth.

'At least you will be quiet now,' said Agatha, as she wrapped the tiny corpse in the blanket before tucking it under her arm to carry back to Ben.

'Time to see your dad. I did say he could have you back.'

*

We have finished our paninis and the bottle of wine.

'Time for bed,' says Tom.

'Sure. Let me get us some drinks for the room. I guess a man like yourself would like a whiskey with a little water. I understand adding water allows the aromas to open up.'

I give him a flirty smile.

Tom doesn't like whiskey. He only drinks wine and the odd real ale.

'That would be lovely, thanks.'

Maintaining eye contact, he slips a room key across the table. 'Your key. I'll see you in bed. I'll settle the lunch bill on my way out.'

Without another word, Tom leaves the table and the restaurant. I wait to make sure he won't be at the bar. I'm going to order a bottle of wine for the room and a neat whiskey for him.

I will add the water.

Chapter Twenty-Seven

Agatha took her time retracing her steps back to Ben and the stone outhouse. Ava was slumped under her arm.

'You are heavy,' said Agatha, to the lifeless infant as she switched arms and sides.

She was at the blood trail. She knew that rain was forecast for the following day but not that day.

'Look what your mammy did. She's made a mess of the field. Never mind. Tomorrow, the rain will wash her away.'

Agatha was humming the French lullaby, 'Are You Sleeping?', known to her as 'Frere Jacques'.

'No, you are not sleeping, are you? You're dead.' She gave Ava a little shake, before shrugging her shoulders. Outside the stone outhouse, she dropped the baby on the ground.

'Back in a moment,' she said. 'I have to check on your mammy, as you say in England.'

She ran happily towards the pigpen.

'Did you enjoy your late breakfast, piggies?' she asked, as she climbed on the bottom rung of the enclosure to take a closer look.

'Wow, you were hungry. I have my very own meat processing facility!' she squealed with maniacal excitement.

There was very little of Emma left. There were chunks of her raven hair tangled on some of the pig's bloodied trotters and many had rosy snouts from her gore. Most were still foraging and crunching her remaining bones.

Agatha watched for a few moments.

I love living on a rural farm where screams go unheard, and bodies are devoured.

Climbing down, she headed to see Ben and unite him with his baby daughter.

She pushed the large rock back into position behind the heavy door allowing enough gap, when it opened, to pass Ava through but keep Ben in. Next, she turned her attention to the lifeless body of the baby, whose face was now pale and waxy.

'You are not a pretty baby,' scolded Agatha, wrapping the blanket tightly around the small frame to make it easier to pass her through the gap. Satisfied the baby would fit, she unlocked the door.

Ben was there, looking through the small gap. His eyes burned against the light after so much darkness.

'Where's Ava?' He sounded jittery.

'Relax, she's here. Stand back and I'll pass her through.'

'What about Emma?'

'In pieces,' grinned Agatha.

'What do you mean?' he asked, confused.

'Literally, she's in pieces. Been torn apart and eaten by some very hungry pigs. You can't blame them, Ben. I was late with their breakfast.'

It was then that Ben vomited. His stomach was cramping as he hadn't had anything to eat or drink in two days.

'Yuk! You have to live in there, Ben. Stop it,' she scolded. She waited until the retching noises had stopped.

'Put your arms through the gap, Ben. Take your baby. My work here is done.'

Two dirty arms appeared. Agatha placed the small body in them and then watched as Ben carefully drew it to himself.

Quickly, Agatha closed the door but not before saying the words.

'She's dead.'

*

I head back down the stairs to the bar.

'What can I get you?' It is the same waiter who greeted me earlier.

'Can I get some drinks for the room, please?'

He tries to keep the smile from his face. I can't help thinking he sees me as another notch on Tom's bed.

'Of course. Would you like to see the drinks menu?'

'No, thanks. Can I have a bottle of Malbec and a whiskey on the rocks, please? I'll leave the type of whiskey to you. Can you charge it to the room?'

I show him the key and he smiles and nods before turning to get the drinks.

This is such a lovely place. Three couples are sitting at tables, eating and drinking. One couple is leaning into each other in their own world of happiness. The other two are eating in silence. They look bored with each other and life.

'I've put them on a small tray for you. Can you manage?'

'Yes, I'm good. Thank you.'

'Do you know the way to your room?'

'Yes, through the door and up some stairs.'

I smile as I take the tray. I've had enough of talking. I want some privacy.

Leaving the bar, I head towards the room. There is a set of drawers in the corridor. Placing the tray down, I remove the water bottle from my bag. Let's see what water contaminated with Lily of the Valley does to an adult. I carefully add two finger widths of the toxic liquid.

Concealing the bottle in the bottom of my bag, I head to the room, carrying the tray carefully. The door is ajar and I push it open with my foot and remain in the doorway.

The room is smaller than I expect. My own bedroom is bigger. There is a small dressing table, a built-in wardrobe and, what I presume is, the door to the bathroom. There's a small table with two chairs in the corner with cups and saucers on it.

There is a double bed with white bedding and a large high brown headboard. A naked man is lying on top of it.

Tom's 6' 3" frame is toned and tanned. His brown eyes are locked on my face and his arms are bent behind his head. He is a very handsome man, and he knows it.

'Take your clothes off.'

It is a command.

I do not like being told what to do. When the Grey Trench Coat Man captured me, nearly two decades ago, he had drugged and abused me. He had been in control. Since then, I have always been in control.

'Shall I close the door first?' I ask, as I stall for time.

'If you want to.'

I enter the room and push the door firmly with my foot. It clicks shut.

'I'm not sure what school of romance you went to, Tom Quick, but I prefer a drink first.'

Walking over to the bed, I place the tray on one of the bedside tables. There's not much room because of a large bedside lamp. Focusing on the tray, and not the naked man on the bed, I pour two small glasses of red wine which was corked at the bar. I pick up one red wine and the whiskey.

'I hope you like it,' I say, handing Tom the whiskey.

'I know I will,' he responds, his eyes indicating that he isn't talking about the drink that I've placed in his hand. He tries to grab my arm but I'm too quick for him.

'Strip and get on the bed,' he demands, smiling.

'Cheers,' I say, slowly taking a sip.

He sniffs at the whiskey before holding the glass up to the light. 'Do you know what I find strange?' he asks.

Just drink the whiskey, Tom. Then we can play a game of cat and mouse. But I am not the mouse.

'What's that?' I ask, smiling.

'This stuff costs a fortune and all it does is burn your throat.'

Not that whiskey, Tom. That is special whiskey. Now, drink it.

'Cheers,' I say, for a second time, and take another sip of the rich red liquid.

Tom gulps the whiskey down.

'In the future, only ever buy me red wine and only when I tell you to.'

He looks annoyed.

I hold his gaze and give him my best 'sorry' smile. Maintaining eye contact, I slowly start to unbutton my white shirt. He watches.

I let it slide from my shoulders and drop to the floor. Slowly, I unbutton my jeans and slip my feet out of my sandals. I push the jeans down my legs and step out of them. I stand facing him in my white lacy underwear and slowly crawl onto the bed to kiss him.

'And your underwear,' he says.

'When I'm ready.'

He looks annoyed with my lack of compliance. Without warning, he moves away from me and picks up a black backpack from his side of the bed. He brings out a navy tie and leaves the bag on the bed.

'Put your hands together in front of you.'

Another command.

'That's not my thing,' I respond.

'Trust me,' he smiles. 'It's fun.'

With his free hand, he reaches forward and pulls my face towards him for a kiss. The chemistry is captivating. I hold out my hands.

'Good girl,' he murmurs. He binds my wrists, tightly.

I go to kiss him again but he pushes me back onto the bed.

'Lift your hips.'

I oblige and he slowly removes my knickers. I can see that he is aroused. He lowers his weight onto me. I can't move and my arms are pinned under his chest. I can feel that he has reached for something. It's the backpack.

'This is part of the game, Faith, do not resist.'

I'm confused, as this is alien to me. It's gone dark. He has pulled the bag over my head. I hear the zip being pulled around it. I'm panicking and I can't breathe.

'Stop!'

It's hard to talk, as his weight is crushing my chest.

Roughly he enters me and I'm powerless to stop him.

Chapter Twenty-Eight

After a shower and change of clothes, Agatha was in high spirits.

It's late afternoon and she's going out. Preferring the solitude of the farm, going out is a rare occasion unless she is on the hunt for vulnerable, accessible and powerless victims.

Emma's blood-stained dirty underwear, clothes and bag were hidden underneath her bed with Ben's work T-shirt from The Swan. Only her Volkswagen Up had to be disposed of.

Agatha knew a place about fifteen minutes' drive away where tourists parked and did long country walks. The small car park was free and had no CCTV. It would take her about an hour to walk back. Picking up her bag which contained the killing kit, she headed happily for the door.

Her hair was tied in a ponytail and she was dressed in black leggings, a T-shirt, trainers and a baseball cap. She didn't want to leave her DNA. Emma's car keys lay on her bed, which she had taken from the dead girl's bag.

The car was considerably smaller than her old Land Rover and had two other notable differences, a car seat and a baby bag in the back.

She started the engine and the sound of 'Twinkle, Twinkle, Little Star' filled the car. She immediately pressed the eject button of the CD player with her gloved hand. Raking in the glove compartment, she replaced the nursery rhymes CD with Ed Sheeran's 'Divide'.

The little car held the rural roads well. Agatha loved the views of the expansive green fields, wildflowers and trees. The drive was uneventful and, arriving at the car park, she was pleased to see a few free spaces.

Having parked the car, she put the keys in her backpack and started the long walk home. She knew that there was a little pub about thirty minutes away where she planned to call in for a cold drink. Hopefully, she might cross paths with another vulnerable and desirable male.

Someone to keep Ben company.

*

I can't breathe.

I don't know if it is Tom's torso pushing down on mine, or the large backpack that he's placed on my head. Probably both.

'You are enjoying this, aren't you, Faith?' grunted Tom.

'You are hurting me.'

'It's meant to hurt. It's going to get so much worse for you.'

I try to push him off but he's too strong for me.

Without warning, my humiliation is over. I can hear him moving quickly across the room and the slam of a door.

My wrists are tied but my fingers are free. I feel for the zip and, forcing a finger into the bag, I push it back and free my head. I can hear Tom vomiting and what sounds like the loss of his bowels.

Using my teeth, I quickly undo the knot which binds my wrists together. I dress with speed and head for the door, taking the backpack, whiskey glass and his clothes with me.

Explain that one, Tom Quick.

Outside, I inhale large gasps of fresh air into my lungs. When my breathing has calmed, keeping my head down to avoid any eye contact, I head for my car and home.

I hope Agatha isn't too disappointed that I'm not staying out all night.

*

Tom Quick lay on the bathroom floor, holding his stomach. He had crippling stomach pains, diarrhoea and vomiting. It was coming from both ends onto the floor.

It must have been the BBQ pulled pork and cheddar panini.

He lay for a while, in vomit and faeces, until the pain subsided. Pulling himself upright, he turned and stepped into the shower. Housekeeping could clean the floor. It was their fault that he was ill.

Wrapping a towel around his waist, he went back into the bedroom. He did not feel too good.

'Faith?'

He was confused that there was no sign of her or his clothes.

How dare she leave when he was ill and steal his clothes, especially since he had paid for the room and had been showing her a good time. He would call her and demand her to come back. He needed someone to look after him.

He couldn't call her as she had taken his phone.

*

Agatha had walked for longer than she had anticipated. She had been reliving Emma's killing. How the blood had gushed from the wound and how fear had frozen her face.

It was about another twenty minutes from Crow Springs Farm. Thirsty, she decided to stop at the Blackcock Inn in the pretty little village of Falstone. The name meant 'speckled stone' which most of the buildings, including the two churches, were made of.

Agatha had only been to the Blackcock Inn a couple of times because Maman said it was too close to home and she didn't want people getting to know them. It was a shame, as it did great Sunday lunches.

The large bar and restaurant were quiet. It was a mild day and most of the customers had chosen to sit in the beer garden. Agatha made her way to the bar and planned to sit in a quiet corner.

Until she saw him, sitting on his own.

A large Bergen rucksack rested against his chair. He looked in his early twenties and was wearing tracksuit bottoms and a black trench coat.

Her father's signature look.

Agatha's gaze remained fixed on the stranger as she ordered a glass of red wine. She had been drinking it with meals since she was a child living in France. Having paid the bartender, she made a beeline to her next victim.

'I've never seen you in here,' said Agatha, making out that she was a regular.

The stranger was surprised to see a pretty willowy girl speaking to him. Usually, girls ignored him. He didn't feel confident around them, although his fifth pint of Black Sheep ale was helping.

'I'm just passing through. I'm staying at a B&B in the village.'

'I'm Agatha.'

'Philip Daw.'

'Are you travelling on your own, Philip Daw?'

'Yes. I'm travelling around Northumberland, then I'm going to visit Wales before starting university in London. I love backpacking. I usually can find a cheap B&B or youth hostel on my travels.'

I like it when people don't have any ties. No one notices they are missing after a day or two. You are also a couple of years younger than I thought. Availability and vulnerability are two of my favourite things.

'Please, join me, if you want,' said Philip, gesturing to an empty seat.

Agatha sat.

'That's an unusual coat you are wearing. You don't get many young people wearing trench coats.'

'I bought it in a charity shop, I get all my clothes in charity shops.'

You can tell.

'So how long are you staying in Falstone, Philip?'

And would you like to share some free accommodation with Ben Stark?

'I'm flexible. I have the B&B booked for two nights, then I'll see. Do you live here?'

'Not too far. I've just been for a walk as I had some car trouble,' smiled Agatha, happy with her little joke.

She had already nearly finished the wine.

'Do you want to see the farm I live on? It's about a twenty-minute walk.'

'I'm not sure. We've only just met,' replied Philip.

'It's up to you. It's quite safe. I'm not a murderer!' Agatha laughed again at her perverse humour.

'Okay, I'll just nip to the gents. Can you watch my bag, please?'

'No problem,' she beamed.

She watched as the long-haired skinny Philip Daw headed for the gents. Once he was out of sight, she opened her backpack and rummaged inside for her sock.

She found this part of the killing game exciting.

She slipped her hand in and counted each piece of paper. There were four. Perfect. Selecting the one nearest to her hand, she opened it slowly.

Number 2. Blindfold them, have sex and then stab them repeatedly

It's the lucky dip of death. It will be the second time today that I will have killed someone with a knife. I hope Maman doesn't want it back.

Philip appeared back from the gents, wiping his hands on the outside of the trench coat.

I'm going to cut you to shreds, Philip Daw. While wearing that trench coat.

'I'm ready to go,' he said, smiling.

'Come on then. Can I ask you a question?'

'Sure, Agatha. What is it?'

'Do you like pigs?'

*

My mind is in a whirl. I can't believe that Tom Quick tried to suffocate me.

Or maybe he didn't. Maybe it is a game that I'm not aware of. I haven't dated or slept with many men.

I feel so angry and so violated. I said no and he continued.

I have been suppressing the urge to kill since I was a child. I now have an excuse to let the demons out once more. I realise that I know very little about him but I will, in time. I'll research him in the days to come. Then I will create a premeditated killing plan.

I'm about five minutes from home and I see Agatha. She is walking with a young boy.

Pulling over as far as I can on the narrow road, I beep my horn. She turns around. She doesn't look happy. I watch as she says something to him, and then heads in my direction. He waits.

'Maman, I thought you were staying over in Alnwick.' She sounds irritated.

'Something happened to me. I will tell you about it when we are home. Who's your friend?'

'I've just met him. I was going to show him the farm.'

'Maybe tomorrow, Agatha. I don't want any visitors.'

Agatha forces a smile and says, 'Okay, Maman. I'll tell him.'

I watch as my daughter slopes off to tell the young boy that the one-night stand is off. I don't believe that she was going to show him the farm. Her bedroom, yes. Not the farm.

He continues walking and Agatha jumps into the car.

'Was he okay when you told him?' I ask.

'Yes. I'm going to meet him tomorrow in Falstone. I have to go. I can't cancel. I don't have his number and I wouldn't give him mine.'

You have an extra day left to live, Philip Daw.

'What happened in Alnwick, Maman?'

I was going to wait until we were home, but the story spilt out, including the part when Tom tied my wrists together and zipped a bag around my head.

'Shall we kidnap him, Maman, and put him in the stone outhouse?'

I pause before thinking what that would mean. Recreating the death of William Channing.

'Yes, Agatha. Eventually, we'll put him in the stone outhouse.'

'He won't be alone. There's already someone in there.'

Chapter Twenty-Nine

Lil Hunt was in a deep sleep when rough hands shook her shoulders, waking her with a start. She recognised the angry face immediately.

Tom was standing, glaring down at her. She watched in fear as she knew what was about to happen. Again.

He threw off unfamiliar clothes, a black T-shirt with 'The Plough' logo and trousers, before roughly pulling the bedcovers from Lil's battered body.

'Lie on your stomach,' he commanded.

Lil did as she was told, shutting her eyes tightly. She knew that he enjoyed deliberately inflicting pain on her. She mentally readied herself, waiting for the hands which would soon be compressing her throat as he roughly entered her.

'Move your hair out of the way,' he ordered.

She did as he instructed.

His hands slid slowly across the back of her naked neck, finding her throat. Then he started to squeeze. He loved the sensation and having control over if, and for how long, he allowed her to breathe freely. The weight of his naked body, bearing down, trapped her. He felt his body reacting to this huge turn-on.

Before he could forcibly take her, his stomach cramped again, followed by an eruption of his bowels. Diarrhoea flowed down his legs and onto Lil.

He fell from the bed, clutching his stomach and groaning in pain.

Lil lifted her head and gazed towards the floor, in time to see another gush of diarrhoea leave him. The odour was strong and unpleasant.

'I'm going to sue them!'

Lil wasn't sure who 'them' were. She watched as he struggled to their ensuite, covered in excrement.

She didn't care that it was on her too as she lay back and laughed. She laughed as she hadn't laughed in the last five years. She wrapped her arms around her bruised body and belly-laughed.

He had looked pitiful. Which was what he was.

Composing herself, a smiling Lil gently lowered her legs out of bed and slinked towards the ensuite. Even through the door, she could hear that Tom was still having trouble with his lack of bowel control. Grinning, she quietly left their bedroom and headed for the main bathroom. There she was going to lock the door and have a long hot soak, after she had showered Tom's faeces from her back.

Chapter Thirty

Detective Sergeant Harriet Pickle was appropriately named. She was unorganised, uncommunicative and lazy. Somehow, she got away with her underperformance because, when things mattered and Detective Chief Inspector Aaron Webb wanted answers or results, her Detective Constable Amelia Earle delivered, and she took all the credit.

Now DS Pickle felt irritated.

At 47 years old, she wanted a quiet life and was only three years away from reaching her 30 years of service and retirement. But three missing persons had just been reported. Nothing unusual there as, in the UK, someone goes missing every 90 seconds; 180,000 people a year. Out of those, about 79% either return or are found safe. Most people who are reported missing often have some sort of mental health issue.

Not this time.

DS Pickle looked around the small room at her team before briefing them. She was thankful to see DC Earle present. While the rest of her colleagues were discussing the usual who was about to go on holiday, who wanted a bacon bap ordering from the canteen, and what brain trash they watched on television last night, DC Earle sat in silence with her notebook, waiting for her boss to speak.

DS Pickle walked in front of the huge whiteboard and waited for her colleagues to give her some attention. It took a while. She was about 5' 6" tall, three stones overweight, with mousy bobbed hair and a beige personality. When she started to speak, it was usually by the tenth word before the team realised that she was there.

'I'm going to keep this brief,' was always her opening line and style.

'A mother and her baby have been reported missing. Emma Beale is twenty-two years old, white, with raven shoulder-length hair, brown eyes and a large build. PC Hodgson, you went to interview her parents. Do you have a photograph yet?'

PC Edward Hodgson nodded, opened up the file on his knee, and retrieved a photo of the missing girl and her baby. He passed it to DS Pickle and she stuck it on the whiteboard.

'The baby in the photo with Emma Beale is four-month-old Ava Beale. Dawn Perry reported them missing yesterday. She and Emma are good friends; they go to yoga together and meet regularly for coffee. It was when Emma didn't respond to her messages on Saturday, or turn up for Monday morning class, that Dawn rang us. She last saw her on Saturday; that's three days ago.'

'Do we know who the father of the baby is? Couldn't Emma be with him?' The question was asked by DC Earle.

'Also reported missing by his roommate, Peter Hutchinson, is 23-year-old Benjamin Stark. He is the father of Emma Beale's baby. Peter should have gone to an indie concert with Ben on Saturday night but couldn't go, so Ben took a date instead. Peter doesn't know who. According to him, Ben hasn't had contact with Emma in about a year. Here's a photo of Ben with Peter, taken about three weeks ago. Peter messaged Ben on Sunday morning and again yesterday. He also tried ringing him. The phone is either flat or switched off. Ben also failed to turn up for a shift yesterday at The Swan.'

The photo, taken on a night out, was placed next to Emma's.

'DC Earle, can you go to The Swan and speak to Ben's boss, Rose Parks? Ask for any CCTV and speak to any regulars.'

'Yes, Boss,' she replied.

'DC Sterling, can you check out the mobile phone records of the missing persons?'

'Yes, Boss.'

'Any questions?'

The team remained silent.

DS Pickle left the room.

'Do you fancy going to the pub?' DC Earle asked DC Sterling.

'At this time of day? Absolutely,' he grinned.

DC Earle and DC Sterling had worked together for several years. Their relationship was no longer purely professional.

They had been the first detective constables to attend the horrific crime scene of two prisoner officers. Daryl Sinnatt and Sue Aldine were slayed and mutilated in Sue's home, allegedly by missing suspect William Channing, the Grey Trench Coat Man.

They knew, from the DNA evidence found at the crime scene, that William Channing was highly likely to be responsible for the crime. Detective Chief Constable Aaron Webb had led the investigation, and it was his first and only unsolved murder. Two years later, much to his frustration, they were still unable to trace the Grey Trench Coat Man's whereabouts.

The drive to the pub had been pleasant. The country roads had been reasonably clear with, thankfully, not a caravan in sight. 'Sheds on wheels' the locals called them. It was never a pleasant experience being stuck behind one, mile after slow mile.

The Swan was a typical rural pub. Six large hanging baskets, abounding in colour, lined the white frontage. Begonias, dangling fuchsias, petunias and lobelia created a line of vivid welcoming colour. Inside, it was quiet with a couple of punters sitting with a Full English breakfast and a pint. A black Labrador sat at his owner's feet, waiting patiently for any leftovers. Dark mahogany chairs and tables filled the space, the floor was stained a chestnut brown and pictures of the pub over the years hung from the stone walls.

'Smells good. It's making me feel hungry,' said DC Sterling.

'Maybe they'll do you a bacon sandwich to go,' replied DC Earle.

'I fancy the Full English.'

DC Earle didn't respond to her colleague. She had switched to work-mode and was heading towards the bar. Showing her police ID, she introduced them to the middle-aged lady behind the bar.

'Morning. I am DC Earle and this is DC Sterling. Do you mind if we ask you a few questions?'

The lady looked disinterested. 'If you must. But I'm in on my own, so do you mind if I continue cleaning the glasses?'

'Sure,' replied DC Earle. 'Can I ask you your name and position here?'

'I'm Penelope North and I'm bar staff. My manager, Gareth Gregory, will be in after lunch.'

'Do you know Benjamin Stark?'

'Yes, I've worked a few shifts with him. Nice lad. Why?'

'He's been reported missing. When was the last time you saw him?'

'About a week ago.'

'Can you tell me who was on shift with him on Saturday?'

Penelope retrieved a lever-arch file from under the bar and flipped it open to last week's roster. She still had a disinterested air about her. Ben being missing was not her concern.

'He was on his own. We were short-staffed due to Covid. He worked until 5 pm and then Gareth took over. I came in about an hour later and we worked until midnight.'

'What can you tell us about Ben?' DC Sterling asked. He found Penelope cold and robotic.

'Not much. Good-looking lad. He's popular with the locals,' said Penelope, as she placed a pint of pale ale on the bar for a customer. The black Labrador sat at his master's feet as he paid cash.

'I was in on Saturday afternoon. We were sat right there, at the end of the bar, weren't we Maximus? Ben had given him some crisps. You love a bag of crisps, don't you, boy? Ben was in no hurry to leave after his shift. He was sitting with a girl,' said the man, as he affectionately rubbed the dog's head. 'They left the bar together.'

'And you are?' asked DC Earle and DC Sterling in unison.

Chapter Thirty-One

Lil Hunt lay in the hot bubbly bath, feeling finally at ease. The thought of Tom incapacitated and covered in his faeces still made her smile.

Hopefully, whatever bug he had caught would last a while. Even better, he might be hospitalised. The thought excited her.

Stretching her sore limbs, she submerged her head under the water. She was in no hurry to leave her sanctuary.

*

Tom lay on the bathroom floor, gripping his painful stomach. He retched but there was no vomit left to come out. Gently, he pulled himself to his feet, cursing as he slipped in the diarrhoea. They had a cleaner, Althea, who came in on Wednesdays and Sundays. She could clean it up.

Stepping into the shower, he washed his body down. The smell was intensified by the heat of the water. He felt weary.

Turning off the shower felt too much of an effort. Wrapping a towel around his waist and avoiding his bowel contents on the floor, he headed for bed. He didn't care where Lil had gone. He knew she would be in the house somewhere as he had locked all the doors, and she didn't have a key.

Thanks to Faith stealing his clothes, he had to use the spare key which he kept hidden in the garden. He had yet to decide how to punish her.

But now, he needed to sleep off whatever was wrong with him. He had to go to work the next day and his first meeting was with one of his young managers, Katherine Kendall, in his private bathroom.

Chapter Thirty-Two

'What do you mean, 'there's already someone in there'?' My voice has risen and Agatha gets very angry when I raise my voice. I'm afraid of her response.

'Maman, don't get cross. He isn't dead. Yet. But the baby…'

'What baby? And who is 'he'?'

My heart rate increases. For the past two years, we have got away with the murder of William Channing. For months, I have waited for the police to call. They haven't. My confidence has grown that they never will, until now.

The Land Rover feels too enclosed for this conversation. I need to get to the outhouse and see for myself what lies behind the heavy door and stone walls. The farmhouse is only a few minutes' drive away and I continue on the journey. Thoughts of Tom Quick are, for now, paused in my mind.

'Slow down, Maman.'

I ignore her request.

'His name is Benjamin Stark and he is my boyfriend. Well, he was, until his ex-girlfriend turned up with his baby. I drugged him and put him in the outhouse to teach him a lesson.'

'When did you put him in there?' I ask.

'Saturday. It's only been two days. He's fine.'

'Why, Agatha? Why in there?' I know the answer before she says it.

'It's where we put William. I'd rather not call him 'Father'. I wanted to see how long it would take Ben to die.'

We are home. I park the Land Rover but, before I let Agatha out of my sight, I have questions.

'Did you kill the baby?'

'There was no need. A fox got it. I gave it back to Ben. At least it's quiet now.'

I take a steady breath before asking the next question.

'Where is the baby's mother?'

Agatha is grinning at me. Her eyes sparkle with delight.

'She tried to escape so I had no option but to kill her. Max ate most of her when I put her in the pigpen.'

I have not seen her this happy since she helped me feed her father to the pigs after I left him to die of hunger. I try to remain calm. I do not want the police searching my farm.

'Was that her white car parked here on Sunday?'

'It was,' she smirked.

'How did she find you?'

'She tracked Ben's phone. I only turned it on to check his messages.'

'I want to meet Ben.'

'Okay, Maman, but you're not mad at me, are you?'

'No, Agatha, I'm not mad. I'm furious. You have put us at risk of the police turning up.'

'Don't worry. I can kill anyone who turns up. It's fun.'

I remain silent as I climb out of my vehicle and head towards the stone outhouse. Agatha is next to me, looking excited.

'I hope you like him, Maman. But you aren't going to let him go, are you?'

'No, Agatha, I'm not! You will be arrested for kidnapping and murder. You will go to prison.'

'I'm too smart to get caught. Of course, I'm not going to prison!' she laughed.

I can see the stone outhouse. There is a large rock in front of it. 'Can you explain that one, Agatha?' I ask, as I point to the unfamiliar small boulder.

'That is so that, when I open the door, Ben can't push it open to escape. I bet you wish you had thought of that, Maman.' She looks pleased with herself.

She is her father's daughter.

I notice that the padlock is open and that only the large bolt is holding the door closed. I pull it back.

'Maman, wait. It has to go here.'

Agatha pushes the large rock about six inches from the door and I cautiously open the door.

'Hello.'

There is no response and I can't see anyone. Only rock-solid darkness.

'BEN!' yells Agatha.

'Agatha! You made me jump,' I say.

'Sorry, Maman,' she giggles.

'Help me.'

I can hear the voice but can't clearly see the face which has appeared at the agape door. I dare not push the rock out of the way. I can't allow this unfortunate boy to escape as he must die.

I won't let my daughter go to prison.

'She's killed my daughter,' he whimpers. He holds a baby's lifeless face to the door. Dried blood covers the small delicate features.

'No, Ben, I didn't kill your baby; a fox did. I promised to give you your baby back and I did. Don't be so bloody ungrateful,' Agatha hissed.

'Are you thirsty?' I ask.

'Yes, very,' he replies.

'I'm going to close the door now, but I will be back very soon with some water and food.' I mean every word I say.

'Why, Maman?' asks Agatha. 'I want him to die like Father.'

I ignore her.

'Please let me out,' pleads Ben.

'I will let you out, but not yet. I'm going to close the door now,' I say with a calmness that I don't feel. Ben moves from the door, and I slide the bolt back into place.

'Why are you going to feed him, Maman? I want him to die slowly.'

'You are not going to let him die slowly, Agatha. Someone will be looking for him and they can't find him here. I will drug the food and water and, once he's unconscious, we will put him in the pigpen.'

'But he will still be alive!'

'Not for long he won't be.'

'Maman! This is so exciting.'

Chapter Thirty-Three

DC Earle and DC Sterling left The Swan after taking a statement from Tony Archer. As a thank you, DC Sterling bought Maximus a packet of beef crisps. He bought salt and vinegar flavour for himself as a small consolation for not having a bacon sandwich.

Inside the police car, Amelia Earle rang their boss, DS Pickle, who answered on the second ring.

'DS Pickle.'

She always answered formally, even though Amelia's name came up on her phone screen.

'Hello, Boss. I have an update for you on the missing persons' case from this morning.'

DS Pickle smiled. She could always rely on DC Earle.

'I'm all ears, Amelia.'

'DC Sterling and I went to The Swan and interviewed a member of staff, Penelope North. She confirmed that Benjamin Stark was a nice guy and a good worker but didn't have anything else to add. However, we also took a statement from Tony Archer, who was in The Swan on the Saturday afternoon when Ben was working.'

'What did he have to say?' asked DS Pickle.

'He said that when Ben finished his shift, he spent about an hour talking to a girl with black hair, slightly plump and looked in her early twenties. Mr Archer said they seemed close, and his guess was that they knew each other and hadn't just met that afternoon.'

'Interesting,' interrupted DS Pickle.

'I showed him the picture of Emma Beale and he confirmed that she was the girl he had seen Ben with. He also said they left together. So, our intel wasn't correct. They had recently seen each other.'

'Good work. Is there any CCTV we can check to see where they went?' DS Pickle asked.

'No, it hasn't worked for months. Do you think they might have just gone off together and will turn up in a few days?'

'Did Emma have the baby with her?' DS Pickle was trying to piece together this new information. 'Maybe they have gone off to play happy families.'

'No. Mr Archer confirmed that there was no baby.'

'That's a mystery. PC Hodgson has contacted Emma Beale's parents, and they haven't heard from her in weeks. She hasn't left the baby there. Her close friend, Dawn Perry, often babysat but, as we know, she was in Manchester on Sunday and reported Emma missing on the Monday. She has confirmed that Emma didn't leave the baby with anyone else but her.'

'Is there anything else you would like us to look into, Boss?' asked DC Earle.

'Not at the moment. I'm less concerned about this case than I was this morning. Sounds as if the pair of them are together, having fun somewhere. I've asked PC Hodgson to see if he can track Emma's car.'

'Okay, Boss. We'll go and interview Farmer Wilson up at Sunnybrook Farm. He has reported that someone has stolen another ten of his Cheviot sheep. That's twice this week.'

'I'll let you know if there are any updates on the missing persons' case. I really do think they are together having a good time somewhere. Good work, Amelia,' said DS Pickle as she ended the call without saying goodbye.

DS Pickle was right. Ben and Emma were about to be reunited but, in spirit, in the pigpen.

*

I know I should feel worse than I do. That's the darkness within. I am going to feed someone's son to a sounder of pigs to save my own daughter. Is that technically murder? I don't think so. It is not me doing the killing. The pigs will tear him apart and I am just setting up the scene. I will not let my daughter go to prison.

I'm about to put the heavy bolt back that keeps Ben trapped. Agatha is next to me. She was very animated as I prepared Ben's last meal. You would think she is about to watch a West End theatre show, not see the person she still refers to as 'her boyfriend' eaten alive.

With the bolt removed, I open the door but Agatha insists on using the rock to stop it from opening too wide.

'Ben, I have something for you to eat and drink. Come nearer so that I can pass it to you. You will need it.'

You don't want to be awake when the powerful teeth tear the flesh from your bones.

'Thank you, I'm parched.'

He took the water bottle first. I can hear him noisily consuming the drink. It contains a lethal dose of Rohypnol and Triazolam, which is a central nervous system depressant tranquilliser. Often taken for insomnia, I've given him four times the 0.25mg recommended dose.

His hand appears and I pass the sandwich through to him. It contains a ham and pease pudding stottie, which is a favourite in the North of England. It was Agatha's idea to feed him ham as she said he could get his own back before the pigs devour him.

He ravenously swallows the sandwich. According to Agatha, he last ate a few days ago, at the indie concert on Saturday.

'Thank you,' he says.

'You're welcome,' I respond.

'Can you let me out, please? Even for a short while. I need to bury my baby,' he beseeches.

'I give you my word that I will let you out shortly.' I mean every word.

'I can't wait!' Agatha gleefully says, with an enormous smile on her face.

'Agatha! Please, be quiet,' I scold.

Her face has changed. She is irritated. No one tells Agatha what to do and there are always consequences.

'I can't wait for you to come out, Ben. We are going to feed you and your dead baby to the pigs. And it is all your fault because you kept me waiting when you were with her. Your ex-girlfriend,' she says, emotionlessly.

'Please, no. I won't tell anyone. Just let me live or, at least, let me speak to my mam,' he pleads.

'Not happening,' she snaps.

'Agatha, please. Let me handle this,' I say.

This is not how I had planned Ben's final moments. My daughter has callously told him how he will die. He knows he will be eaten along with his baby. He is crying.

'Please let me tell my mam that I love her and my family. Please!' he weeps.

'Sorry, Ben, I can't allow you to do that.'

I hold my finger to my lips as a warning to Agatha to say nothing.

'Will you tell her? Will you tell her how much I love her and Dad?' he implores.

'No, Ben.'

I wish our conversation would end. I wish that the poor boy would go into a drugged sleep and end his misery.

'They'll never know what happened to me.' His words are slurred.

I glance at Agatha, giving her permission to add her thoughts about Ben's last request. Maybe we can allow him to write a note to his parents. She shrugs her shoulders.

Ben has gone quiet. Glancing into the darkness, I can see him near the door. He is lying on the ground trying to get up. He is moments away from his final sleep.

'Can I see him?'

Without waiting for my response, Agatha pushes me to the side so that she can see Ben.

'He's not moving, Maman. Open the door and let's get him out!'

'Wait for a few more minutes.'

She is restless and starts to pace. She is singing 'La Vie En Rose' or, in English, 'Life in Pink'. It is a love song, and she is using theatrical arm movements to mimic a broken heart. I'm not sure if the performance is reflecting her feelings towards Ben or his towards not seeing his parents again. She stops singing because she is laughing to herself.

I have heard and seen enough.

Without warning, I move the stone and open the door wide. Ben is lying motionless, and Agatha bounds over to take a closer look. It is so cold in there and dark, even with the door open. It seemed a perfect stone tomb for William Channing but not for a young boy with his life ahead of him.

'Ben.'

I gently say his name and shake his bare shoulder.

No response.

'It is time,' I say to Agatha.

I take his arms and Agatha takes his feet. He is very heavy, and we have to regularly put him down, even though the pigpen is only a short distance away. I open the gate to the pig's enclosure. They start to squeal in unison as they sense what is about to come.

Max nudges Ben's torso while we are still carrying him. Before we place him down, Max takes a bite from his left side.

'Max don't be greedy,' laughs Agatha.

Gently, we place him down and have to move swiftly out of the way as the pigs tear into their meal of human flesh.

Ben is still wearing his boxer shorts. The pigs won't eat those. I make a mental note to look for them tomorrow and burn what is left in a steel drum, along with the baby blanket and clothes. The thought has just reminded me.

'Agatha, please go and get the baby and place her with her dad.'

'Okay, Maman.'

I am going to head back to the sanctuary of my kitchen for a flat white coffee. I will return to the stone outhouse in about an hour. I need to clean it with bleach and water as it smells of bodily functions.

Whilst I have found the last hour mentally challenging, I'm thinking of getting the outhouse ready for my next guest.

It is time to visit Tom Quick at his office tomorrow.

I need to return his clothes.

Chapter Thirty-Four

Tom Quick woke up, feeling out of sorts, in an empty bed. Standing up to go in search of Lil, he felt weak and nauseous. He had to go to work that day as his diary was back-to-back with appointments, including a one-to-one meeting in his private bathroom with one of his senior managers. He felt too weak for full sex but she could have the pleasure of relieving him. He was, after all, the chief executive.

Heading to one of the guest rooms, and without knocking, he opened the door. Lil was fast asleep. He'd deal with her tonight; she knew better than not to sleep in their bed.

Skipping his usual morning workout, he headed for a shower in the main bathroom and planned to go straight to work. He couldn't stomach any breakfast. As the cleaner was due that day, he would leave her a note to thoroughly clean the floor in the ensuite as a priority.

Feeling slightly better after a cold shower, as he didn't like hot showers, he dressed in a pale grey Ted Baker suit with a white shirt and queen pink tie. Even though he was not feeling his best, he still liked what he saw in the mirror. Narcissistic sociopath Tom Quick thought he looked handsome to women and men.

As he headed for the door and, hopefully, a day of no surprises, a small dark figure appeared. Opening it, he greeted 60-year-old Althea. She had a key to the property and looked after it when they were on long holidays.

'Morning. Lil's not been too well so the ensuite and bedroom carpet needs a clean. I've left you a note.'

'No problem, Mr Quick.'

He was out the door and heading towards the car before she stepped foot inside the luxury house.

Althea was glad that he had gone to work, as she found him creepy. She would start on the kitchen and, in four hours, the whole house would be clean. There was usually hardly any mess. It was an easy job and, apart from Mr Quick, she enjoyed working there. She thought the house was beautiful. Often, she and Miss Hunt enjoyed a chat and a cup of tea.

She would put the kettle on and take one up for her.

*

He was roughly pulling her hair. It really hurt but, as he reminded her on many occasions, he was the chief executive. She had already had a promotion because they were sleeping together, and she also knew that it wouldn't go on for much longer. She was right.

Tom Quick cried out and immediately let go of her hair.

'Go,' he commanded.

Getting up from her knees, Katherine Kendall left immediately as she knew his personal assistant would soon be starting work.

Tom washed his face. He still didn't feel great even after Katherine's efforts. Buttoning up his trousers, he glanced at his TAG Heuer watch. He had seven minutes before his first meeting of the day. It was in the Chief Executive's Conference Room.

It was also a delicate meeting. Central governments were asking all local authorities to home more asylum seekers. They wanted Northshireland County Council to house one hundred and fifty and they would receive funding for this. Where to put them and how to win over the locals was another matter.

If Tom thought that meeting was going to be the biggest challenge of his day, he was wrong.

*

After cleaning the stone outhouse with bleach and burning the items belonging to Ben, Emma and their baby, including Ben's T-shirt and Emma's clothes from under Agatha's bed, I wake feeling refreshed.

I'm in my favourite place; my kitchen, with a large mug of flat white coffee. Guzzle is at my feet, happy as he's just been fed.

I've washed and styled my hair and I'm wearing a summer dress with white trainers. Tom's clothes and mobile phone are in a box, ready to be returned by hand to him today.

The drive will take me about thirty minutes, which means that he'll have them back within the hour. It's now 10 am.

'Morning, Maman.'

'Morning, Agatha. Are you okay? It's still a bit early for you to be up.'

'I'm good. I was thinking I'd clean the pigpen out this morning, and I've got a date at teatime remember? With Philip Daw; the guy you sent away yesterday.'

'Try not to kill him.' I wasn't joking.

Agatha put her head back and roared with laughter.

'Maman, you are so funny! Will you be cross if I do?' as she laughed again.

'Agatha, you can't just kill people and expect to get away with it.'

'Yes, I can! CCTV only operates in public spaces, not on the rural lanes where we live. I have checked.'

She is right. We live in such a rural part of Northumberland and our only surroundings are sheep and fields. It is only when we go to areas such as Alnwick or Falstone that we have to be careful.

Agatha still wants to put her point of view across.

'Around here, the main crime is stolen sheep or farming machinery. The police can't even find missing tractors, and they are huge!'

She is right. There is a Northumberland Police Farm Watch scheme for members of the rural community. It is designed to alert residents to criminal activity in the area. The police also use the scheme to appeal for information. I didn't sign up.

My daughter is right. In this rural setting, it is easy to commit murder. Disposing of a body is harder.

Unless you have a pigpen.

'I'm off out for a couple of hours to drop some things off. Thank you for cleaning the pigpen. If you find any teeth, hair or bones, please bury them.'

What a weird request to my daughter. What is becoming of our lives?

'I will. I'll do it now.'

Kissing me on both cheeks, she heads off.

Washing my coffee cup and putting it neatly away, I head for the bathroom to check my appearance before surprising Tom.

*

Althea entered the master bedroom with a cup of English breakfast tea for Lil. The room smelt of blocked drains. She placed the tea on the bedside cabinet.

The bed was unmade and there was no sign of Lil.

Frowning, she went to tap on the door of the ensuite when she realised that the door was open. The smell made her retch. Switching on the light, she looked in and saw that the floor was covered in bloody diarrhoea.

Groaning, she headed back downstairs to get her bucket, mask and gloves. Mr Quick's note now made sense. She was humming to herself as she climbed the stairs once more and headed towards the bathroom. She stopped as she heard movement coming from one of the guest bedrooms.

'Hello,' she called, knocking at the door. She stood back as the door opened.

She gasped.

Lil stood before her with a friendly smile, despite her bruised and swollen face.

'Hello, Althea.'

'Miss Hunt, have you been in a car accident? Can I help you?' Althea wanted to hug her employer but knew that it probably wasn't acceptable.

Lil paused before answering. She knew the correct response was to say 'yes', as it was what she had told Althea many times. Her cleaner must think she was the most accident-prone woman walking. In the past four years, she had fainted and slipped on a wet floor, fallen down the stairs and fallen off a ladder. Every time Tom abused her, she had covered for him.

'Yes, you can help me, Althea.' Lil smiled before continuing. 'Can you drive me to the train station, please?'

'Yes, no problem,' replied Althea.

'To answer your question, I didn't have a car accident. Tom did it. It's always been him and I'm not coming back.'

Althea remained silent as she watched her employer go to the master bedroom. Opening the large wardrobe, Lil removed a small overnight case. She packed what she could fit into it. Pulling out her bedside drawer, she removed an envelope containing the cash she had been accumulating over the years, ready for this day. It was nearly £1,000. Tom only ever gave her what she thought she needed. She had thought of taking money from his drawer, but she knew there would be consequences if he found out.

She dressed quickly in a pair of jeans, a long-sleeved cream top, a short waterproof jacket and white trainers.

'Let's go, and Althea...'

'Yes?' Althea enquired.

'I highly recommend that you look for a new job.'

Chapter Thirty-Five

This is the first time I have visited the Northshireland County Council building. With its stone walls and single-glazed windows, it looks like a listed building, similar to an old bank.

I confidently stride through the large entrance, carrying the box as if I am one of the three kings about to present gold, frankincense and myrrh to Baby Jesus. When, in reality, there is nothing saintly about Tom Quick.

A very smiley lady is at the reception and a nearby security guard, who is so big that he probably can't tie his shoelaces. Maybe he just sits on anyone who causes trouble. He certainly can't run after or apprehend them.

'Hello, can I help you?' asks the smiley lady, with a matching smiley voice.

'Yes, I'm here to see Tom Quick.' I match her smile.

The smiley lady is now looking serious.

'Do you have an appointment?'

'No.' Now it's my turn to laugh. 'I don't need one. Can you let him know that Faith is here? Thanks.'

'Mr Quick is the chief executive. You'll need an appointment. Can you tell me what it is regarding? Then I'll get someone else to help you.'

I have a power issue. It is simple - power corrupts. To me, people are people. I don't put them on pedestals.

Miss Smiley is not being very helpful. Turning, I see two men in suits behind me. Sometimes, I love an audience. I raise my voice to make sure they can hear.

'Could you please give Tom Quick a call? Tell him it is Faith. I'm returning his clothes and mobile phone. I hope he didn't have to go home naked from The Plough. See, I have his boxer shorts too!' I'm really enjoying myself as I hold up a pair of navy blue Emporio Armani cotton boxers.

I hear laughter from the two gents behind me. I give them my best smile and shrug my shoulders as if it is normal to be returning the chief executive's clothes.

Miss Smiley picks up the phone, while Mr Security moves closer to me. I hope he doesn't sit on me. That would be a couple of broken ribs, for certain.

'Sarah, there is someone at reception to speak to Mr Quick. Could you come down please?'

'No, I don't want to speak to Sarah. I want to speak to Tom.' I give Miss Smiley a warning look and take the phone from her. 'Hello, Sarah. You must be Tom's secretary. Can you tell him that Faith is here with his clothes? Thanks. I'll just wait here as you ask him.'

There is silence from Sarah. I look at Miss Smiley, who now looks furious with me.

'I won't be long, and then I'll leave you in peace,' I say to her.

There is a short silence before Sarah is back on the phone.

'Thank you, Sarah. See you soon.'

I hand the phone back to Miss Non-smiley.

'Isn't Sarah helpful?' It was a rhetorical question.

I continue, 'It seems that Tom would like his underwear back.'

I turn away from the speechless receptionist and security guard, and head for the third floor where Sarah said she would meet me. I take the stairs. I avoid lifts as I hate confined spaces. It goes back to my days when I was captive in a small bedroom.

On the landing of the third floor, I am met by a young attractive redhead, dressed very professionally in a tight-fitting black dress and nude heels.

'Sarah?' I ask.

'Hello, yes. Mr Quick said he will see you in his office. He only has fifteen minutes until his next meeting. Can I get you a tea or coffee?'

'No, I'm good, thanks.'

Sarah uses her security pass to open a set of double doors. They lead us down a very long corridor. It is very quiet, and all the office doors are shut tightly. I can't tell if people are working behind them or maybe having a nap.

Another set of security doors.

The carpet changes from a thin grey floor covering, as we head down the corridor, to a deep rich red. It is the Executive Suite.

'This way, please.'

I follow Sarah into a large office which is very tidy. There is a desk, a set of trays and a small sofa with a large plant in the corner. There is an adjoining door to the right and Sarah knocks on this door before opening it.

'Mr Quick. Faith is here.'

She turns to Faith and says, 'You can go in.'

'Thanks, Sarah.'

I enter Tom's office.

It is very spacious with a door to his left, which I presume is his private bathroom. His large mahogany desk is tidy and the room also includes a settee, coffee table and two chairs. Pictures of Northumberland decorate the walls. Various large pot plants are dotted around the room. It has an air of power.

Tom is sitting at his desk. He looks enraged.

'Hi, Tom. I'm returning your stuff,' I say, trying to lighten the mood.

He rises slowly and comes directly towards me. I stand my ground. I know the lovely Sarah is on the other side of the door. Surely, if I scream, she will help me?

We are standing eye-to-eye, with the box between us.

'How dare you show up here, trying to humiliate the chief executive,' he hisses.

I remain quiet. He has referred to himself in the third person, which is a typical trait of a narcissist.

'Sometime very soon, you will get your punishment. Now get out, you bitch.'

I head to the safety of the door but, just before I leave, I turn to face him.

'I hope you are feeling better. I wonder what or who caused you to shit yourself like a baby?' I ask with a smile.

I watch his face change as he realises it was not food poisoning. It was me.

'Be careful, Tom Quick. I am no victim,' I say, before heading for the door.

Chapter Thirty-Six

Agatha kept her word and cleaned out the pigpen. She smiled as she saw the pigs with their red snouts; substantiation of yesterday's feeding frenzy.

The fenced-off area was attached to a stone building which gave the pigs protection from the elements. Placing fresh food and water inside, she watched contently as they happily wandered in, allowing her to close the door. That left the outside area, the death site, free for her to explore and sanitise.

The pigs were voracious feeders and would eat any flower or weed that tried to grow in their enclosure. The ground became nothing more than mud, which provided a natural sunblock for their pale skin, and they loved rolling in it. Usually, it was light to dark brown but Ben's blood had turned parts of the earth a shadowy black.

Taking a shovel, Agatha started to move the stained soil as she looked for any remains of Ben and his baby. Apart from his hair, boxer shorts and some of his lower jaw, there was nothing. Taking a high-pressure hose, she aimed it at the contaminated earth and watched the water flow down the large drain, along with Ben's hair and jaw. She placed his boxer shorts in the steel drum where Faith had previously burned the other garments belonging to him, Emma and Ava.

Maman said she will burn them later.

Her maman always cleaned the pigpen thoroughly using a disinfectant solution. Agatha couldn't see the point, as pigs were actually very clean animals. A quick hose-out should do it.

Glancing at her watch, she made a mental note that she had two hours before she met Philip Daw in the Blackcock Inn, about 20 minutes away on foot.

She smiled as she remembered pulling Number 2 out of the lucky dip of death while Philip had gone to the men's room. If her maman hadn't come back from Alnwick early, he would have been blindfolded, they would have had sex and she would have stabbed him to death by now.

Agatha decided that she enjoyed killing people. It was like a job to her.

Letting the pigs back into the open-air enclosure, she headed back to the farm for a shower and a change of clothes. She didn't want to wear anything that would make her memorable to the staff or customers of the Blackcock Inn.

She didn't want people to remember a serial killer.

*

Althea dropped Lil off at Alnmouth Station.

'Take care, Miss Hunt.'

'Thank you, Althea. You too.'

'Where are you off to?'

'I've always wanted to go to the Snowdonia National Park, but now I'm not sure. I'm not even sure which train to catch or which direction I want to head in,' Lil confessed.

I've finally escaped from Tom. I didn't expect to have my freedom so soon.

'Just leave me here. I'll be fine. Again, thank you,' Lil said, as she hugged Althea.

'If you are sure. Message me if you ever need anything.'

'I will,' Lil replied, as she took her small case and started to walk; to where she wasn't sure. It was years since she had been on a train.

In her pocket, she felt her mobile phone, which she had retrieved. There was also Tom's American Express Gold credit card which she had taken from his bedside table. He kept most of his credit cards there as he only carried a debit card and some cash, unless he was going out on business or holidays. The credit card did not have a spending limit, which was handy.

Turning away from the station, Lil headed for the taxi rank. She would be comfortable in a taxi. The driver of the next available cab got out and opened the boot, ready to take her small case.

'Where you off to?' He had a local accent.

'Wales, please.'

'Wales? That's about a six-hour drive. Sorry, I can't take you that far.'

Pausing, she thought for a moment. She loved zoos.

'How about Chester?' she asked, hopefully.

'That's about a four-hour drive. My sister and nephews live there. It would be good to see them,' he admitted.

'Chester it is then. Near the zoo,' she added.

'You do know that's about a £400 fare?'

'Do you take credit cards?'

'I do.'

'That's okay then.'

'My name is Bill. We might as well get to know each other as it's going to be a long drive.'

'I'm Lil. It's nice to meet you, Bill.'

'Have you been in an accident?'

'No, Bill, it was no accident.'

'I'll not ask you any more about it,' he said, sensing her discomfort.

'Best not,' she agreed. 'Can you put 'Absolute 80s' on the radio, please? The best era for music.'

Without another word, Bill found the radio station. He soon wished he hadn't, as Lil sang tunelessly along to 'Karma Chameleon' by Culture Club.

I hope she tips well.

*

As Lil was happily singing her way to Chester, Tom Quick was on his way home. He had told his secretary, Sarah, that he was feeling unwell. Which was true.

But he wanted some time alone and he wanted revenge.

How dare Faith do that to me! Poison me and then humiliate me at work! I am the chief executive! I am the highest-paid member of staff!

Pulling onto the driveway, he immediately noticed that something was wrong. Althea's car wasn't there. She had at least an hour left to work.

Unlocking the front door, he went straight to Lil's favourite part of the house, but the conservatory was empty. Taking the stairs two at a time, he headed to the master bedroom. The bed was still unmade, and his bowels were still on the floor of the ensuite. Not that he had to check, as the odour hit him when he entered the room.

The wardrobe door was open and Lil's overnight case was missing.

He smiled.

Well done, Lil.

Tom had expected her to leave him one day and had even prepared for the occasion. Inside the front pocket of Lil's overnight case was a device that looked like a metallic black keyring.

It was an Apple AirTag.

Retrieving his phone from his back pocket, he fired up an app and found Lil's location. She was moving.

Maybe Althea is giving her a lift.

He had already decided to sack the cleaner for not cleaning the ensuite.

Watching the red dot move along the map, he started to undress. It was time to get changed into something more comfortable and plan a relaxing evening. It seemed that he had a long drive ahead of him the next day.

To bring Lil home.

Chapter Thirty-Seven

Agatha was ready to slaughter Philip Daw.

Studying her reflection in the bedroom mirror, she thought she looked beautiful, although she was probably more in the 'pretty' category. Her blonde hair was tied into a high ponytail and a dusting of brown eyeshadow accentuated her green eyes. Her willowy frame was dressed in jeans, a black T-shirt and a hoodie.

Her kill bag was packed and ready to go, with cable ties, a kitchen knife (still bloodied from Emma), a blindfold, Rohypnol and the sock which contained the four pieces of paper.

Each finalising her victim's fate.

Finally, she took £20 from a drawer and stuffed it in her back pocket. She never paid by credit card. It made it not so easy to get away with murder.

Checking her appearance once more, she blew herself a kiss. She wanted to get to the Blackcock Inn before Philip, to make sure they sat at a table out of the way. Usually, she wouldn't meet in a pub when she knew her date would be dead within a couple of hours, but the pub had a bar and restaurant and a steady flow of people. As long as she didn't do anything to draw attention, they wouldn't be particularly noticed.

Picking up her backpack, she headed for the door. Maman still wasn't home and Guzzle was waiting near his food bowl. He gave an excited wag of the tail, hoping to be fed.

'You can wait until Maman gets home,' Agatha snapped.

The Golden Labrador's tail immediately stopped wagging, and he lay down again.

Locking the door, she set off on foot singing Talking Heads' 'Psycho Killer' to herself. When she got to the chorus, she added her own twist.

Psycho killer, qu'est-ce que c'est?
Fa-fa-fa-fa, fa-fa-fa-fa-fa-fa, better
Run, run, run, run, run, run, run away
Philip, Philip, Philip Daw

For Agatha, life was full and exciting.

She entered the Blackcock Inn feeling energised, as the fire which burned within her to kill was soon to be ignited.

At the bar, she ordered a small glass of Malbec and took a seat in the corner to watch for Philip arriving. Once he was there, she would switch chairs so that her back was to the bar and the punters.

With ten minutes to go until they agreed to meet, he walked in, still wearing the black trench coat. He saw Agatha immediately and headed in her direction. This time, he didn't have the Bergen rucksack.

'Agatha, you came! You look lovely.'

She gave him her best smile but didn't stand up as she didn't want him to hug her.

'Of course, I came. I'm sorry you didn't get to see the farm. Maman wasn't feeling too good.'

'No worries. Can I get you another drink?'

'No, I'm good, thank you. Just get yourself one.'

He gave her a shy smile before heading to the bar to get himself a pint of Black Sheep ale. At eighteen years of age, this was his first date and he had never even kissed a girl. He was usually invisible to them.

Back at the table, he noticed that Agatha had switched seats, but he didn't say anything.

She got straight to the point. 'Do you have a girlfriend, Philip?' It was a rhetorical question as she didn't care if he did or didn't. She was setting him up so that she could give her rehearsed response.

'No, I don't. Do you have a boyfriend?'

Theatrical tears swelled in Agatha's eyes. Philip went to comfort her, but she quickly held her arm out. Pausing for effect, she took a deep breath before speaking.

'No, I don't. He died. He was only twenty-three years old. He died along with his baby daughter, although she wasn't mine,' she sniffed.

I'm so good. Give me your pity, Philip Daw.

'I'm so sorry, Agatha. Can I ask how long ago?'

'It was recent.'

It was yesterday. But it's okay, I'm over it.

'Was it an accident?'

'It happened on a farm. At least he is still with his daughter now,' she said, as she managed to shed another tear.

'It's obviously upsetting you. I'll not ask any more questions.'

'Thank you. Last night, when I was lying in my bed, I felt he was nearby.'

In the abdomen of a sounder of pigs.

'You must have loved him.'

'I always say, "Don't cry because it is over. Smile because it happened".'

Well, that was what Dr Seuss said.

'Let's not let my sorrow sour our afternoon,' she said, shrugging off the act of grief. 'Tell me all about yourself, Philip Daw.'

I want to check that no one will come looking for you immediately.

'I'm eighteen and I will be starting university in September, studying Culinary Arts.'

Culinary arts! Isn't that rated as the number one most useless degree, followed by fashion design?

'Culinary arts. Isn't that dietary requirements and menu planning? My maman does that every day and she doesn't have a degree,' she mocked.

Philip's face fell at the insult. 'I want to be an award-winning chef.'

I can promise you that you won't achieve your dream.

'I'm just teasing,' she said, backtracking, as she didn't want him to leave. 'I love food. What's your signature dish?'

'Meatloaf.'

I should kill you now.

'Mine is bouillabaisse,' she said. Seeing the puzzled expression on his face, she added, 'It's a classic French soup.'

'This talk of food is making me hungry. Shall we order some food?' asked Philip.

'I thought we could go to your B&B and get to know each other better,' she replied flirtatiously.

Philip paused. He had never been with a girl before. A mixture of ecstasy and terror swept through him. He needed another drink.

'Shall we get another round in first?' he asked, hopefully.

'How about you get us a bottle of Malbec and we'll take it with us. Make sure it has a screw top.'

'Okay,' said Philip, as he headed for the bar. He had no idea if he liked Malbec. He just knew that he'd gladly drink it for Dutch courage.

The bottle of red wine cost him £18, which left him with £12.

I will have run out of money once I've paid for my accommodation. I might see if there are any temporary chef jobs locally and stay another couple of weeks. That way, I could be near Agatha.

'Let's go then,' said Agatha, as he returned from the bar. 'You lead the way.'

It was a pleasant walk to Hill House B&B. Agatha smiled as Philip took a swig from the wine bottle to calm his nerves.

Drugging your victim is easier if they are tipsy.

The B&B was typical for the area. A small stone-fronted house with a 'Welcome' sign in the window. The property looked dated. Philip explained that the owner, Miriam Hill, was in her early seventies and had been widowed for three years. She let out three bedrooms, with a shared bathroom, for only £48 a night. They would have to be quiet as he wasn't meant to have any visitors. Miriam took a nap in the afternoon as she was up early doing the breakfasts.

The front door was unlocked and led straight to a set of stairs. Agatha followed Philip up to his room. They passed two closed doors before stopping at the third. Unlocking the door, Philip stepped aside to allow Agatha to enter first.

'Cosy,' lied Agatha.

The room had an MDF pine wardrobe and dressing table and smelt of mould. There was a double bed with a country rose-garden quilted bedspread and matching curtains. The carpet was deep pink and heavily stained. A small television was mounted on the wall, and Philip's Bergen stood in the corner.

I don't feel sorry for Miriam that she will have to redecorate this room after you've died. I'll have done her a favour.

'Get your clothes off, Philip,' she demanded.

'What! Already?' he asked, nervously.

Agatha laughed. She loved playing games.

'I'm joking, let's have a drink first. I'll pour. Where do you keep the Waterford Crystal wine glasses?' she teased.

'I won't be long,' he replied, before leaving the room.

Agatha seized the chance to place the cable ties, knife and blindfold under one of the two pillows. The Rohypnol was, as usual, in her back pocket.

Philip returned with two tumblers. 'I couldn't find any wine glasses,' he apologised.

'These are fine,' she fibbed, taking them from him. It was her pet hate; not having the right glass for her drink. Turning her back to him, she poured the wine.

'At least, take your trench coat off,' she said, to distract him from the extra liquid she had added to his glass.

Handing him a tumbler of Malbec, she gave him her best seductive smile. He really was a funny-looking boy. She felt no attraction towards him.

'Can I try your coat on?' she murmured.

'Sure,' he said, as he emptied his glass in three gulps.

Agatha slowly removed her clothes, while Philip watched in amazement. She stood before him wearing white lacy underwear and a deceitful smile. Stepping forward, she slowly leaned across him, picked up the black coat from the bed and put it on.

A trench coat. It didn't matter that it was black and not grey. She felt like her father's daughter. It was his signature look.

She gently pushed Philip onto the bed. His arms reached for her waist as he tried to kiss her but she moved her head, denying him the tenderness he sought.

'Not yet. Lie down,' she admonished.

He did as he was told.

'Do you like it rough?' she asked.

'Sure,' he replied. At that moment, he'd take anything.

Gently, she took his arm and placed it above his head. Discreetly, she reached under the pillow and pulled out the first cable tie. She secured his wrist to the headboard.

'What are you doing?' he slurred.

'Quiet,' she smoothed. 'Trust me. You'll never have another experience like this again.'

Philip was starting to feel unwell. He was not used to drinking red wine. He felt dizzy and confused, and was finding it hard to speak. Reaching out for Agatha, he accidentally pulled her hair.

'That hurt!' she snapped.

Annoyed, she roughly secured his remaining wrist to the headboard before placing the blindfold over his eyes. Seeing him tied helplessly to the bed excited her. She started to kiss his neck.

Removing the knife, she slowly cut his grey T-shirt with the words 'Culinary Gangster' decorating the front in large yellow lettering.

I'm doing the world a favour by removing it from you.

Her hands moved down his body and her nimble fingers unzipped and removed his jeans, exposing his black boxer shorts with '100% Pure Beef' on the front.

She rolled her eyes out loud.

'Would you like me on top, Philip?' she asked, as she climbed into position, still wearing the black trench coat.

No response.

'Philip?' She shook him.

No response.

'Merde!' she cursed. She had given him too strong a dose. He had already passed out.

Climbing off his chest, she stripped him naked before lying on top of him. She lay still, listening to his heartbeat and feeling the warmth of his body. She started to kiss his neck and then worked her way down his torso.

His body didn't respond.

Frustrated, she climbed off the bed and stood for a moment, watching him. Anger raced through her body. She didn't try to control it and it discharged into seething fury.

'You are no good to me now, Philip Daw.'

The first stab wound was in his shoulder.

She watched as the blood ran over the country rose-garden bedspread. Leaning forward, she licked the warm blood that flowed down his arm, before forcing the knife leisurely into his other shoulder; then his stomach, legs and chest. Judiciously, she inflicted fifteen lacerations but she was careful not to get any blood on her new coat.

Happy with her work, she kissed the deceased Philip Daw on the top of his head before tidying up the scene.

After dressing, she placed the knife, blindfold, tumblers and bottle of wine in her kill bag. Using the T-shirt she had cut from his body, she wiped down any surfaces she had touched. She didn't want to leave any DNA or fingerprints.

Finally, she put on her new trench coat.

She loved it. She planned to wear it again the following day when she went on the hunt for another victim. At least, this time, she hadn't brought her work home with her. She didn't want to make her maman cross.

Pausing, she admired her work. Philip's torso was a mixture of crimson, scarlet, burgundy and ruby reds. She thought he looked striking.

Using her new coat to open and close the door, she felt exhilarated as she headed for home. Her killing kit was slung over her shoulder, ready for her next prey.

She was unaware that a single strand of her hair lay on Philip Daw's chest.

Chapter Thirty-Eight

Lil woke, feeling relaxed. She smiled to herself as she stretched out in the king-size bed. In the taxi, on the way down, she had booked the DoubleTree Hotel and Spa online. It was less than two miles from Chester Zoo, and she had paid for four nights' accommodation with Tom's American Express Gold card.

It had also paid the £400 taxi fare, plus the £100 tip for Bill. So far, Tom had spent over £1,000, without knowing it.

Climbing out of bed, she headed to the bathroom. She was pleased that the hotel provided complimentary shampoo and shower gel, as she hadn't brought any. On arrival, the receptionist had provided her with a toothbrush and mini toothpaste.

Mirrors were used to make the small bathroom feel larger. As she stepped into the bath to use the overhead shower, she could see the bruising on her torso and face. Lil, like many women, was a master at disguising imperfections with the clever use of makeup. She may not have packed many clothes or toiletries in her overnight case, but she did have her makeup.

Feeling refreshed by the shower, she started to get ready for the day ahead. She applied her makeup carefully, hiding most of the bruises from her old life, dried her hair straight and dressed in jeans, trainers and a long-sleeved cream top.

She felt free, for the first time in five years, as she headed for breakfast. She hoped that a Full English and breakfast tea were on the menu to set her up for the day.

Breakfast was served in the Garden Room and Terrace Restaurant which overlooked walled gardens. A waiter showed her to a table for two, where the leather-backed seat was comfy, and the napkins were white and crisp. As he offered her the menu, Lil raised her hand.

'Could I have a Full English, please, and a breakfast tea?'

'No problem. Anything else?'

'No, thank you.'

Breakfast was delicious and filling. Glancing at her Rolex Datejust, a Christmas present from Tom, she noted it was 9.15 am. She had pre-booked her Chester Zoo ticket for when it opened in forty-five minutes. The twenty-minute walk would burn off some of her breakfast.

She finally felt that she was living her life. She had always wanted to go to a zoo and now it was happening.

It was day one of 'life without Tom' and she planned to enjoy every minute.

*

Tom had slept well.

He had managed his early morning workout and was feeling better. His stomach pain had gone. Not that he was going to let his work colleagues know the truth.

He had rung Sarah at 7 am to say that he still wasn't feeling well and told her to either reschedule or ask the relevant director to cover the day's meetings. He would, however, be available to take any urgent phone calls. With the day job taken care of, he checked the Apple AirTag location on his iPhone.

Lil was 219 miles away at the DoubleTree Hotel and Spa. Tom felt riled that it was a fancy hotel.

She had better be alone.

He had not expected her to be such a distance away, as she knew the rules. She wasn't allowed to go too far from home without him.

Going to his bedside cabinet, he removed a tie for her wrists on the journey home.

Tapping the destination into his phone, he discovered that the drive would take about three hours and thirty-nine minutes in light traffic. It would give him a chance to listen to one of the many audiobooks he had downloaded and never got around to listening to. 'The Hobbit' by J.R.R. Tolkien was at the top of his list.

Driving all day didn't fill him with elation. Perhaps he could stay overnight in Lil's hotel room? Opening the drawer above where he kept the tie, he took out his credit cards. He instantly saw that the one with no credit limit was missing.

LIL …!

She was starting to become a liability. She might have an accident in the next few days.

She was easily replaceable.

Chapter Thirty-Nine

Agatha was in a light sleep. She was aware of her head, cushioned softly on her pillow, the cosy warmth of her body in bed and the silence in her bedroom. She didn't want to wake up. She was willing the dream, that she had earlier, to return.

In it, she had started work in an office. Her colleagues seemed egotistical and fatuous. They were gathered around a meeting table, with someone she presumed was their boss. The middle-aged figure, with short dark hair and nondescript clothes and personality, started shouting at her without reason. Then she was threatened with dismissal.

Agatha rose from her chair and, without warning, grabbed her boss's head and pulled her backwards onto the floor. Her hands gripped tightly as she smashed the head repeatedly into the floor, stopping only when the skull had cracked, and blood trickled from the mouth.

Her four colleagues sat watching, motionless. From behind her back, Agatha drew her maman's kitchen knife, which she had used to kill Emma Beale and Philip Daw. Merrily, she gripped the hair of the next victim to die and slowly moved the knife across her throat. Still, the others didn't move. She repeated the process until she was the only living person in the room. With blood on her hands, she took her seat and drank coffee that had appeared from nowhere. She felt formidable, strong and alive.

The visual of the dream had gone but the feelings remained.

Opening her eyes, she stretched her long limbs before kicking off the bedcovers. Swinging her legs to the floor, she left the bed with the dream still vivid in her mind.

Her thoughts drifted to Philip Daw, and how she had slowly, yet firmly, inserted the knife across his body. It gave her a sensation that was hard to describe. She believed that she carried a flame within her which, when she killed, became a blaze.

She needed to kill again. She wanted to experience a firestorm. The flames of Hell.

First, she would eat. Yesterday had given her an appetite and, pulling on her robe, she headed for the kitchen.

'Morning, Maman,' she greeted her mother, with kisses on both cheeks.

'Morning. Although, in half an hour, it will be lunchtime,' laughed Faith.

'Is there any coffee?'

'Sure. Would you like that with pancakes and strawberries?'

'You are the best!'

She watched as her maman left the homemade jam orders, which she had been packing ready for delivery, to make pancakes and coffee for her. Agatha wondered if she should tell her that she had committed another murder.

She decided she would.

'Did you meet your date yesterday?' asked Faith.

'I did,' Agatha replied.

'Did you have a good time?' probed Faith, as she started to whisk the batter mixture.

'I had an amazing time. Him, not so much.'

Faith laughed.

'Me too. You know when I went to Alnwick and I met that guy for lunch?'

'The one I said I'd help you put in the pigpen?'

'Yes, that one. I went to see him at work but the receptionist wasn't very helpful. So I showed her his underwear and said I wanted to return them. I finally got to see him, and he was furious. I'm not sure what he's capable of. I think he may be a problem.'

'Let me know if you want me to help you.'

'Thank you, Agatha,' said Faith, as she served the pancakes and placed two cups of fresh coffee on the table.

'Merci,' said Agatha, stabbing a strawberry with her fork.

'What did you mean when you said that your date didn't enjoy themselves as much as you did?'

Agatha paused. She wanted to tell her maman but she wanted to eat first.

'I took his coat,' she admitted.

'Did you steal it?'

'Not really. It's a black trench coat. I saw it and I wanted it. He didn't say I couldn't have it.'

Agatha felt irritation rise within her.

I shouldn't have to explain myself to anyone.

Dread seeped through Faith's body, yet she had to ask.

'A trench coat. Why did you want a trench coat?'

She sensed what her daughter was about to say.

Agatha was already hungrily on the last pancake. The conversation was ruining her breakfast. She just wanted to be left alone to savour the sweet pancakes, mixed with strawberries and cream on the side.

'If I tell you, will you promise not to ask any more questions until I've finished eating?' she demanded.

'I promise.'

Agatha placed her knife and fork down and looked boldly at her maman.

'I wanted to know how my father must have felt, in his grey trench coat, taking all those lives. And now I do. I wore the black trench coat, my trench coat, while I stabbed some stupid boy who had allowed himself to be tied helplessly to his bed,' she said, nonchalantly.

Faith stared at her daughter. She began to speak.

'No, Maman! You promised. Shush!' Agatha scolded.

Faith remained silent and nodded her agreement to her daughter who had just confessed to yet another murder.

Agatha smiled before picking up her knife and fork to resume her breakfast. She planned to eat it slowly.

Faith watched her eat every mouthful.

Chapter Forty

Miriam Hill was agitated.

It was now 1 pm and her guest, Philip Daw, had not vacated his room. The rules, which were laminated and clearly displayed on the back of all three bedrooms, stated clearly, 'Check in after 3 pm and check out at 10 am.' She had just taken another booking for the room and needed to get it ready.

At seventy-two years old, she didn't like any stress. She still missed, and thought of, her dear husband every day. He had died three years ago of a heart attack, in the very room Miriam was sitting.

She only kept the small B&B going because it was a distraction from acute loneliness. She had more than enough money to last for what was left of her remaining years … or minutes.

There were no children, no siblings and no family. She was the only one, and her will stated that her house and all her savings were to go to her neighbour, Sally Newburn. She was a single mother with two small children, and she always checked that Miriam was okay. The poor girl was living in poverty, yet her kind ways made her priceless. She always refused when her elderly neighbour offered her money.

Exhaling deeply, Miriam made her way upstairs to Philip Daw's room. He needed to either pay her for an extra day or leave immediately. She didn't mind if he wanted to stay on as he hadn't been any trouble and she could ring the potential guest and apologise.

She gave a little knock.

No response.

She knocked louder.

Gavin Coles came out of the shared bathroom. He was staying in the room opposite Philip Daw.

'Hello, Gavin. Have you seen the guest staying in Room 2?' Miriam asked.

'No, sorry. I haven't.'

Miriam removed the spare key from her pocket but, first, she tried the handle. The door was not locked.

'Hello! Philip?' called Miriam, as she pushed the door open.

She didn't enter the room. She could see that the young man was naked and covered in gore, with his wrists secured to the bed. A metallic scent filled the air.

Miriam felt her blood pressure plummet. Her heart hammered in her chest as it battled to pump enough blood around her body. She felt faint and she couldn't breathe.

Gavin tried, but failed, to catch her before she hit the floor. Dead.

Chapter Forty-One

'What is the difference between Asian and African elephants?' shouted the overzealous zookeeper to the large crowd.

Lil knew the answer. She had been watching David Attenborough, King of Conservation, for most of her life.

'Their ears,' she yelled. 'Asian elephants have small round ears compared to the large ears of the African elephant.'

'That's right. Their ears are different and, while only male Asian elephants have tusks, both male and female African elephants grow tusks,' explained the zookeeper.

Lil was having a great time. She had planned her day carefully as she didn't want to miss seeing any part of the 128-acre site. She had already heard the talk about the giant anteaters and, after the elephants, she was off to see the tigers, penguins and then, her favourite, the Komodo dragon. The talks were spread out during the day and, in-between, she would see the red apes, lions, bats, red pandas, cheetahs, zebras and warthogs. The zoo had reportedly spent £150m on conservation over the last ten years and was home to around thirty thousand animals and five hundred different species.

Smiling at the excited faces of the children around her, who were still enthusiastically answering questions on elephants, Lil decided that it was a good time to head to June's Food Court for a coffee and, hopefully, cake. She was having such a good time that she was even thinking of coming back and doing it all again the next day.

But every minute that ticked by, Tom Quick was getting closer.

*

Tom didn't stop until he got to his destination, the DoubleTree Hotel and Spa. It was lunchtime when he pulled into the car park. He had to hand it to Lil. She knew how to book great hotels. It was actually an impressive 18th-century manor house, surrounded by twelve acres of landscaped grounds.

He decided he would have lunch and then surprise her.

Walking into the double-door entrance, with a white balcony above, he was immediately greeted by the concierge.

'Afternoon, Sir. Can I help you with anything?' asked the well-groomed man.

'I'm meeting my partner here; Ms Hunt. Could you tell me which room she's in?'

'Sorry, Sir. We have to protect the privacy of our guests. I would need Ms Hunt's consent to give out her room number or allow you into her room. She hasn't left any messages at reception. I hope you understand,' replied Mr Well-Groomed.

Tom wanted to beat him to the ground.

How dare he doesn't do what I have asked!

'Can I have lunch in the restaurant, and could you phone her room and tell her I'm here?' replied Tom, glaring at the concierge to make him feel uncomfortable.

'Of course, Sir. The restaurant is this way.'

Tom followed in seething silence.

The restaurant had a sophisticated air about it, with a mixture of circular booths and tables.

'Scarlet will take care of you,' said the concierge, who couldn't wait to leave the aloof, angry man. 'Can I take your name, to let Ms Hunt know you are here?'

'She knows my name. Most people know my name. I'm the Chief Executive of Northshireland Council,' snapped Tom.

The concierge remained silent and headed back to reception to call Ms Hunt's room. Sadly, he dealt with egos on a daily basis.

Tom ordered the duck and a bottle of Rioja. As Scarlet returned with the wine, she handed him a note, written in the hand of the concierge. It simply said, 'No answer from Ms Hunt's room'.

Tom screwed the note up and threw it on the floor. He would enjoy his meal and then he would sit in reception and wait for as long as it took.

The concierge was also keeping an eye out for Ms Hunt.

He recognised danger when he saw it.

Chapter Forty-Two

There was one piece of pancake left on Agatha's plate.

She swirled it through the remaining cream, before slowly savouring its taste and texture. She had her faults, such as killing without compunction, but she did appreciate her maman's cooking.

Faith watched her baleful daughter, conscious that their lives had perpetually changed. She was her father's daughter and this was just the beginning. There would be more victims.

'Yum!' declared Agatha, breaking the silence between them. Faith remained silent.

Agatha grinned.

'Maman don't look so serious. He was just some dumb boy that no one is going to miss. And he was wearing a trench coat. It was his own fault. He was lucky that it was black. If it had been grey, I might have killed him right there in the pub!' she chuckled. 'I'm joking. I would have at least waited until we were in the car park!'

More laughter.

'Agatha, you've murdered an innocent boy, and you find it funny.'

'I find it exciting,' Agatha smirked.

'What about prison? Will you find it funny being incarcerated for years and years?' Faith snapped.

'I'm far too intelligent to get caught. Chill out, or do I have to kill you too?' she threatened.

Mother and daughter locked eyes. Without moving her eyes from her mother's face, Agatha slowly picked up the knife from her plate and raised it to her own throat.

'I wonder if it is easy to pierce the windpipe with a blunt knife?'

Faith's stare remained fixated on her daughter but she didn't respond.

Without warning, Agatha threw the knife up into the air and it clattered down onto the kitchen table. Guzzle raised his head at the loud interruption and started to bark.

Faith remained motionless.

'What if I slaughter you, Agatha? To stop you from becoming your father. How do you know I haven't poisoned your coffee?'

Agatha's face changed. It showed apprehension.

'Maman! I was teasing you. I could never kill you,' smiled Agatha. 'You haven't poisoned my coffee, have you?'

'Not yet,' came Faith's icy reply.

'There's no need to worry about me, Maman. I won't get caught. I only choose people who are vulnerable and easy to get close to.'

'Agatha, I'm not worried about you! It is the innocent people you've slayed that I'm concerned about.'

'No, Maman. They are not innocent!' yelled Agatha. 'Benjamin betrayed my trust. Emma was in the way, and Philip had a coat I wanted. I would have thrown Ava to the pigs alive, but a fox got to her first. That baby cried too much.'

'I want you to return to the Carmans' vineyard. Just for a few months, in case the police come looking for you.'

'I can't go back yet. You don't understand the feeling of watching someone take their last breath. It makes me feel formidable. Knowing someone is going to die because I've chosen them. My father was a serial killer and you, Maman, let him die deliberately. Your birth mother murdered her boyfriend. You both made me who I am.'

Agatha's words struck hard. She had a point.

Faith thought about her own dark thoughts growing up. She used to fantasise about what it would feel like to murder someone. The abduction by William Channing had given her that chance. Then there was Tom Quick. She had planned to poison him, but wasn't that different? Agatha killed the naïve. She killed those who needed to be taught a lesson.

Maybe psychopathy did run through Agatha's genes. It was possible. MAOA L, or monoamine oxidase L to give its full title, is a gene linked to augmented levels of violence, aggression, impulsive behaviour and mood swings. When combined with environmental triggers, this could increase the likelihood of psychopathic traits.

Faith felt responsible.

Did witnessing and abetting Faith, when she had taken cold-blooded revenge on her captor, trigger something within Agatha to hunt and kill?

'I hear you, Agatha. This has to stop. Right now!'

Agatha remained tight-lipped. She had no problem lying. She was a natural at it. She wanted to know that her maman was on her side. Otherwise, she would have to kill her. It would be a shame, as she had just cleaned the pigpen.

'Tell me what happened, and do not leave out any details,' said Faith.

Her only child obliged.

She happily explained about her killing kit and the sock. She was very proud of the sock. It was exciting to unfold the small piece of paper which predestined their fate. This, she elucidated, was why Philip Daw had to be tied and blindfolded to the bed. But she had got the dosage wrong, and he had passed out before she could have sex with him. She had to move to the final phase of repeatedly stabbing him. It had felt like pushing a blunt knife into a raw pork chop. She took her time as she didn't want to bloody her new trench coat. She got dressed, cleaned up the scene and left. No one saw her leave.

Agatha recounted the scene with excitement in her voice.

If she hadn't earlier confessed to murder, I might have assumed that she was describing a top-ten must-watch movie. And don't forget the popcorn!

Faith felt bilious.

She didn't want her daughter to spend her youth in prison. She would protect her when the urge to kill became too much.

She couldn't allow Agatha to continue these premeditated killing sprees. B&Bs carry too many risks. She must use the stone outhouse and then dispose of the bodies in the pigpen.

Or to give it a more fitting name, the Killing Pen.

Chapter Forty-Three

After five years of feeling trapped, Lil felt content. She had loved exploring Chester Zoo and she still couldn't believe the size of the critically endangered black rhinos. Huge powerful beasts. Something had happened within her as she watched the pair move their giant statures gracefully across the mud. She felt their dominance and saw the faces of the other visitors as they also looked on with respect and awe. She wanted others to look at her in the same way and, at that moment, vowed never to return to life with Tom.

What happened next cemented her decision.

'Impressive, aren't they? They can weigh up to 300 stones. That's roughly 1900 kilograms in new money! And they've been known to reach speeds of up to 34 mph in the African savanna,' said the stranger.

Lil turned and saw kindness in his dark blue eyes. His blonde hair was cut short and his face was clean-shaven.

He looks in his mid-forties and hot.

'They are imposing creatures,' she replied.

She felt self-conscious next to the attractive stranger. Her face, even with makeup, showed Tom's handiwork.

'Are you on your own?' he asked.

Lil nodded.

'Me too. Would you think it odd if I asked if you would like to grab a coffee?'

'I love coffee,' she said, smiling.

'Great. I'm Boston. Boston Winter.'

'Lil Hunt.'

'Nice to meet you, Lil.'

'You don't sound as if you are from Boston.'

Boston laughed.

'No, I'm not and neither are my parents. They are from Eccleston in Lancashire. My mam is a huge Bee Gees fan and she named me, sort of, after their first number-one hit, Massachusetts. Boston is the capital of Massachusetts.'

Lil burst out laughing. 'Did she ever consider calling you Massachusetts?'

'Thankfully, no. But Dad wouldn't allow her to name me Barry, Robin or Maurice.'

'I think Boston is a great name,' smiled Lil.

'Thank you. Can I ask you a question?'

'Sure,' she smiled.

'Have you been in an accident? I don't want to pry, but your face looks sore.'

Lil thought about telling him the truth.

'Car accident and I'm fine, thanks. Although I am a little thirsty!'

'We can't have that. Coffee and maybe cake, it is,' smiled Boston.

For the next two hours, they didn't leave each other's side. Boston told Lil he was forty-five, a pilot for commercial flights currently flying from Liverpool airport, and never married. He had rented a flat in Liverpool but was staying with his parents for a few days, as his mother was recovering from knee surgery. He made the hour's drive to Chester Zoo as he loved their conservation work and the animals.

Lil could not face telling the humorous and gentle Boston Winter about the narcissistic sociopath Tom Quick.

How do I explain why I didn't leave before now?

Instead, she lied and told him that she was staying in a hotel until she found permanent accommodation in Chester.

'Does that mean you are free for dinner tonight?'

Lil didn't hesitate. She had no desire to see Tom again and, even if she did, he deserved some of his own medicine. She felt no guilt about cheating.

'That would be lovely. Thank you,' she grinned.

'Which hotel are you at? I'll pick you up.'

'The DoubleTree Hotel and Spa. It's about two miles from here.'

'I know it. Would 8 pm be okay? We could meet in the bar and eat at about 8.30 pm?'

'Great, thank you. I could book us into the restaurant there. The breakfast was lovely.'

'Sounds like a plan. Then I can take you out another night, or day, or lunchtime!' grinned Boston.

Four hours before their date, he dropped Lil off at her hotel. They had exchanged mobile numbers and shared an affectionate kiss in the car. There had been an instant spark and neither of them wanted to leave.

Boston parked the car and walked Lil to the hotel entrance, to give them a few more moments together. He hugged her before she headed inside and she paused to blow him a kiss.

She had plenty of time to nip back out and buy something nice to wear before getting ready. She was picturing what to buy as she headed into the foyer.

That was when she saw him, waiting.

Tom Quick.

Chapter Forty-Four

'Police emergency. What is the address of the emergency?' asked the calm female voice.

'She's dead and he's dead! He's been murdered,' came the distressed response.

'I'm going to get help for you but I need you to answer my questions.'

'Okay,' he snivelled.

'What is the address of the emergency?' she asked, empathetically.

'Hill House B&B, Falstone. I don't know the postcode,' he apologised.

'What's your name?'

'Gavin Coles.'

'And your telephone number?'

He gave the operative his mobile number.

'Do you know the name of the deceased?'

'Miriam. She owns the B&B. Sorry, I don't know her surname and I don't know the guy's name. He's tied to the bed, naked and covered in blood.' Gavin started to sob heavily and his body shook.

'You are doing great, Gavin. The police are on their way. Just take some deep breaths for me,' she soothed. 'You said one of the deceased is on the bed. Where is Miriam?'

'She's at my feet. She opened the door to his room and saw the body, covered in blood. Then she went very pale and, literally, dropped down dead.'

'Have you checked for a pulse?' asked the operative.

'Yes! Just get someone here!' shrieked Gavin.

'They are only minutes away. You are doing great.'

'I can hear the siren,' said Gavin, hanging up.

Within the hour, the scene had been cordoned off. Police constables were making door-to-door enquiries and forensics were photographing the room and every part of Philip Daw's corpse.

PC Hodgson was taking a statement from a traumatised Gavin Coles.

Senior Investigating Officer, DCI Webb, was at the scene, trying to run the rewind button in his mind. What events led to a young male being tied to a bed and mutilated? Had he known the murderer? They usually did.

'What are your thoughts, Sir?' asked DC Earle.

She had been standing next to DCI Webb, taking in the gory scene. The stench of faeces and blood permeated the small room.

'Maybe revenge or some kind of sexual game gone wrong. Has to be personal and doesn't fit in with the area. We mostly deal with livestock and vehicle crimes around here. We'll have to wait and see what forensics come up with. What are your thoughts?' he asked.

'Maybe sexual. It's interesting that the victim has so many knife wounds, but his throat hasn't been cut. Maybe the perpetrator was trying to avoid blood splatters. Which means perhaps they have done this before,' she replied.

As DCI Webb stared at the remains of Philip Daw, something stirred in his memory. The last time he had investigated such a crime was when two prison officers, Daryl Sinnatt and Sue Aldine, had been mutilated. The prime suspect, William Channing aka Grey Trench Coat Man, had disappeared.

They had never found him.

Chapter Forty-Five

Life can be cruel.

Happiness can be whipped away and replaced with desolation in a trice. When Lil set eyes on Tom Quick, as she walked into the hotel's foyer, her recent exhilaration was forgotten.

He was immediately on his feet and heading in her direction. Lil stood, rooted to the spot, with fear pulsing through her body.

'Darling, there you are. Surprise!' declared Tom.

He wrapped his arms around her and pulled her into a painfully tight embrace. That was the first warning.

'We are going to your room. Now!' he hissed into her ear. The second warning. She could see the wrath in his eyes as she nodded in compliance.

'Good girl,' he murmured. 'Now, show me the way.'

Lil's room was on the first floor. She headed for the stairs, with Tom's hand grasping hers tightly. The silence between them was palpable. In less than one minute, they would be in the room. Chatting over coffee and Boston's laughter seemed a lifetime ago.

I was foolish to think I could be free of Tom. Free from his cruel and manipulative ways.

Lil unlocked the door with the plastic key card. Tom pushed her inside.

The punch connected with her abdomen and she doubled over, clutching the pain. His kicks struck her legs, over and over and over. She curled into the foetal position and pictured herself, playing with her dad at the beach when she was about 8 years old. They were building sandcastles and she was safe.

Her mind snapped back to the present. Not because of the beating. Someone was at the door.

The knock grew louder.

Tom stopped and pushed his hair off his face. He was sweating from the exertion.

'Stay there and don't make a sound. Or I swear, I will kill you,' he warned Lil.

She lay still and defenceless on the floor as he opened the door a few inches.

'Hello, can I help you?' smiled Tom, as he switched on the artificial charm.

'Can I speak to Miss Hunt, please?'

'She's lying down. You can speak to me,' Tom replied, forcing a smile.

'Miss Hunt reported an issue with the shower. Do you mind if I come in and take a look?' asked the man, hopefully.

'No need. We are checking out in half an hour.'

Tom didn't wait for a response as he shut the door.

'Get up you, stupid bitch. I'm taking you home. Now!'

Lil rolled onto all fours. Tom helped her to her feet by her hair.

Outside the door, the concierge paused before heading back to reception. He had seen the expression on Lil's face when she saw the man who had insisted on waiting for her. Fear. He had wanted to check that she was okay.

Something didn't feel right, but all he could do was wait until she checked out.

Inside the room, Tom watched Lil's every move as she packed her few belongings.

He was deliberating how to get away with murder.

Chapter Forty-Six

Agatha was in a killing mood.

Her maman had spent the morning giving her tasks to do around the farm and in their home, to keep her busy. One hundred jars of homemade jam were boxed and ready to be dropped off at the post office. She had also very firmly told her that there was to be no more killing of young men in B&Bs.

Ever.

They agreed that, if the urge became too great, she could use the stone outhouse. Maman didn't understand the fire of her urge that burned deep within.

Today, the flames needed to be fanned.

Alone in her bedroom, Agatha checked her killing kit. Gloves, Rohypnol, cable ties, a knife, her new black trench coat and her favourite item, the sock. She threw the backpack casually over her shoulder and put it in the boot of her car before heading to the kitchen to find Maman.

She found her, cleaning the already-clean kitchen.

'I will take your orders to the post office. It will keep me busy.'

'Thank you, Agatha. Can I trust you to behave?'

'Maman. Stop worrying! The police aren't knocking at the door, are they?'

'Not yet.'

'You killed my father and they didn't come. I'm cleverer than you,' she beamed.

I am my father's daughter. I now understand the sense of euphoria watching someone take their last breath. My face is the last one they see.

Faith ignored her daughter's joviality and offered to help her load the car.

'I don't need any help, thanks. You finish the cleaning.'

I don't want you to see my killing kit in the car.

It took Agatha twenty minutes to transfer the boxes to her Land Rover.

Merde! This is taking longer than expected. I have my own work to do.

After saying goodbye to her maman, Agatha sped down the rural country roads to the post office. It was usually a thirty-minute drive but she was there in twenty-three.

The post office was divided into three sections: the actual counter, a small shop selling arts and crafts, and a coffee shop. The ice cream was always popular with tourists.

The door was already open, Arjun Chopra was behind the post office counter and his wife, Diya, was busy serving tea and cake. They had run their business for five years and Diya was expecting their first child, after three years of trying.

Agatha stood in the doorway.

'I have a number of boxes for delivery. Can I bring them in?' she asked.

Arjun smiled politely. He found the young girl unnerving and much preferred to deal with her mother. 'Yes, of course. I'll get Noah to help you. He's in the back, unloading stock. One moment please.'

Agatha had seen Noah before. He had worked there for about two years, was in his mid-twenties, already balding, lived at home with his parents and was about four stones overweight. Agatha had no desire to kill him. He didn't meet her profile of available, vulnerable and desirable. He was safe.

The next target to meet her profile was only feet away from her but she had been so focused on getting rid of the boxes of jam that, at first, she hadn't noticed him.

Theodore Forst was oblivious to Agatha and her numerous boxes. He was mindlessly drinking his coffee and working his way through a tuna-melt panini while reading 'The Five Stages of Grief' on his Kindle. From the age of three, he had been raised by his grandparents after his parents had perished in a car accident on their way to the airport to celebrate their fifth wedding anniversary. A drunken lorry driver had collided with their car after he fell asleep at the wheel. The high-speed collision had engulfed their car in a fireball. Young Theodore had been dropped off, to spend the weekend with Grandma and Grandad, only minutes before the tragedy.

He had been too young to remember his parents. But he could clearly picture his grandmother whom he lost eight months ago to nephritis, an inflammation of the kidneys after a bacterial infection. His grandfather couldn't cope without his companion of fifty-nine years. He became isolated as the sadness and depression took a strong grip.

'The pain never stops,' he would say and, two months later, he died of a broken heart. He had left his only grandchild financially stable, with a home, but also alone.

Theodore now found himself in a café, having something to eat, as there was nothing in the cupboards or fridge at home. He had just returned from a week in Crete the previous day. He needed to have a break from the house, where he expected his grandfather to walk in from the garden and make them both a sandwich for lunch.

His week away had created new memories and helped him to think of his grandparents with love, rather than melancholy.

He had stayed in the Attalos Boutique Studios, a family-run business in Agia Pelagia. His spacious room was clean and a lemon tree grew outside, near his balcony, adding dabs of bright colour to the view. The staff were caring, welcoming and attentive. In the afternoons, he would walk into town to visit the bay of the small coastal town which was lined with bars and restaurants. The turquoise water was so clear that you could see the fish as you swam.

In the evenings, he would go to his favourite seafood restaurant, Bravo. The food was delicious and the view over the bay was stunning. He would order what Tomas recommended as the 'catch of the day' and watch the sunset over the bay. At the end of his meal, Adonis would bring him the bill and a shot of complimentary Ouzo. He had loved the buzz and camaraderie of the restaurant.

Back in Northumberland, he had swapped red snapper and sangria for a panini and white coffee.

'Can I join you?'

At first, he thought the pretty girl with green eyes was talking to someone else. He looked up from his Kindle and saw that other tables were free.

'Sure,' he replied.

Placing her coffee, she pulled out the chair next to him.

'I'm Agatha.'

'Theodore.'

'I've never seen you here before, Theodore. Do you live locally?'

'Not too far away, and you?'

'Not too far away,' she grinned. 'What are you reading?'

'How to cope with grief. Not a very cheery subject.'

'Someone you know has died?'

'My grandparents. I live with them. I mean, I used to live with them.'

'And now you are on your own?'

'I am. Just taking each day as it comes,' he said, with sadness.

Vulnerable, available and desirable. Theodore, you tick all my boxes.

'You look tanned. Have you been on holiday?' she asked, deliberately changing the subject and building up to the part where she would prey on his susceptibility.

Theodore told Agatha about the warmth of the Greek people, the great food and the beautiful views surrounded by azure water. She told him very little about herself, adeptly turning the questions and attention back to him.

After another round of coffees, paid for by Theodore, she knew where he lived and how the loss of his grandparents had left him utterly bereft.

'Theodore, you need cheering up. How about I show you the farm where I live? My maman will prepare us dinner tonight.'

He didn't need to think about his decision. He didn't want to be alone.

'I'd love to. Thank you, Agatha.'

'Did you drive here?' she asked.

'No, I walked. I wanted to clear my head.'

'Perfect. We will go in my car.'

Agatha felt the anticipation build as they headed to her Land Rover. She had another victim. It was only yesterday that she had taken the life of Philip Daw.

'Climb in,' she said. 'I just need to check something in the back.'

Theodore did as she said.

She went to the back of the vehicle and retrieved her killing kit. Opening the backpack, it was there, lying ready on the top.

The blue sock.

Inserting her hand, she felt the four pieces of paper before choosing one and withdrawing it with anticipation. She loved this part.

Death by numbers.

Carefully she unfolded it. She smiled at the number. Theodore Forst's end of life had been determined by the number 3.

Death by drowning.

Chapter Forty-Seven

The drive home in Tom's spacious BMW X5 should have been one of comfort.

Lil watched the clock. She should have been getting ready for her date with Boston. In an hour, he would be arriving at the hotel to meet her at the bar. Instead of having dinner with a kind gentleman, she knew that, once she arrived home, she would receive the biggest beating of her life.

Tom had behaved as if nothing had happened. It was part of the game he played. He had spent the last hour on work calls which came straight through to the car. He was obsessed with power and control. Lil was forced to listen as he spoke to some of the callers as if they were inconsequential.

He had sworn at and belittled David Morrison, Director of Highways and Transportation, over a report which had to go to full council, demanding that he reconsider the funding proposal.

Then his manner changed.

His boss rang. Councillor George Shakespeare, Leader of Northshireland County Council.

'Leader! How were your birthday celebrations?' he gushed.

'They were good, thanks. I hear you're not feeling very well.'

Councillor Shakespeare did not like Chief Executive Tom Quick, who had been recruited before he had been elected as leader. Egocentric and arrogant were descriptions that came to mind when he thought of Tom Quick. However, so far, he hadn't stepped over the line and the county council was in a good financial position.

'Just a stomach bug. I can't be too far from the bathroom,' lied Tom.

'You sound as if you are in the car,' stated his leader.

'No, I'm in the bathroom,' responded Tom.

The leader knew when he was ringing someone in their car, as the sound was amplified. He did so numerous times a day.

'I want an update on how many empty social housing properties we have in Northshireland, along with costs of refurbishment and housing needs.'

'Sure, I'll …,' started Tom.

'I want it tomorrow. I'll see you in my office at 5 pm. Don't worry, you can use my private bathroom, if needed.' The leader ended the call without bothering to say goodbye.

The next call Tom made was to his director of housing.

*

Boston was feeling a mixture of nerves and excitement. There was something about Lil that drew him in.

He was fifteen minutes early but he didn't care if he seemed too keen. He was.

Making his way up the steps of the DoubleTree Hotel and Spa, he headed to the bar, carrying a large bouquet of bright and vibrant sunflowers for Lil. On reflection, he would deliver them to her room.

Heading back to the reception, he was greeted by the concierge.

'How can I help you, Sir?'

'Hello. I know you can't give out guests' room numbers. However, would you be able to ring Lil Hunt's room please, and ask her if it is okay if Boston drops off a gift?'

'You are correct. We can't give out room numbers but unfortunately, I can't call Ms Hunt for you,' replied the concierge.

'It's okay. I'll wait for her at the bar. I'm a little early.'

'You will have a long wait. Ms Hunt checked out this afternoon.'

Boston felt a crushing disappointment. 'Are you sure?'

'Are you a close friend of Ms Hunt?'

'We only met today. We were supposed to meet here at 8 pm for dinner.'

'I am overstepping the line, but I think Ms Hunt may be in some kind of trouble.'

*

They were on the drive outside their luxury home, or prison, as it was for Lil.

'Get out,' snapped Tom.

She did as he asked and followed him into the house. She stood still and silently as he locked the front door.

No escape.

'Look at me,' he ordered. Lil looked at him. He was seething.

Time passed between them. Lil could feel her heart beating in her ears as she waited to learn what retribution Tom would choose.

'You are to go to our bedroom and immediately clean the ensuite. Use only your hands. No cloth. We need a new cleaner, but you already know that after Althea helped you escape.'

He smiled as he said the words. He was enjoying having Lil hang on his every word. Standing there, like a naughty child, not knowing what her punishment would be.

'Then,' he continued, 'you will go to bed. You are not permitted to have anything to eat or drink. I have to work this evening until late. Tomorrow night, you will be whipped. You will receive one lash for every hour you were away from home.'

Lil had been gone for thirty-six hours.

Chapter Forty-Eight

Agatha actually liked Theodore. She found him easy to talk to.

On the drive back to Crow Springs Farm, they had sung along to the radio. He was a very good singer and, when Agatha sang along to 'Dancing Queen' by Abba in French, he discovered she was bilingual.

She had learned that he was a freelance graphic designer for websites, brochures, advertising campaigns and electronic media. She told him about her previous life in France and the freedom of picking grapes in the vineyards.

He had made fun of her old Land Rover Discovery and said that it reminded him a little of the television programme 'Vera', where DCI Vera Stanhope, played by Brenda Blethyn, drove around in a similar vehicle. But he told her that, apparently the model was automatic because Brenda Blethyn didn't have a manual licence and just pretended to change the gears.

Agatha confessed that she had never seen an episode of 'Vera'. She rarely watched television, preferring to spend her free time outdoors, walking across the lands. She would have to check out the programme. But not tonight. It was bath night with Theodore.

Agatha parked her car next to Faith's. She was excited to see what her maman thought of Theodore.

'Come on then, and I'll introduce you to Maman,' she smiled.

Faith was in the kitchen, making shepherd's pie for their evening meal, when Agatha walked in.

'Hi, Maman. I'd like you to meet Theodore.'

Faith turned and saw a young innocent man. She knew instantly what his fate would be.

'Hello, Theodore. I'm Faith.'

'Can I get you a drink?' asked Agatha.

'A cup of tea, please. Thank you,' he replied.

'No,' said Faith. 'You two both make yourselves comfortable at the table and I'll make it.' Mother and daughter locked eyes. Faith didn't want her daughter drugging him.

'Is it okay if Theodore stays for something to eat?' asked Agatha, sweetly.

'Yes, of course. There's plenty. Do you like shepherd's pie, Theodore?'

Faith saw sadness creep into the young boy's eyes.

'It's one of my favourites. My grandma used to make it for me. She died eight months ago and my grandfather two months later.'

'I'm sorry,' said Faith. 'You must miss them both.'

'I do,' he admitted.

'Theodore is all alone in the world, Maman,' explained Agatha. 'I thought he could eat with us and then I will show him the farm and the pigpen. Do you like pigs, Theodore?' she grinned.

'I like most animals.'

Faith gave her daughter a steely look. Agatha ignored her and carried on, 'You did say the pigpen area was fine, didn't you, Maman?'

'Yes, Agatha. Showing Theodore around the farm is fine.'

'I don't want to intrude,' he said.

'You are not. We don't get many visitors. You can stay the night if you wish. We have a spare room, or there's always my bed,' Agatha winked.

Theodore felt his cheeks redden. At twenty-two, he had been in relationships but the longest had only lasted six months. He had been too busy working and helping his grandparents around the house.

'I'll just check the oven and then I'll make a pot of tea. Agatha, would you mind helping me with the vegetables please?' asked Faith.

'I would mind. I'm talking to Theodore.'

Faith tried another tactic. 'Did you manage to post my parcels?'

'Yes, that's where I met Theodore.'

'I have some more orders to go out which are boxed up and ready. Would you mind putting them in your car and dropping them off tomorrow?' she asked, trying to remove her daughter from Theodore's side so that she could ask her nicely not to kill him.

'I'll do it tomorrow,' smiled Agatha, knowing that her maman wanted to give her a lecture on not randomly killing young boys. She didn't want to hear it.

Shaking her head, Faith switched on the television as she waited for the kettle to boil. She needed the distraction of some background noise.

The news was on. The reporter was outside a B&B called Hill House in Falstone, about a ten-minute drive, or thirty-minute walk, from the farmhouse.

'Yesterday afternoon, two bodies were discovered here at Hill House B&B. One is believed to be the owner, 72-year-old Miriam Hill, and also 18-year-old Philip Daw, who was staying at the accommodation. The police are treating one of the deaths as murder and the other, at the current time, as unexplained. They are appealing for any witnesses and keen to speak to anyone who may have seen Philip Daw in the local area.'

A photo of the young man flashed up on the screen.

Faith turned the channel over and focused on making the tea. Her daughter's handiwork was on the local news and her next victim was about to have his last meal at her kitchen table.

'Wow! A murder! That's not too far from here,' said Agatha.

'It's tragic,' agreed Theodore.

'It also means that there is a murderer on the loose,' continued Agatha. 'You need to be careful. It could be me, for all you know!'

Agatha started to giggle, followed by Theodore. 'You are too nice to murder anyone,' he said.

Faith listened and observed her daughter as she flirted and playfully teased Theodore.

You are so wrong!

After the shepherd's pie, with root vegetables on the side, Agatha announced that she was going to show Theodore the pigpen.

'Great idea,' said Faith. 'I'll come with you. I want to collect some eggs for breakfast tomorrow and Guzzle can stretch his legs.'

'I'll get them for you,' said Agatha, challengingly.

'You have already helped me today by going to the post office. I'll come with you and then I'll drop Theodore off home, safe and sound.'

'I'll drive him.'

'It's not open to negotiation,' replied Faith.

Together, they walked across the fields to the pigpen and Faith collected some eggs. She watched as Agatha took great pleasure in showing Theodore the stone outhouse and pigpen.

Before dropping him home, Faith grabbed her mobile phone and turned it on. When it was late, or getting dark, she took it with her in case she ever broke down on the winding rural roads.

It vibrated as a text message came in. She checked the time. It had been sent at 9.12 pm, about one hour ago.

'Let's meet at noon on Saturday at The Plough.'

Tom Quick was back on the scene.

Chapter Forty-Nine

Two days had passed since the bodies of 72-year-old Miriam Hill and 18-year-old Philip Daw were discovered. Miriam's death was being treated as heart failure due to trauma.

DCI Webb wanted the case solving. He had failed to find the killer of two prison officers and he didn't want another unsolved case on his record. He had called a briefing and was firing off the questions.

'What do we know about Philip Daw? Anyone?' he asked.

'The parents have been tracked and contacted in Manchester. He was their only child. His mother, Sophie Daw, said he was travelling around Northumberland before going to do a culinary arts degree at the University of West London,' replied DC Sterling.

'What about any CCTV in the area?' asked the DCI.

'Nothing yet, Sir,' replied DC Earle. 'We tracked the victim's phone signal to the Blackcock Inn but the manager said that the CCTV hadn't been working for weeks. Also, the bar staff, who were on shift when we think he visited the pub, can't remember him. They said they serve too many people and can only remember the drunks that get a little too loud at times.'

'Any text messages or leads on his phone?'

'No, Sir,' continued DC Earle. 'The cybercrime unit confirmed that, for a young person, he rarely used his phone. Wasn't on any social media sites. The last text was to his mother, saying that he had found a B&B and was staying in Falstone.'

'A young man has been tied to a bed and stabbed multiple times. Someone, somewhere, must have seen or known something,' said DCI Webb, not hiding his frustration.

'There was one thing,' said DS Pickle.

'Which is?' asked DCI Webb, not holding out much hope from his lazy detective sergeant.

'The contents of his backpack have been examined and, oddly, it didn't contain a coat or jacket. There wasn't one found in his room. He was either travelling without one or it has been taken.'

'And how likely, DS Pickle, do you think anyone would go travelling without a coat or jacket? In the UK, where it rains constantly at times, even in the summer?' scolded the DCI. 'DC Earle, contact the parents and ask if they can remember what Philip was wearing the day he left home.'

'Shall I step outside and make the call now, Sir?'

'Yes, please do. Does anyone else have any updates for this particular case?'

Those present remained silent.

'Any other updates?' asked the DCI.

'Sir, just before this briefing, I received a message that traffic have located Emma Beale's car, a white Volkswagen Up. It was found, with a baby seat in the back, in the car park of one of the popular nature walks, about 45 minutes from here. It was unlocked but the keys weren't in the car,' reported PC Hodgson

'DS Pickle, can you arrange for forensics to take a look at it? Find out how long it's been there and if anyone saw the driver.'

'Yes, Sir. I'll do that today.'

The DCI rolled his eyes out loud. He wasn't asking her to do it next week.

All heads turned when DC Earle re-entered the room. She didn't bother to take her seat. Instead, she spoke to her boss from the centre of the room.

'Sir, I've spoken to Sophie Daw, and Philip was wearing a coat on the day he left. An unusual coat for a young person. It was a black trench coat.'

'I hope it will be easier to find than a grey one,' muttered DCI Webb.

Chapter Fifty

I haven't slept well.

Tom Quick and Theodore dominate my thoughts. You can't find two people so different. Tom has darkness running through his veins and Theodore has humanity.

They have one thing in common though. They will both be deceased, very soon.

When I dropped Theodore off at his home, I tried to warn him about Agatha. I told him that she wasn't quite what she seemed and it would be best if he didn't see her again.

His response was that she was young and had time to change. He pleaded with me to let them see each other, as the previous few hours had been his happiest in months. Plus, my shepherd's pie is nearly as good as his grandmother's. We agreed that he could come to the house again, as long as I was at home.

It is only a matter of time before Agatha seals his fate.

I haven't responded to Tom Quick's message from yesterday and I am not planning to meet him at the weekend. There is something dangerous about him that I find exciting, but I will meet him when I am ready. In the meantime, I want to know more about him. There is a lot of information online regarding him as a chief executive but very little about him personally. I plan to fill in the gaps.

I'm not making jam today, even though I have orders to fulfil.

I'm making poison.

For thousands of years, our ancestors have known about the power of plant toxins In hieroglyphics. The Egyptians recorded numerous recipes for poison and the Romans used poisons to get rid of their subjects and opposition. Poisoning for personal benefit became a status symbol in the first century AD. The most popular are vegetable poisons, which include plants with belladonna alkaloids, such as hemlock, deadly nightshade and colchicum autumnale, commonly known as autumn crocus.

Today, I'm using conium maculatum, also known as poison hemlock, which is attributed to the death of the famous Greek philosopher, Socrates, in 399 BC.

I've done my research and know that all parts of this plant are poisonous. Symptoms appear thirty minutes to three hours after ingestion, depending on the amount consumed. It causes paralysis of the central nervous system, which leads to respiratory failure.

I'm wearing plastic gloves to chop the plant before I drop it into the juicer, along with the leaves and stalk.

It has to taste good, so I chop cucumber, celery, spinach and ginger and add some frozen pineapple chunks. I switch the juicer on and watch the ingredients become green liquid in under ten seconds.

Now I need to try it out.

Chapter Fifty-One

For the third time that morning, Boston tried Lil's phone. It went straight to voicemail. Again.

He had been drawn to her compassionate spirit and easy-going way. Something had sparked between them when they met. His instinct told him that their paths would cross again. But when?

A man had checked out on Lil's behalf. Boston's mind went back to the concierge's belief that she might have been in trouble. There had been bruises on her face. What if she hadn't been in a car accident and someone had assaulted her?

Disappointment swept over him. He knew so little about her; only her name and mobile number. The next day, he would be back at work, with forty-five flying hours spread over six days. He had some commuting to do as he was also piloting flights from Newcastle, Liverpool and Manchester.

Hopefully, Lil feels the same way and will contact me.

*

Tom Quick was exasperated as Faith hadn't responded to his message. That had never happened before.

Women always messaged him back.

He also had to deal with Lil that night, as soon as the housing meeting with the leader of the council and his director of housing was over. 'The Leader', as all staff formally referred to him, wanted residents to live in a healthy thriving community. He wanted boarded-up properties refurbished and low-income families rehoused. Tom didn't agree. He didn't care about the residents but only about his own salary and status.

He was extremely bothered that someone had called Lil the previous night.

He had gone to his office to prepare for the housing meeting, while Lil went to clean the ensuite floor. He had confiscated her mobile phone and it had lain discarded on his desk. He was surprised when it rang and was even more surprised not to see his mother's name come up on the screen.

He had turned the phone off to end the call.

Who the hell is Boston?

He reached for his mobile phone and sent another message. 'I have a proposal for you. The Plough. Noon on Saturday.'

He clicked 'Send'.

There was a knock at his office door. His personal assistant appeared. 'The clients are here for your next meeting. Shall I show them in?' she asked politely.

No response.

'No, not yet,' he snapped, continuing to look at his phone.

Sarah hesitated, waiting for further instruction on how long to keep the chief executive of another local authority waiting. None came.

She closed the door.

Faith smiled at the message on her screen. Usually, she kept her phone switched off but she knew that her silence would prompt Tom to send another message.

She typed her response and pressed 'Send'.

'I'm busy Saturday. What's the proposal?'

Tom glared at the reply. This was new territory. His looks and status always got him the women he wanted. He had never been turned down. Even as a teenager, he got or just took who he wanted.

His retort was instant.

'I want to offer you a job.'

Faith raised her eyebrows. She didn't need another job. Financially, she still had the money from her late parents and her business, which generated enough income to cover the running of the farm.

She messaged back.

'Doing what?'

Tom didn't have time to play table tennis text messaging. He got straight to the point.

'Housekeeper, my house.'

Faith frowned at his answer.

What is he up to?

It would be much easier to poison him if she had access to his fridge.

Her special poisonous green juice had been a success. She had tried it on one of the Kentish sheep that roamed on the top field. Using a funnel, she poured the green liquid down the animal's throat. The ewe had been fine at first. Then she watched as it dropped to the ground, convulsing. Satisfied that she had the mixture right, she headed back for a cup of coffee before returning a few hours later while walking Guzzle.

The sheep lay dead. Its eyes were shut and white spittle remained around its open mouth.

She was intrigued to see where and how Tom Quick lived.

You can tell a lot about a person and their mind from how they live.

She replied.

'Call me later.'

Tom shook his head at her ingratitude. He would call her that night from home. Then he would deal with Lil after she explained who Boston was.

Walking towards his office door he threw it open.

'Tobias! Great to see you again. Sorry about the delay. I was on an urgent call,' he lied, as he switched to his charming and charismatic mode.

Chapter Fifty-Two

DC Earle and DC Sterling made their way towards DCI Webb's office.

'Anything you are currently dealing with can wait,' he had said when he called them.

He hadn't informed DS Pickle.

While the DCI waited for them, he read the case notes of the unsolved murders of the two prisoner officers, Daryl Sinnatt and Sue Aldine. When you are the lead investigating officer, and no one is charged with the crime, it never leaves your mind. No matter how many years pass, you continue to pursue justice for the killer and closure for the family.

Their murders, nearly three years ago, were always in his thoughts. He remembered vividly walking into the crime scene, Sue's bedroom. They had been having an affair. Both bodies had been mutilated, the bed seeped in blood, and the room was a stark bloody contrast to the sanitary condition of the rest of the house.

The lovers had been purposely splayed naked and crudely carved open, with their intestines exposed. Neither had been sexually assaulted and only Daryl's semen had been found at the scene. His bowels had opened, and the room had smelt of death, faeces and gore.

There were no fingerprints or fibres left at the scene. The murderer had been careful, apart from the hairs found by forensics. One was on Daryl's torso and the other in Sue's bathroom sink, where they believed the killer had cleaned himself before leaving the scene. The one in the bathroom contained root pulp and had come back as a match for 51-year-old William Channing. He had just been released from HMP Frankland, where both of the deceased had worked. He had served nearly seventeen years for kidnap, false imprisonment and murder.

Eighty-three-year-old, Ellen Haden, was Sue Aldine's neighbour and had confirmed that she had seen a tall man in a grey trench coat and hat entering the smart semi-detached property, on the day of the murders. He was then on parole, never to be seen again. He had literally vanished.

The knock on the door was firm.

'Come in,' he called. DC Earle and DC Sterling entered the room.

'Take a seat.' DCI Webb nodded to the vacant chairs opposite his organised and tidy desk. The detective constables sat down and remained silent. They could feel the tension radiating from their boss.

'I have the coroner's report,' said DCI Webb. 'Miriam Hill died from acute coronary failure. Philip Daw had fifteen stab wounds, nine of which were not life-threatening. They were inflicted with care to his shoulders, legs and arms. The other six were in his stomach and chest. The fatal one passed through his ribs and straight into his heart. Death probably took three or four minutes. He also had Rohypnol in his system.'

The detective chief inspector took a cold mouthful of coffee before asking, 'Any questions or observations?'

'You said that the wounds were inflicted with care which probably indicates that the killer was having fun, rather than carrying out a revenge attack,' commented DC Earle.

'That's one theory, indeed,' replied DCI Webb. 'Now for the interesting bit. Forensics have confirmed that there were no fingerprints or fibres found at the Hill House B&B crime scene. But there was a single strand of hair found lying on Philip Daw's chest. It contains root pulp and the nuclear DNA has been compared with all the samples on the database.'

There was a pause and another slurp of coffee.

'There was no exact match. However, the sample is a close match to a wanted offender. Whoever carried out this murder is likely to be related to the alleged offender of another unsolved case.'

DCI Webb drained the last of the bitter beverage.

'Who is it, Sir?' asked DC Sterling.

'Someone whose case you both worked on and whose work you witnessed first-hand. William Channing, the Grey Trench Coat Man.'

The detective constables turned to look at each other. They were thinking the same thing.

'There will be more murders!'

'There's more,' said DCI Webb. 'The DNA result showed the Hill House suspect to be female. It is highly likely that William Channing and the accused are father and daughter.'

'The apple doesn't fall far from the tree,' muttered DC Sterling.

Chapter Fifty-Three

Something was scaring Agatha.

Fear was unfamiliar to the emotionally manipulative and deceptive young girl.

She actually liked Theodore.

Her maman had asked her not to leave the farm because of the social media coverage of Philip Daw's murder. Agatha's thoughts returned to the feeling of having him powerless and bound to the bed and the sensation when the knife drove into his skin, causing the warm ruby blood to spill.

She would keep her word and not leave the farm.

But then again, she didn't need to. She had invited Theodore over for the afternoon. It was a lovely day for walking over the fields and having a picnic. She had never prepared a picnic for a boy before.

She had made a little hamper in one of the cardboard boxes that her maman used to package her homemade jam. There was fresh bread (made in the bread maker the previous day), ham, cheese, olives, fresh fruit and three bottles of blueberry juice. Two were safe to drink and the third had a slight tear to the label. That bottle contained Rohypnol.

Agatha had yet to decide which one she would give to Theodore.

A small piece of neatly folded white paper was in the back pocket of her jeans. It had the number 3 written on it. Death by drowning.

There was someone at the door. She would have to answer it as her maman was feeding the pigs. Agatha wondered if her day would end with a visit to the pigpen.

Theodore had a grin on his face, from ear to ear.

'Hello beautiful,' he said to Agatha as she opened the door.

'Hi,' she beamed.

'These are for you. Too cheesy?' he asked as he handed her a bunch of wildflowers which he had handpicked on the walk over.

'A little,' she teased. Another first. No boy had bought her flowers before.

'Come in,' she said. 'Head through to the kitchen.'

Theodore took a seat at the kitchen table and smiled when he saw what Agatha had prepared. Placing the flowers in the sink, she ran the tap. She didn't want them to die but felt too self-conscious to place them in a vase.

'I thought we could wander across the fields and have a picnic. I never tire of the view,' she suggested.

'Sure, can I carry the box for you?'

'It's okay, thanks. On second thought, I am going to leave the box here and just put the food in my backpack. Wait here and I'll get it.'

Agatha left the kitchen and took the stairs two at a time. Once inside the privacy of her bedroom, she retrieved her kill bag.

She felt conflicted.

I do like you, Theodore. But I also have a compulsion to kill. If the urge intensifies, you will die.

Back in the kitchen, she carefully packed their lunch into her backpack.

'Can I carry it for you?' Theodore asked.

'No!' she retorted sharply.

'Sorry. I was just trying to help,' he said, slightly unsettled by her reaction.

'Are you ready?' she asked, moving away from the subject of her kill bag.

He nodded.

'Let's go!' she said, with a false smile, as she pulled on her black trench coat.

*

I have spent most of the morning tending to the pigs and chickens. My favourite pig, Macy, has had numerous head rubs; she is so affectionate and loving. Yet she, too, plays her part in devouring the corpses. The big boar, Max, continually tries to nudge me out of the way as I check the welfare of the pigs.

They all seem fine and my focus is now elsewhere. I am watching Agatha and Theodore as they walk across the fields, side by side. I feel a sense of dread as he takes my daughter's hand. She hasn't rebuffed him. He has no idea of the danger he is, literally, holding on to.

Is this pigpen about to become a killing pen once again?

I will give them an hour before I take the boy home and save his life.

My back pocket is vibrating. I knew he would call. I swipe to answer but remain silent.

'Hello, Faith. Can you hear me?'

'I can. I can't talk for long as I'm busy.'

I smile as I know my dismissive tone will exasperate him.

'I'm lost, where exactly is your farmhouse?'

'You are not to come here, Tom. How do you know the name of the farm?'

I am not on the open electoral register which is available to anyone who wants to buy a copy. I registered as anonymous.

I can hear him laughing.

'Faith, I'm the chief executive and have contacts and influence. However, your farm isn't showing up on the Satnav. I'm near Stannersburn.'

I can hear my heart beating. My farm is in Stannersburn.

'There is a hotel called the Pheasant Inn. I will meet you in the bar in half an hour,' I say, hanging up before he has the chance to say anything else.

I never go into the Pheasant Inn. It is too near and I don't want my face to become familiar.

I jog back to the farmhouse to wash the scent of swine from my skin and put on a clean change of clothes. The inn is only a few minutes' drive. I will walk. Tom Quick will just have to wait until I get there. I am not comfortable with his intrusion.

The shower is hot, yet far from relaxing. It is over in a minute. I regret my decision not to meet Tom on Saturday.

Drying my body quickly, I pull on a pair of jeans, dark trainers and a sweatshirt. I haven't washed my hair, so I redo it into a ponytail and add a little makeup.

I'm ready to see what is so important that Tom Quick has nearly tracked me down.

I grab my bag and keys, before leaving a scribbled note for Agatha on the kitchen table.

'Gone for a long walk. I will drop Theodore off when I get back. DO NOT take him to the outhouse or pigpen. XX'

I pray for the boy's safety.

*

Agatha and Theodore had enjoyed their walk across the land. She had even taken him to the top field where the Kentish sheep and their lambs roamed. Theodore was sad to discover a dead ewe, with a woolly form covered in flies. Agatha had looked on apathetically.

They had enjoyed their lunch. Bread and cheese was one of Agatha's favourites, especially with a glass of red wine.

'Are you thirsty, Theodore?'

'A little.'

'Would you like some blueberry juice?'

'Please,' was his fateful reply.

Agatha pulled two bottles out of the kill bag. The one in her left hand had a slight tear to the label.

RIght or left? Life or death?

'Here you are,' she smiled, handing him one of the bottles. 'Do you fancy going back to the farmhouse to watch a movie?'

'Sounds perfect,' he grinned, as he took a long drink of the blueberry juice before getting to his feet. He stretched out his hand and helped Agatha to hers.

They stood face-to-face. Slowly, he leaned in for a kiss. She responded. Wrapping his arms around her, he didn't want the moment to end.

It was Agatha who broke the embrace. Taking his hand, she led him back towards the farmhouse and they walked in contented silence.

She was surprised to find the front door locked. Her maman should be back by now but she hadn't seen her on their way back past the pigpen.

Agatha unlocked the door and called out, 'Maman! I'm back. Theodore is here too.'

No response.

Walking into the kitchen she saw the note. Her maman's veiled threat of not harming Theodore made her smile. She placed her hand in her jeans pocket, feeling the folded piece of paper with its number sentencing Theodore to death by drowning.

'It seems my maman has gone out, Theodore. We have the place to ourselves. How about we freshen up after our walk and then maybe watch a movie.'

'What do you have in mind?'

'Let's have a bath.'

Chapter Fifty-Four

I have never been here before. I have driven past it but have never stopped.

The front of the Pheasant Inn looks inviting. It is a large stone building covered in trailing ivy and hanging baskets bursting with multicolours. There are a few tables outside, all occupied with people enjoying a few drinks. Avoiding eye contact, I head towards the entrance.

Inside looks rich and welcoming, with a red tartan carpet. The bar looks traditional for the area, made from heavy wood and offering draft local ales and cider.

Tom is sitting at a table next to the bar. He is dressed in a black shirt and jeans. His appearance is a combination of handsome, dangerous and smug. I can see that he has already ordered a bottle of Rioja and poured two glasses.

'Darling, it is good to see you.'

He moves from behind the table and squeezes me into him. I can feel the pressure on my ribs.

'Sorry I can't stay long,' I say, glancing at the wine. 'I have to be somewhere.'

At home, making sure my daughter doesn't feed her new friend to the pigs.

His eyes narrow and, to hide my smile, I take a seat and a sip of wine.

'There can't be anything more important than spending time with me,' he smiles, flashing his perfect white teeth.

A typical Tom Quick statement. He can't bear not being the most important person in someone's life.

I ignore his remark. I'm starting to understand how he works. He ramps up the charm, charisma and humour to get you to like him. Part of his ruse to take advantage of others.

'I can spare you twenty minutes of my time, Tom. Now it's nineteen. What do you want to tell me?'

He leans forward, inches from my face.

'I want you to work part-time for me. As my housekeeper, and you can choose the hours.'

'I don't need a job.'

'This is special.'

I raise my eyebrows. I can't see what is special about cleaning up after a narcissistic sociopath.

'There is something in the house I want rid of. I know it was you who was responsible for me lying on a bathroom floor in vomit.'

And your own faeces.

I smirk at him and shrug my shoulders in response. He glares at my insolence. I'm enjoying myself. It's interesting watching a narcissist's reaction when you dent his deluded ego, refusing to be controlled and are unimpressed by his power.

It disarms him.

'What exactly is it you want rid of?' I ask, jadedly.

'You will find out when you accept the job. I will pay you in cash. Once the house is purged, I will pay you £5,000.'

'And if I manage to purge your house in a week, I will still get paid?' I query.

'Yes!' he says, excitedly.

'I will accept the position of housekeeper. I will start on Monday, and I expect to be paid £5,000 in cash. Once your house has been cleaned to your satisfaction, you will pay me another £5,000. Do we have a deal?'

'£8,000,' he responds.

'Bye, Tom,' I say, rising from my seat.

'£10,000 it is.'

I sit back down and say, 'Text me your address and I will be there by 9 am on Monday. How do I get in?'

Tom passes me an envelope and I can feel that it contains a key.

'The address and further instructions are in there.'

'Thank you. Will you be there?'

'No, I'll be at work.'

'Okay, I need to go. I really am dealing with a life-or-death situation at the moment.'

'Shame. I thought maybe we could get a room here, or go back to yours,' he said, hopefully.

'Do you want to spend the evening being sick again with crippling stomach pains?' I ask sweetly.

'No!' he responds, alarmed.

'Well, you aren't coming back to mine. I'll be there on Monday. Enjoy the wine.'

I push my chair back and head for the exit. Alone.

He remains seated and the superficial charm has gone. I've bruised his ego by turning down his offer. There is no need for him to pretend anymore. He has achieved his goal by presenting me with the envelope.

I walk swiftly past the outdoor drinkers and head to the country track which leads back to Crow Springs Farm. It is so quiet, surrounded by field after field of jade green. Cabbage

White butterflies momentarily flutter amongst the brambles before elegantly moving on.

Curiosity has got the better of me and I just have to tear open the envelope.

It contains a key, a small passport-sized photo and a folded piece of paper. Tom has taken the trouble to type out the information.

KEYCODE FOR MAIN GATES: 86678425

There is something familiar about the sequence of numbers. Taking my mobile phone from my bag, I check the keypad. The numbers spell out Tom Quick.

I'm not surprised.

Underneath the keycode, it reads: ALARM CODE 311069

I guess that is his date of birth.

'House to be purified. I know you have the skills and knowledge. See photo.'

The photo is of an attractive female who looks in her late-40s or early-50s, with shoulder-length hair. I think back to Tom's words and read the note again. By purifying the house, it seems Tom expects me to commit murder.

At least, this time, I will be getting paid for it.

Chapter Fifty-Five

In the last twenty-four hours, DCI Webb had only slept four of them. One of the benefits of being divorced, and living on your own, is that you don't have to answer to anyone and can be at home as little as you wish.

His desk told the story of work, work and more work. Discarded mugs of cold coffee, empty packets of his favourite shortbread biscuits, and prepacked tuna and sweetcorn sandwich wrappers.

When he wasn't giving in to sleep, the detective chief inspector was methodically reading the documentation and evidence relating to the Grey Trench Coat Man's case. At the age of thirty-four, William Channing had been convicted at Newcastle Crown Court for the murders of 18-year-old Helen Boleyn and 27-year-old Rebecca Bixby, and the kidnap of 28-year-old Faith Taylor. He had served nearly seventeen years for his crimes.

DCI Webb suspected that these were just the ones they knew about and that there had been other victims. Could he have fathered a child with one of them?

He had murdered Rebecca Bixby within a day or two after kidnapping her. He ruled her out. The postmortem report on Helen Boleyn did not mention that she had recently given birth. Which left Faith Taylor. The press photos of the trial showed a young slim blonde-haired woman. DC Earle had searched the records at the General Register Office and there was no record of a 28-year-old Faith Taylor having given birth in 2005.

Neither was her DNA on record.

DCI Webb made a note of her parents' old address. He would send someone out to see if any of the neighbours had been living there at the same time as the Taylors. He wanted to check if any of them remembered hearing or seeing a baby.

The only other theory was that William Channing had been offending for many years before he was finally caught and had conceived a child during that time. So the alleged offender of the Philip Daw case could be aged between 19 and 38, if not slightly older. The Office for National Statistics (ONS) records showed that in 2005, there were 357,517 live female births in England.

PC Hodgson had been asked to search the records of the fifty-one Faith Taylors and twenty-one William Channings who were registered in England.

'Come in,' he said, as he heard someone knocking on his door.

It was DC Earle and DC Sterling.

'I hope you two are here to tell me that you have someone in custody for the Philip Daw murder.'

'Not quite, Sir,' said DC Earle. 'It is about the records PC Hodgson has been searching.'

'Go on,' said the DCI.

'A Faith Taylor is living at Crow Springs Farm in Stannersburn and her age matches one of William Channing's victims. The location is roughly one mile from the Philip Daw murder site,' reported DC Sterling.

'Are you saying that you think Faith Taylor may have been related to William Channing and it is her DNA at the scene?' asked their DCI.

'We don't know, Sir. I think it is worth paying her a visit to see if it is the same Faith Taylor,' replied DC Earle.

'Who else is registered as living at the farm?'

'No one. Just Faith Taylor,' replied DC Sterling.

'If it is the actual Faith Taylor, I think it is worth visiting her and asking if she knows the whereabouts of her abductor, William Channing. Because, if it is her, my instinct is telling me that she'll know,' said DCI Webb.

All of a sudden, his day had just got brighter.

Chapter Fifty-Six

Thirty minutes ago, the large freestanding bath had been too hot. The temperature had dropped and the bubbles had dispersed, but the bath stood untouched.

Agatha and Theodore lay naked in her bed. The quilt had slid onto the floor but neither of them had noticed. They lay content and entwined.

It was Theodore who broke the comfortable silence. 'Agatha, would you like to officially go out?'

'Officially?' she laughed. 'It's not the 1950s.'

'Would you like to be my girlfriend?' he asked.

Ben had been Agatha's only boyfriend. Since she had abducted him, and her maman had poisoned him, he may have described their relationship differently.

She thought for a moment. She did like Theodore.

'Yes, Theodore. I will be your girlfriend.'

The young man cuddled his girlfriend tightly. He never thought it would be possible to feel any happiness after the death of his grandparents. Tears fell from his eyes onto her head. Maybe she was his guardian angel and their paths were meant to cross to help him deal with the endless pain.

'Come on, let's have that bath. Maman will be due back soon.'

They shared a final kiss before walking naked, hand-in-hand, into the main bathroom. Like the rest of Faith's home, it was white and pristine.

'You climb in. You might need to add more hot water. I'm just getting us a drink.'

Before Theodore could say that he didn't need a drink, she had left the room.

He climbed in. The water was tepid. He pushed back the large square lever of the waterfall tap. Water flowed and swirled in the bath. At that moment, he felt he would die of happiness. He was about to be joined by the girl he could see himself falling in love with. Hopefully, in time, she would move in with him and they could create new memories in the house that was sentimental and comforting for him.

Agatha walked boldly and naked into the bathroom. She was carrying a bottle of blueberry juice which had a slight tear visible on the label.

'I thought you could do with a cold drink after all your hard work,' she winked. Closing the door, she slid the bolt along. 'We don't want Maman walking in on us.'

Walking to the top end of the bath, she climbed in behind him as she placed the blueberry juice on the side. The lethal dose of Rohypnol was concealed within.

He rested his head against her chest. She placed her head back against the bath and closed her eyes. Theodore's mobile phone rested on the windowsill, playing various tunes from his playlist on YouTube.

'I've never been as happy as this, in the last twenty-four hours, Agatha.'

I've enjoyed them too. Maybe we could make this work. As long as you never enter the stone outhouse. But I can't promise that it won't be occupied.

'Would you like to go on holiday sometime?' he asked. 'I want to get to know you better. My treat. I thought we could fly to Charles de Gaulle airport and spend a few days in Paris, then hire a car and you can show me where you grew up. We could go travelling when we wanted and where we wanted.'

The thought of going back to France appealed to her. However, she had no intention of ever taking him, or anyone else, back to the Carmens' vineyard. They might find out that her maman had secretly given birth to her and concealed her identity so she wouldn't forever be known as the daughter of a sexual predator and serial killer.

'Maybe, one day. We've only just met!'

'It feels as if I have known you for a long time,' he replied. 'I feel so comfortable with you. When I went to Crete, I felt that there was very little meaning to life. I feel fortunate to have met you.'

Agatha opened her eyes and reached for the shower gel.

'Let me wash your back,' she said, pushing herself upright.

That was when she noticed that the bottle of blueberry juice was no longer full. With the music playing, she hadn't heard him open the bottle and drink it.

'Theodore, it is very warm in this bath. Are you feeling okay?'

'I feel great, and thanks for the cold drink. It was very thoughtful of you.'

She opened the shower gel and started to wash his back. He was merrily chatting away but she was no longer listening. She had a decision to make.

To let him live or die.

If they got out of the bath now, she could get him into her bed before he became unresponsive. In twenty-four hours, he would have slept it off and maybe, one day, they could go to France.

Or she could keep him in the bath.

Agatha made her decision.

She was her father's daughter.

It wasn't long before the effects of the drug took hold. Talking started to become difficult and Theodore's words slurred.

'I don't feel good. I feel very drunk,' he garbled.

Agatha held him up out of the water but his head flopped back and forth as he slipped into unconsciousness. She felt the familiar excitement of what she was about to do creep through her body.

'I do like you, Theodore. It's just that I can't help it; killing people. You should have seen what I did to Philip Daw and my work was on the local news. How exciting is that?' she squealed. 'I have a special sock and I select a number out of it. The lucky dip of death. For you, I chose number 3. Drowning. Bye, Theodore.'

She climbed out of the bath.

Theodore's head rested back. His nose and mouth were out of the water. Leaning forward she kissed him but there was no response.

Walking to the end of the bath where his feet lay, she grabbed his ankles and watched as he slipped under the foamy water. With his face submerged, she placed his legs over the side of the bath. Gently, she pushed away the soapsuds that were bobbing on top of the water as she wanted a clear view of his face.

She watched until the last bubble of air had escaped from his nose.

Feeling cold, she left the bathroom and headed downstairs to the coat stand, where she covered her naked chilled body with the black trench coat.

She was heading back upstairs when the front door opened, and Faith walked in. She turned and smiled at her maman.

'You are back,' she said.

Faith immediately noticed the black trench coat and her daughter's bare legs.

'Are you just wearing a coat?' she asked.

'I am.'

'Why?'

'I've just got out of the bath.'

'Where is Theodore?'

'He's still in the bath.'

'Why is he in the bath? Ask him to get out and I'll take him home,' said Faith, annoyed at the intrusion of her personal space. She would have to clean the bathroom now.

'He can't get out of the bath,' Agatha said, not bothering with an explanation.

'Why?'

'He's drowned. Well, I think he's drowned. I pulled his head under the water, but I was starting to get cold so I nipped down to get my coat,' she said, matter-of-factly.

Faith pushed past her daughter and ran up the steps as fast as her legs would allow. She stopped at the threshold of the bathroom. Theodore was still in the same position where Agatha had left him.

'Why, Agatha? Why?' she yelled.

'You said no more killing in B&Bs. This isn't a B&B. What is your problem?' shouted Agatha.

Faith slid to the floor with her head in her hands. She knew at that moment that her daughter would never stop. Agatha had liked this boy, yet she still had no qualms about taking his life.

'Don't be mad, Maman,' Agatha said, bending down to give her a hug. 'Can you help me with something?'

'What?' snapped Faith.

'Can you help me to get Theodore to the pigpen?' she grinned.

It was then that they both heard a knock at the door and Guzzle's forewarning bark.

Chapter Fifty-Seven

We never get visitors. Our location is remote and we don't invite people over. The odds of anyone leaving here alive are currently very low.

'Agatha, I'll get the door. You stay up here.'

'Okay, Maman. I'll talk to Theodore,' she grins.

I leave her in the bathroom, and I head downstairs. Guzzle is barking and telling me that the outline of two people that I can see belongs to strangers. I open the door partially and Guzzle pokes his head out.

I recognise them and my heart is pulsating.

Nearly three years ago, when my daughter took the brief job at the Butterdish Café to entrap William Channing, I called to speak to the owner and Agatha's boss, Beryl Monroe. It was just after we had kidnapped William and left him to die of malnutrition and thirst in the stone outhouse.

I had to check if there had been any CCTV or if Beryl knew Agatha's surname. She had given her name as Agatha Hamilton at the interview and the job had been cash-in-hand as Agatha didn't have a UK bank account. Beryl knew nothing but, as I approached the café, I saw a police car parked nearby. Two plain-clothed officers stood in the doorway, ready to leave but I could tell by their clothes and manner that they were police. Our paths crossed as I entered the Butterdish Café.

Now they are at my home.

'Faith Taylor?' asks the man.

'Who is asking?' I reply.

'I am DC Sterling and this is DC Earle.' They show me their identity cards.

'Yes, I'm Faith.'

'Can we come in?' asks DC Earle.

Do you want to live? If you do, that's not a good idea.

'Sure, come into the kitchen. First door on your left, after you've taken your shoes off.'

They follow my directions and they both take a seat at the kitchen table, shoeless.

'Wow, what a lovely kitchen,' says DC Earle.

I know what you are doing. Saying something nice to win me over.

'Do you live here alone?' DC Sterling asks.

'No, there is Guzzle,' I say, stroking his head, 'a sounder of pigs, which I look after for Farmer Childs, and twelve chickens.'

'Have you lived here long?' asks DC Earle.

'About three years. Why?'

The two detective constables exchange a glance.

'Before then?' they ask in sync.

'Can you please tell me what this is about? I've had a long day and I've still got work to finish and animals to tend to.'

'We are investigating a murder. Less than a mile from here, a young boy was viciously stabbed multiple times,' says DC Earle, pausing for effect.

'That's sad. And you are here, because?'

'DNA found at the scene has been linked to an old case,' continues DC Sterling.

My disobedient daughter has brought trouble to our home. She is, at this very moment, upstairs with yet another dead boy. I hope neither of them wants to use the bathroom. I'm not sure how I will explain a naked drowned boy.

'I need to ask you some personal questions,' he says. 'When you were younger, were you a victim of William Channing?'

I let my face crumple, form tears and discharge sobs. I put my head in my hands to emphasise my heartache. I can only keep the charade up for so long, or I will start to laugh. I take deep breaths before speaking.

'Sorry. Is that why you are here? To tell me that he has been released from prison?'

The detective constables look baffled and I keep a straight face.

'Prison? No …' starts DC Sterling, until DC Earle interrupts him.

'Faith, do you have any children?'

'No, I never settled down. After the abduction, I found it hard to trust people. That's why I live here, with just nature and green space,' I say, giving them my best 'I'm a kind and caring person' smile.

'Can you call into the Hexham station tomorrow and give a statement on your time with William Channing? It would really help us if you did,' asks DC Sterling.

'Am I under arrest?' I ask, feigning shock.

'No, just helping us with our enquiries,' again said in unison.

'I gave a statement at the time and buried all the vile memories deep inside. Now you want me to travel twenty miles to your station and relive them?' I don't hide my displeasure. This time, I'm not acting. I don't like them or their questions.

'We can arrange transport,' replies DC Earle.

'You will need to give me a few days. I need to prepare myself mentally to be of any help to you. It has taken me many years to get over those days locked inside that house.'

I've just played the mental health card. Now what are you going to do? I got over William Channing by feeding him to the pigs. It was the best therapy ever.

'Okay. Here's my number and extension. Can you call the day before and we'll arrange a mutually convenient time then, for Tuesday?' asks DC Earle.

It will have to be Tuesday. I'm busy on Monday. Tom Quick wants me to kill Lil Hunt that day.

'Sure, let me show you out. Sorry, you've caught me at a bad time. I really need to get on.'

I show them to the door and, just as I think the interrogation is over, DC Sterling asks another question.

'You said you live alone. Yet there are two Land Rovers parked outside.'

'Yes, one is mine and the other belongs to Farmer Childs. The pig farmer left it there after having a few too many whiskeys.'

'We'll need to check that it is registered to him,' said DC Earle.

'You do that,' I respond.

I bought that vehicle from Father Childs for Agatha's 18th birthday. I purposely didn't change the ownership of the logbook as he's too sick and old to care. I will always keep Agatha untraceable and safe.

I close the door and turn around to find Agatha standing in the kitchen doorway. She had been listening from the hall.

'Maman, what shall we do? I'm too pretty to go to prison. Do you think they will arrest you for Father's murder?'

'What you will do, Agatha, is stop killing people. I now need to dispose of two detective constables and get the police off my back.'

'Exciting times, Maman! Can I help you get rid of them?'

I ignore my daughter's remark and head to bed. We will get Theodore out of the bath tomorrow.

Closing my bedroom curtains, I can see the detectives talking in their car. They seem to be embracing.

Life is never dull in the countryside.

*

DC Earle started up the Vauxhall Astra and turned to her colleague.

'Do you think she is involved in the murder of Philip Daw or the disappearance of William Channing?'

'No, she's too nice,' replied DC Sterling.

'I do,' said DC Earle. 'I think she knows much more than she is letting on. Our shift is over. Do you fancy a Chinese takeaway and a bottle of wine at mine?'

'Sounds great, Amelia.'

She leaned over and kissed him on the lips before heading home.

Amelia Earle and Jeremy Sterling were in a secret relationship. It had been going on for three months. For Amelia, it was just fun. They worked together and Jeremy was the person she spent all her time with so, to her, it made sense. Jeremy had been in love with Amelia for about two years and he had hoped that one day, his feelings would be reciprocated.

Neither knew that Faith was now planning their deaths.

Chapter Fifty-Eight

It's not often you spend some of the weekend helping your daughter dispose of a body. It is a lot harder than in the movies. A corpse is very heavy and hard to manoeuvre.

On the night of Theodore's drowning, Agatha drained the bathwater and we left him there for the night. He wasn't going anywhere and we had already had a visit from the police, so couldn't risk being caught, feeding poor Theodore to a sounder of pigs. I covered him with a bedsheet and we both slept well that night.

His clothes were placed in the metal drum to be burned the next day. It is starting to become a familiar pattern, destroying mobile phones and burning any items belonging to the victim.

On Saturday, we are having breakfast, as usual. Agatha has her pancakes and I opt for healthy poached eggs on toast with a sprinkle of chilli flakes. The hens are laying well and I can't help thinking that the nutrient-rich maggots they peck on in the pigpen may be the reason.

Agatha insists on using the shower in the main bathroom instead of taking up my offer of using my ensuite. She says it is because she likes the idea of being near to Theodore.

During the day, I keep her close to me. We do the necessary chores on the farm and in the house together. In the afternoon, she refuses to go for a walk. As an alternative, we watch a movie called 'Paradise' which is set in a futuristic world where you can transfer years of your life to others. One of the main characters has to transfer forty years of her life to pay off a debt, which robs her and her husband of the chance of being parents. It makes me think of my life, and Agatha's future, when I am no longer around to clean up the bodies after her.

By 9 pm, dusk is edging in. It is time.

In the bathroom, I pick up the discarded sheet and spread it out neatly on the floor. Agatha had removed it from Theodore earlier that morning when she showered.

On the count of three (I'm not sure why it is that number, but Agatha thinks it is very funny and yells, 'Number 3, drowning!'), we each grab an ankle and haul Theodore out of the bath and onto the sheet.

I wrap the sheet around most of his body and secure it with long lengths of duct tape, leaving from his knees down exposed. This way we can grab and drag the sheet. This process takes an hour and a lot of hard work. Wrapping up a dead body is tiring.

I'd like to say that we are handling his body with dignity and respect. It isn't the case. We push him head-first down the stairs before dragging him across the field and into the pigpen. They are ready for poor Theodore, as it is their first meal of the day. They also have to wait while Agatha and I cut through the tape to remove the sheet. Another item for the steel drum.

*

Today will bring its own challenges.

It is Monday, and I am parked on Tom Quick's drive in Felton. A forty-five-minute drive from my door to his.

His house from the outside is beautiful. A large, detached property with views of green lands and hills. His BMW isn't here but there is a silver Mercedes-Benz. Perhaps I am about to meet the owner of the car and the face in the photograph.

I head for the double main door and try the key. I have the alarm code ready.

I unlock the door but there is no need for the alarm code. She must be at home.

'Hello,' I shout, 'housekeeping.'

Silence.

The entrance hall is airy and pristine. I pick up my cleaning caddy, bought especially for my new role, and wander in search of the kitchen. I will start there.

I love my white kitchen at home but Tom Quick's is something out of a Country Living magazine. I'm standing in a vast space with traditional white country-kitchen units and black granite worktops. You could easily fit eight people around the white granite island which leads onto a large orangery, where three white sofas fill the space. There is a woman, with her back towards me, asleep on the middle one.

I presume she is asleep and not dead.

I hope you haven't set me up, Tom Quick.

I need to find out, so I gently nudge her shoulder and say, 'Hello, I'm housekeeping.'

She is beginning to stir. I'm relieved she isn't dead. I'd like a day off from dealing with the dead.

'Who are you?' There is a hoarseness to her voice.

'Sorry, I didn't mean to give you a shock. I'm Faith. Tom hired me as your housekeeper. Is there anywhere you'd like me to start?'

Slowly, she pulls herself into a sitting position. She is dressed in baby-blue pyjamas and a navy silk dressing gown. Her face is a mass of bruises. Finger marks are clearly visible around her throat and there are deep red wounds around her wrists.

I recognise the wounds from my own work; they are from cable ties.

'What happened?' I ask gently, even though I'm certain of the answer.

'Tom sent you?' asked Lil.

'Yes, to clean,' I reply.

'How do you know Tom?' Her eyes are fixed on me.

'We recently met in Alnwick. I don't know him well.'

'Have you slept with him?'

Wow, Lil, you are direct! I wouldn't say I've slept with him. He started to take me by force, if that counts.

'Have you?' she persists. 'Are you yet another one he's added to his futile pile of conquests?'

'Did Tom do that to your face?' I ask, changing the subject.

'Yes.'

'Why?'

'I tried to leave him, and he tracked me down.'

'How long have you been together?'

'Just over five years,' she says, sadly.

Then it all comes tumbling out.

Lil tells me how life really is with the narcissistic sociopath, Tom Quick. There are extravagant holidays, expensive pieces of jewellery, nice cars and the luxuriant house, or 'residential prison' as she describes it. I don't see it as the latter. I love it. The only thing missing is a pigpen since I need somewhere to dispose of the bodies when Agatha is around.

Manipulation, obsessive control, hostile behaviour, and verbal and physical abuse are part of everyday life for Lil. Escape, she feels, is hopeless.

'Why does he want you dead?'

She might as well know that things are actually worse than she believes.

'What? Why would you say that?' she asks, shocked.

'He wants me to purge your house for £10,000. Look.' I hand Lil the photo of her face that Tom gave me. 'It seems that he wants to add you to his futile pile.'

Lil tenses.

'You are going to kill me? Today?' she shrieks.

'Calm down. I can't deal with hysterics.'

I like Lil and I have no personal reason to kill her. I never had any intention to. I want to see where and how Tom Quick lives. Now I know.

'I'll pay you double to get rid of Tom.'

Poor desperate Lil. I don't kill for money. I kill for fun and I have every intention of killing Tom Quick for what he did to me at The Plough. He is no different to William Channing.

'I have two questions. Number one, where will you get £20,000 from? Number two, just so we are both clear, what specifically do you mean by 'get rid of Tom'?' I ask.

'I have been secretly moving money into a bank account. Tom doesn't seem to notice. I just take one of his debit cards and transfer £500. If we've been on holiday, I transfer £1,000. He never checks. I'll never be free to live a happy life while he is around. Please will you help me? I can't live like this anymore.'

Her body is wracked by heavy sobs. In a way, her experience is no different to my own with William Channing. We have both experienced imprisonment and abuse.

There is only one problem with Lil. She doesn't have the darkness within. She is too nice, and killing doesn't come naturally to her.

Her tears are subsiding and I need her full attention.

'Lil, I have to kill you.'

'No, please. I beg you,' she cries.

'I will kill you now if you don't stop bawling and listen to me.'

I'm feeling impatient. I still have the cleaning to do.

She wipes her bruised face on the sleeve of her silk dressing gown and takes some deep breaths.

'Sorry,' she mutters.

'This is what is going to happen. We are going to move from this lovely conservatory into the kitchen and you are going to make us both a coffee. Mine is a flat white, please. Then, you are going to help me clean this house.'

I pause as Lil is looking at me as if I am unhinged. Maybe I am, sometimes.

'Sorry,' she says.

'You apologise too much,' I interrupt.

'Sorry, I mean I'm not sorry,' she continues. 'You expect me to make you a coffee, and then help you clean my house, before you kill me.'

'I like coffee and, because I have been talking to you, I'm now running late. Tom will expect your already-clean house to be even cleaner when he gets home. I am not going to murder you today, or any other. We just need Tom to think I have murdered you. I do need you to trust me for this to work. Tomorrow, I need to drug you.'

I give her a little smile and shrug my shoulders.

'I'll make the coffee,' she replies.

Chapter Fifty-Nine

Once again, I am parked on Tom Quick's driveway. Today, I will be paid £10,000 for killing Lil.

Or so Tom Quick believes.

I actually enjoyed my time with Lil at their home. She made a great cup of coffee and, together, we cleaned room by room, and talked. Tom had messaged that evening to meet up but I declined his offer. He immediately rang, wanting to know how it had gone and when I would be back for the final purge.

I confirmed that it would be the next day.

He asked if I had met the lady of the house. I said I had seen her but she had been sleeping in the conservatory. He had asked what I thought of her. I said she was very attractive, even with the bruises. He replied that she had been in a car accident.

We both know that isn't true.

He had asked if I had the envelope which was left in his office. I confirmed that I had. It had contained half my wage.

The agreement was that I would meet him here at 7 pm. I am two hours early.

Picking up my large bag, I head for the front door which is already open. Lil is standing in the doorway, dressed in blue leggings and a white sweatshirt.

She hugs me. I freeze slightly. It is an odd sensation, to have someone hug you when you have been sent to kill them. I don't return the embrace.

'Coffee?' asks Lil.

'Yes, please. How are you?' I ask.

'I'm nervous. What if it doesn't work? He'll want us both dead.'

'It will work. You are not the first person I've drugged,' I confess.

She raises her eyebrows but remains silent. I start unpacking my bag and hold up a tall clear container.

'This is my very own special recipe of green juice. Make sure you don't drink it. If digested, you will feel the effects after thirty minutes to three hours, depending on the amount consumed. You will then have paralysis of the central nervous system, leading to respiratory failure, to look forward to.

Lil's eyes widen. It looks like a regular green health juice, apart from the extra ingredient, poison hemlock.

'It does have some health benefits,' I laugh. 'Cucumber, celery, spinach, ginger and pineapple.'

'How will you get Tom to drink it?'

'Don't worry about that. You will be unconscious at that stage,' I reply, trying to reassure her.

'This is also for you,' I say, as I remove a clear plastic bag containing a revolting mass.

'What the hell is that?'

'Sheep sick. This is what I will be pouring near your mouth and on your chest. We have to make Tom believe that I have poisoned you. In this small bottle is Rohypnol which will render you unconscious. Unless Tom takes your pulse, he will believe that I have poisoned you. That's where the sheep sick comes in. He won't want to touch you.'

'Where did you get the sheep sick from?'

'It is fresh this morning. I gave some green juice to a ewe on my land. It's not the first time. You have to test these things.'

She gives me a strange look.

'How do I know you won't kill me? How do I know that is actually Rohypnol, and not one of your poisons? I will know you have killed Tom. I will know your secret.'

Good point, Lil.

'You don't.'

Lil looks into my eyes as she places two cups of coffee on the kitchen island.

Don't look too close, Lil. You'll see the darkness within.

'If you do kill me, can I ask you to do something for me?' she asks.

'Depends on what it is,' I reply with caution.

'Could you go to the DoubleTree Hotel and Spa in Chester and leave a note at reception for someone called Boston Winter.'

'Who is Boston?' I'm intrigued.

Lil tells me the whole story of how their previous housekeeper, Althea, helped her escape from the house, her thirty-six hours of freedom and meeting the charming Boston.

'You are a quick worker, Lil. Out with the old and in with the new,' I tease. 'It is a shame you didn't make the date. He sounds like a nice guy. Okay, if I do kill you, I will go to the hotel and drop a note off.'

'Thank you. I just want to explain why I couldn't make the date and that those hours we had spent talking were my happiest in years.'

'Lil, you live with a narcissistic sociopath. The electric chair would be more pleasant than time spent with Tom Quick!' I reply.

'No. There once was a connection. A spark. Honestly, there was,' as she defends him.

'If you say so. Let's get on with planning your death,' I say, changing the subject. 'Rohypnol is a powerful sedative so you will not remember much while the drug is in your system. It will slow your breathing and heartrate, hopefully enough for Tom to think you are dead.

When you wake up, it is common for you to feel dizzy, drowsy, with a headache and maybe slurred speech. Go to bed and sleep it off. When you wake up, Tom will be gone. You will never see me or him again.

You need to report him missing. Say that you took some sleeping tablets as you had been awake most of the night before. When you woke up the next day, Tom's car was there but he wasn't in the house. Turn off the security cameras. Say that Tom turns them off when he brings lady friends over when you are out. That will keep the police busy trying to find out who it was.'

'I have Alprazolam to help with my anxiety. I'll leave it next to my bed for the police,' she says, helpfully.

'Do you want me to leave you lying in vomit, or shall I wipe your face and change your top before I leave?'

'Can you change it please, and take the top away?'

'Sure,' I say.

Lil walks over to a cupboard in the kitchen and opens it. Inside is a laundry basket and she lifts out a pink sweatshirt. 'Can you use this one, please?'

I nod my head in agreement.

I'm not sure where the last hour and a half has gone but now it is time.

'Lil,' I say gently, 'we need to quickly wash and put the coffee cups away and clean down any surfaces I've touched. Then, I need to drug you.'

Lil smiles at me and places an envelope from a nearby drawer in my hand. It has one word, written in very neat handwriting, on the front. 'Boston'.

'I promise to give it to him,' I say.

She gives me another hug and, this time, I hug her back. I like her. In another life or another time, we may have been friends.

'Drink this.' I hand her the Rohypnol, mixed with water. 'Then lie down on the floor. I'm not going to kill you, Lil. But, if you ever betray me, I will not hesitate. Do you understand?'

'I understand. I'm frightened.'

'Don't be. It will feel as if you are really drunk. I have had to give you a large dose as we only have twenty-five minutes before Tom is due home. Drink.'

Lil drinks while I replace the Rohypnol in the back pocket of my jeans.

Only ten minutes later, she is unconscious. I hope I haven't given her too much.

Chapter Sixty

I have never covered anyone in vomit before. It isn't pleasant, even when you are wearing rubber gloves.

Lil's pulse is beating, but only just.

Careful not to get sheep's spew on myself, I tip the bag and watch a large gloop slide onto her neck, just under her chin. Then I add a small amount to the corner of her mouth. She looks and smells deceased.

That's half the job done successfully.

I place the almost-empty plastic bag back into my large bag. I don't want to leave anything behind. The large container of green juice is in the fridge. Waiting for Tom Quick.

There's a sound of the front door opening and closing.

Showtime.

Tom is standing in the doorway, watching me. He looks striking in a pale grey suit and black shirt. No tie.

'It stinks in here.'

Entering the room, he keeps his eyes firmly on me, pausing briefly to look at his partner of five years, lying lifeless on the floor.

'You did it then,' he says, with a smile. 'You know she'd met someone else? Called Boston. I got the information out of her eventually.'

I shake my head. Lil's clandestine trysts have nothing to do with me.

He continues in my direction, grabs the back of my hair, and pulls me into a passionate kiss.

'Take your clothes off,' he orders.

I do not want to have sex with Tom Quick. Or do I?

'Do you have an envelope for me?' I ask.

He removes a white envelope from his inside jacket pocket which I presume contains £5,000. It feels like £5,000. I move away from him and place it in my large bag. The one that contains another envelope; a declaration of happiness, for me to give to Boston.

Tom grabs my arm and pulls me towards him.

'Doesn't a girl get a drink first?'

'What would you like?' he asks.

'Something chilled,' I reply.

'There's a Veuve Clicquot in the fridge.' He heads towards it. 'What's this?' he asks, removing my special green juice.

'That was my lunch. I haven't had it yet. Green juice; it's a nutrition hit of goodness. Try it,' I suggest.

There is a look of disdain on his handsome face.

'You first,' he says.

'I'm good, thanks. I'd rather have champagne over green juice. Just the one glass as I'm driving, and I need to dispose of your girlfriend.'

He's onto me. Without warning, he walks over to the motionless Lil and kicks her hard in the side. I hold my breath. She doesn't groan or move. I hope she is still alive.

'Please have some respect for the dead,' I interject.

'I was just checking,' he says. 'What is she covered in?'

'I poisoned her. It's vomit. I'll clean it up before I go.'

'Did she take long to die?' he asks, staring at the body.

'About fifteen minutes.'

'Was she in pain?'

'Yes,' I respond.

'Good,' he says.

He removes the champagne and green juice from the fridge and places them next to two Dartington Crystal champagne flutes. The champagne cork hits the ceiling. I don't flinch at the sound as I am controlling my fear of what is about to happen.

He fills one of the glasses. The bubbles dance up to the surface and slide down the side of the crystal. The other he fills with the green juice. I know which one he is going to hand to me.

'Cheers,' he smirks.

'I'd rather have champagne,' I say, with confidence that I do not feel.

'I'd rather not be poisoned. How dare you try and poison me a second time! In my own home. Now drink it or I will pour it down your throat,' he warns.

Stalemate.

He moves towards me. I'm trapped. The kitchen island is directly behind me and he is inches from my face. I follow his eyes, which are fixed on a kitchen knife block. It contains five knives. He'll only need one.

'Drink,' he repeats.

I pick up the elegant glass. It has a hand-cut design which includes smaller crystals. It is a nice-looking glass and it is a shame what is about to happen.

Before he can reach for a kitchen blade, I smash the end of the champagne flute on the island worktop. Holding the stem with all my fear, I slam the jagged weapon into his trachea. He staggers backwards towards the kitchen cupboards. I follow him, driving the glass in, deeper and deeper. I release my hold as he slumps to the floor.

Grabbing a tea towel, I wrap it around the wound. The glass is still embedded. I don't want the scene to be covered in a sea of rosy blood.

An eerie noise escapes from his severed throat. The death rattle.

I leave him on the floor to die and wash my hands. I focus on Lil and change her vomit-soaked sweatshirt to the pink laundered one. I also clean her face. There is a large bruise forming on her side. I hope she won't think I'm responsible for it. I place the envelope containing my purging fee next to her. She deserves it more than me.

I feel her weak pulse.

A weak pulse is better than no pulse. Stay with me, Lil.

There are bin bags under the kitchen sink. Where else would they be? Even I store mine there, in a nice little plastic storage box along with dusters and furniture polish. More essentially, there is a bottle of bleach.

Tearing off one of the big black plastic bags, I rummage in my large bag for my own supplies. Cable ties.

I remove Tom's mobile phone from his pocket and place it on the kitchen island, along with his house and car keys.

Pulling him up by the front of his shirt, I place one of the bin bags around his head and secure it the best I can with a cable tie, just under the protruding glass. Then I pull him, by his wrists, through the kitchen and out the front door. It takes time and immense effort. My back aches from picking up his lifeless body in a fireman's lift to heave him onto the backseat of my Land Rover.

Hopefully, Agatha will be at home to help me move him into the pigpen. Otherwise, he'll be spending the night in my car.

Wearily, I wander back into the kitchen to clean up. I leave the champagne and one remaining flute behind. I bleach the kitchen surfaces, island and floors through to the front door. I take back everything I brought with me, including the poisoned hemlock green juice.

The room is sterile and clean; just how I like it.

Walking into the conservatory, I remove a large cushion and a white faux shaggy throw. Lil might as well rest her head on something comfortable and be warm until she gains consciousness.

'Good luck, Lil. I hope you find happiness. But, remember, never betray me,' I warn, before I leave her motionless on the floor.

I lock the front door behind me and, when finally inside my car, I select a CD for the hour's drive back home.

'This is a great tune, Tom Quick. Shame you can't hear it in Hell,' I grin, as I press the button for the large gates to open and I pull out at speed.

I can't wait to feed Macy and Max, and then have a hot relaxing bath, now that Theodore is no longer lying in it.

Tomorrow, I will be interviewed by the police. For now, I push that thought from my mind.

It has been a productive few hours. I've rid the world of Tom Quick and set Lil Hunt free. I turn up the volume and sing along to the lyrics from one of my favourite movies, 'Dirty Dancing'.

'(I've Had) The Time of My Life.'

Chapter Sixty-One

The drive home is uneventful, apart from having a body in the backseat. It doesn't bother me. It is the living I need to be wary of, not the dead.

What does trouble me are those two detectives and my interview tomorrow. I am concerned that they will find out about Agatha and charge her with murder. I won't let that happen.

The male detective is clearly in love with the other one and he hangs on her every word. I can use that to my advantage.

I have not passed another vehicle for a few miles now, as I turn into the farm and follow the snaky road. Agatha's Land Rover is there, on its own. We seem to be police-free. Always a positive, when you have just murdered the chief executive of your local council.

Driving around the farmhouse, I stop near the pigpen and kill the engine before jumping out. A mixture of grunting and squealing suggests that the pigs are going to enjoy fresh meat for their next meal.

I'm about to heave Tom out of the car when I stop. I'm not sure what Agatha's reaction will be if I don't include her. She gets mad at me if I enjoy a coffee and don't make one for her, even when she's out in the fields.

Traipsing back to the farmhouse, I have an epiphany. I know how to get the police off my back. I plan the script in my head and the second part of my plan involves killing the two officious detective constables.

'Agatha, can you help me, please?' I call from the front door. Wearing shoes in the house is a cardinal sin and I can't be bothered to remove my trainers, only to put them back on again.

Guzzle rushes forward, pleased to see me. Agatha follows behind, not so cheerful.

'Maman, I'm making something to eat. What do you want?'

'Nice to see you too. It's okay if you are busy. I have Tom Quick in the car and I thought you might want to see him.'

'The one you met in Alnwick? The one who tried to hurt you?'

'That's the one,' I confirm.

'Is he dead?'

'There's a champagne flute jammed in his throat.'

'Maman, you are so wicked,' she laughs. 'Wait there.' She runs upstairs and returns with her backpack. 'Come on then, show me!'

We head across the field with Guzzle happily loping at my heels.

'I hope you didn't thrust the champagne flute in Tom's throat in a restaurant,' jokes Agatha.

'No, it was in his kitchen. He had hired me to kill his girlfriend.'

'Is she dead too?'

'No, she is unconscious but should make a full recovery.'

'What a thrilling day you've had,' says my daughter, with admiration in her voice.

I open the rear passenger door and Agatha peers in.

'Why have you put a bin bag on his head?'

'I didn't want blood everywhere. That's why I didn't pull the glass out. It would have made a scarlet puddle.'

'You are clever, Maman.'

'Let's grab a leg each and get him on the ground. I need to undress him and then burn his and Theodore's clothes.'

'Can I take the bin bag off his head?' she asks.

'If you want to.'

We grab a leg each and Tom thuds onto the earth.

I start to remove his socks and shoes, and then his suit jacket. There is no mobile phone and I remember that it was left on the kitchen island.

Agatha is kneeling at his head. She swings her backpack onto the ground and reaches inside. I recognise what she is looking for. My kitchen knife.

'That looks familiar.'

'It's my killing knife. Just ask Emma Beale and Philip Daw. Ah, I've just remembered, you can't. They are dead!' She laughs at her joke.

She takes the murder weapon and cuts the cable tie around Tom's neck. Carefully, she puts the knife back into her bag before gradually pulling off the bin bag. She stares at the waxen face. Tom's eyes and mouth are open, and the glass is still impaled in his oesophagus.

'Shall I remove the glass?' she asks.

'Yes, then we must bury it.'

Agatha pulls the glass out and exposes muscle, tissue and Tom's severed windpipe. She places the glass down. I will bury it once I have set light to the clothing.

Together, we drag the naked body of Tom Quick, Chief Executive of Northshireland County Council, into the pigpen. The noise is deafening and the pigs are frenzied. As usual, Max is the first to tear flesh from Tom's calf. We move hastily out of the way.

The body is soon surrounded by boars and sows.

*

'Goodbye, Tom Quick,' I say, as I light the metal drum containing the clothing, while Agatha digs a small hole to drop the glass into. It doesn't take her long.

'Would you like some pizza?' she asks. 'I'm starving.'

'Sounds great,' I say. 'We do make a good team.'

Together, we walk back in contented silence.

Chapter Sixty-Two

Something was not quite right.

The bed felt hard, the pillow was too high and the covers were too thin. Waking from her drugged sleep, Lil moved her leg to feel for Tom but he wasn't there. Moving it further forward, it hit something hard and obstructive.

The memories were slowly firing up. Faith, Rohypnol and their pact ... their pact to kill Tom.

Is he here? Is he dead?

She forced her eyes open. She was on the kitchen floor and her leg was touching the kitchen cabinet. Her side felt bruised. She fought against the drowsiness and pushed herself gradually up to standing. In the darkness, she saw a white envelope next to where she had been sleeping. Touching it with her foot, it felt like money.

'Tom? Are you here?' she slurred.

Silence.

She managed to make her way over to the sink and ran herself a glass of water, before gulping it down.

Is Tom dead?

The thought panicked her. She couldn't think straight. She needed to sleep. She could feel her heart beating, not quickly from anxiety but slowly. It felt too slow.

Holding onto the units, she made her way out of the kitchen and towards the stairs. She felt drunk even though she couldn't remember drinking any alcohol. Her last memory was talking to Faith and drinking coffee.

Did Tom come home?

She couldn't remember. Gripping the bannister, she pulled herself up, one step at a time. Even in the dark, she recognised her surroundings and succeeded in stumbling into bed. An empty bed. The bedside clock read 2.43 am.

'I'm sorry Tom,' she murmured, before sleep took her.

*

Amelia Earle was in her cosy front room, wrapped in her fluffy white hooded dressing gown, reading the files on the trial of William Channing.

It was 3 am and Jeremy was sleeping soundly in her bed. There were only seven hours to go before they interviewed Faith Taylor. Her senses told her that Faith knew that William Channing had been released from prison and she also knew where he was now.

Amelia had seen the sullenness in Faith's eyes and she was going to use all her expertise and training to wrench the truth from her. She reread the questions she had prepared and studied the photos from the media coverage. Faith had changed her hair colour since those days and gained weight but there was something familiar about her.

Amelia was certain she had seen her somewhere before.

Chapter Sixty-Three

I slept well. My mind and body feel alert after a hot shower and the first cup of coffee of the day.

I contemplate what to wear for my interview with the police officers. My wardrobe is comprised mainly of jeans, leggings, T-shirts and sweatshirts; the uniform of a rural life. I want to appear casual, with an 'I have nothing to hide' kind of look. Ordinary and uninteresting, rather than the person I am.

A killer.

I feel that the astute Amelia Earle will not make it easy for me. I can feel the ambition, drive and intensity she exudes. She wants to be the one to crack the case of the missing Grey Trench Coat Man. She wants promotion and recognition.

It is up to me to make sure this never happens. It is a secret that I will take to my grave unless Agatha betrays me. She is the only other person who knows.

A dusty-pink blouse, light-blue denim jeans and white canvas trainers is the chosen outfit. There is still time for another caffeine hit and to paint my nails a soft delicate pink. I want my hands to look gentle, not ones which, less than twenty-four hours ago, severed Tom Quick's windpipe. Another secret for the grave.

I'm wearing my hair in a tight ponytail, and I won't accept hospitality. I don't want to leave my fingerprints on anything. The drive will take me about forty minutes but I will leave here an hour before. Surely, an innocent person would turn up early.

For now, I am going to enjoy a leisurely breakfast of freshly poached eggs and a white coffee, while I take in the agrestic views before paying a visit to the pigpen.

Hopefully, Tom Quick will be nothing but a memory.

*

'Jeremy! Get up! I want to be in the office early,' said Amelia.

'It is only 5.30 am,' he moaned.

'I've been up for three hours already. There's tea and a bacon sandwich ready for you downstairs.'

'You've cooked? You never cook. You can't cook!'

'We've got a long day, remember. Faith Taylor is coming in.'

'Amelia, do you really think she looks the type to commit murder? She makes jam for a living!'

'Jeremy. As a detective, sometimes you are gullible. Now get up!'

'No, you get in,' he said, playfully trying to pull her back into bed.

Rejecting him, she headed out the door. 'I expect you downstairs and showered, in fifteen minutes.'

Jeremy kicked off the covers and, cursing, headed for the shower. He knew she wasn't kidding, and it was too early for the wrath of Amelia Earle.

*

I hug Agatha tightly before I leave. Usually, she objects but, this morning is different.

Neither of us knows if our lives are about to be uncovered. Currently, the police don't know of Agatha's existence, and I plan on keeping it that way. If my crimes are uncovered, I will probably serve a twenty-year custodial sentence.

But who will control and cover up the urges she has inherited from her father?

I can't go to prison.

The two-storey stone building looks tired and outdated. I park my car in one of the empty parking bays and head towards the sign saying, 'Northumbria Police Public Entrance'. Two vast conifer trees grow on either side. I smile, as they remind me of two bottle-green soldiers standing guard.

I'm nervous and I lower my head to breathe in and out of my nose, slowly for five counts, before heading to reception. There is another sign. 'Opening times: 10 am to 2 pm. Monday to Friday. Closed on weekends.'

I wonder if that is a sign of cutbacks or if the residents of Hexham are a law-abiding bunch and don't misbehave at the weekend. It's a nice thought.

There's a uniformed officer in reception.

'Morning, I have an appointment with Amelia Earle at 10 am. My name is Faith Taylor.' I refuse to use her job title as I want to keep this equal.

'Take a seat and I'll let DC Earle know you are here,' he says.

I do as he asks and fight the urge to fidget. Hopefully, I will be leaving here in a few hours, if not before.

'Morning, Faith.'

Amelia appears from a door to my left. She is wearing her hair in a bun, with black trousers and an azure-blue blouse. Her natural makeup doesn't hide the tiredness in her eyes.

'Thanks for coming in. Follow me.'

Late night, Amelia? I slept great, so I'm already a step ahead.

She leads us to a small room. There is a table, four plastic chairs and what, I presume, is a device to record the interview. Jeremy is already seated, with a 'Northumbria Police' notepad in front of him. He is chewing the top of a Bic biro.

'Take a chair,' Amelia says.

I deliberately sit in the chair furthest away from the wall, creating the impression of openness.

There's a long beep.

'Testing. One, two, three. 22nd August 2023, Tuesday, at 10.06 am,' says Jeremy, into the tape recorder before pressing the 'Stop' button.

Amelia gives him a nod and the machine starts up again. The same beep confirms it is recording.

Showtime.

'We are going to take a voluntary statement from you. You understand that you are free to leave at any time unless you are arrested or you give your consent to stay. This interview is being recorded, as previously discussed,' says Amelia.

I nod my head in agreement.

'For the tape, can you please confirm that you understand,' she adds.

'I do.'

'Here is my ID. I am Detective Constable Amelia Earle, and this is my colleague …'

'Detective Constable Jeremy Sterling,' Jeremy says, holding up his identification.

'We are here because, on Friday 27th August 2004, you were abducted by Elizabeth Channing and held captive by her son, William Channing. After his release from prison, we have been unable to trace him. We would also like to talk to you regarding a DNA sample linked to William Channing which has been found at the scene of a recent murder,' explains DC Earle.

I say nothing. It looks like this is DC Earle's interview. DC Sterling is taking notes.

'First of all,' she continues, 'can you please state your name for me.'

'Faith Taylor.'

'And your date of birth, please?'

'3rd November 1975.'

I hope I'm celebrating my forty-eighth year by getting away with murder. Or murders, to be technically correct.

'And your home address?'

'Crow Springs Farm, Stannersburn, Northumberland.'

'Postcode?'

'NE48 IDD.'

'Would you like a duty solicitor to be present?'

'No, thank you.'

'Before we start your statement, would you like a tea or coffee?'

'No, thank you.' I have been careful not to touch any surfaces since arriving.

'I have read through your statement from the abduction in 2004. We know you were drugged, starved and kept confined in a cold room, in only your underwear and with a bucket for the bathroom. Sorry, but I need to ask you, as it isn't on record and there doesn't seem to be any medical report, did he ever sexually abuse or rape you?'

Or put another way, do I know who the DNA sample belongs to?

'Not to my knowledge. I was regularly drugged.' I am going to answer the questions with the least amount of information.

'Do you have, or have you ever had, children?'

'No,' I reply.

Keep the closed questions coming. I prefer them.

DC Earle has already checked the records. There are no births recorded for Faith Taylor around July 2005.

'After the trial, where did you go? There is no record of you paying tax, using a credit card or claiming social support.'

'I still lived with my parents so I had no bills or responsibilities. They supported me financially. I closed the world out for a very long time.'

Good luck checking my story with them. They are dead and, for once, I'm not responsible.

'Did you always live with them before moving here, to Northumberland?' DC Earle watches my reaction to her question. I give her none. She will have to conclude that I am either innocent or that deceit comes naturally to me.

You have been digging around.

'No,' I reply. 'After a while, I went to stay in France, away from the media and memories.'

'When was the first time you went to France?'

'Sorry. I can't honestly remember. It was nearly twenty years ago.'

*

Inside, Amelia is excited.

She has no evidence of where Faith Taylor has actually been for many years. She has traced the estate agents who sold the disused farm and found that the sale was handled mainly online via an email address in France.

She tried to obtain Faith's travel details from the French airlines but, at that stage, they wanted an official request for privacy reasons. Last year, 17 million Britons flew to France.

Unless Faith Taylor was on the wanted list, they didn't want to waste resources.

*

I don't like flying, so I took the train and then the ferry to Calais.

'Where exactly in France did you stay? asked the detective constable.

'I travelled around,' I said, smiling.

Keep your nerve. There is no way they will find out about the Carmens.

'Why Northumberland? Why buy a farm?'

It's easier to kill people and dispose of their bodies.

'The views, the rural life and the picturesque views. I was abducted from a city. I thought rural life would be safer.'

'Did you know that William Channing was serving the remainder of his sentence in HMP Northumberland, a category C prison, ready for his release?'

The shock is genuine when I reply. I thought he had been in HMP Frankland. I only found out about the release when I read it online.

'No, I didn't.'

'When was the last time you saw William Channing?'

I take my time with my response. Am I about to find out that this indomitable detective constable remembers me from the Butterdish Café?

'Strangely, I never had the urge to visit him in prison after the trial.'

'Can you confirm, for the tape, that you are saying that the last time you saw William Channing was at the trial?'

It is time to take back some control, so I confirm it was and ask them, 'Have you ever been abducted and spent those days wondering if you were going to live? Have you? Either of you?'

DC Sterling does not respond.

'I haven't,' replies DC Earle.

'I didn't think so. If you had; you certainly would not be going to visit them in prison.'

'Did William Channing ever talk about any of his victims? Do you know if he had fathered a child with any of them?' asks DC Earle and, this time, her tone has softened.

I know he kept a list of us, concealed in his grey trench coat. I was number eighteen. Sorry that I can't give it to you. I burned it as he was being devoured by a sounder of pigs.

'No. I only know about one victim. My best friend. I woke up next to her naked body.'

'Rebecca Bixby,' confirms the detective constable. 'Yes, that is in the file. Have you ever been to Hill House B&B in Falstone?'

Another closed question.

'No.'

I am about to hear exactly what Agatha has been up to.

'An 18-year-old male was found at that location. He had been cable-tied naked to the bed and stabbed repeatedly. Most of the wounds were non-life-threatening. It was the one through his heart that killed him. For the tape, I am showing Faith Taylor the photos of the victim.'

Stay calm. Do not give your only child away.

The photos are horrific. Theodore got off lightly with drowning.

'Why are you showing me these? What have they got to do with my abduction?' I ask.

'The offender isn't as forensically clever as they think. While we are still looking for the murder weapon, we have their nuclear DNA. A single strand of hair, which had been pulled out at the root, was left on the victim's torso. We ran a DNA test. It is highly likely that their father is William Channing.'

'Highly likely? You are not 100% sure?'

'It is not 100% conclusive, no,' admitted DC Earle. 'We would like you to volunteer to provide a DNA sample. To rule out that you are not the mother.'

Shit!

'Am I being charged with anything? Am I being charged for being abducted by someone you think, but aren't 100% certain, may be linked to a crime?'

'At this stage, you are not being charged,' confirms DC Earle.

'Then I am not providing you with a DNA sample. I have spent nearly twenty years putting the past behind me. I don't want to be recognised as 'that woman who was abducted'. I do not trust technology. Banks, police, mobile phone suppliers, airlines and NHS are just a few examples where records have all been, at some time, vulnerable to hacks and data breaches.'

She's never going to cease chipping away. Until I stop her.

'Do you have any more questions? I feel there is nothing more I can add to your investigation. Reliving that time is still very painful for me.'

But DC Earle continues with her questions.

'The room you were held in; did it look like anyone had given birth in there, before you?'

'My memory is sketchy of that time. There was dampness everywhere and the bed smelt of urine. It didn't have a feather-down quilt and pillows. The sheet I had was engrained with dirt. It was hard to tell what grime I lay in.'

'The interview is being terminated at 11.07 am. You are free to leave but we will be in touch with further questions. You aren't planning on going to France anytime soon?' asks DC Earle.

'No. I will be making jam and walking my dog. Will today be a long day for you both?' I ask.

'Twelve hours. We finish at 8 pm,' says DC Sterling.

DC Earle gives him a 'shut-your-mouth' look.

'Thank you for coming in. I will show you out,' she says.

We walk in silence along the corridor before parting ways at reception.

'Thanks again,' she says.

'You are welcome,' I lie.

I keep my pace steady. I know you are watching me, Amelia Earle, as I climb into my car and start the engine. I will head home and come back to watch you both later, but you won't know I'm here.

*

Back inside the interview room, DC Sterling stretched his body.

'My hand aches taking all those notes. Do you fancy a coffee, Amelia?'

'Do you think she knows more than she is saying?' Amelia asked.

'I do,' Jeremy replied.

'Me too. We need more evidence. I want a search warrant for her farm.'

'Why? Apart from sheep, what do you expect to find?'

'William Channing's remains.'

A knock on the door interrupted her theory.

'DCI Webb would like to see you both, now,' said the police constable. 'He's in his office.'

'We are on our way,' replied DC Earle.

Picking up their files and notepads, they made the short walk along the corridor and up the back stairs. The door was open.

'Sit,' said DCI Webb.

They both sat down.

'Anything helpful from the interview?' he asked.

'Just that she had spent some time in France,' replied DC Earle.

'Apart from the food, that is not a crime,' joked their DCI. 'Two missing person cases have come in this morning. One is a 22-year-old Theodore Forst, whose neighbour, Daisy Leadbitter, rang because his curtains hadn't been drawn and she has been keeping an eye on him since the death of his grandfather, six months ago. DS Pickle is investigating this. The other is Tom Quick.'

'That name sounds familiar,' said DC Sterling.

'He's the chief executive of Northshireland Council. His partner, Lil Hunt, rang Alnwick station a few hours ago to say that he didn't come home last night. Apparently, she went to bed early and woke up this morning and his side of the bed was empty.

Also, my close friend and the leader of the council, George Shakespeare, rang me to say that Tom had missed their 8 am meeting. He rang their home and his partner, Lil Hunt, confirmed that she hadn't seen him since the day before. Here is the address in Felton. Can you go and speak to her today and keep me informed? I've already let the Alnwick station know that we are looking into it, as Northshireland is under our jurisdiction.'

'Yes, Sir,' said the detective constables, in unison.

'That's it, for now.'

They left the room and Jeremy was the first to speak. 'Are we ever going to get a coffee?'

'Maybe Lil Hunt will stick the kettle on when we get there.

Chapter Sixty-Four

'You aren't in jail then?' Agatha jokes. I don't return the smile.

'Agatha, they have your DNA and know that I've spent time in France. I think it is only a matter of time before they find a reason to get a search warrant. If they start forensically examining the pigpen, there might be traces of our work. And when they discover your bedroom, they are going to know that you exist.'

'What are you going to do, Maman?'

'I am going to return to the police station and follow one, if not both, of the detectives who interviewed me. I think they are in a relationship. I need to know where Amelia Earle lives.'

'Then what?' asks Agatha.

'I will find a way in and add a little something to whatever she has in the fridge.'

'Good plan, Maman, as long as you can get in unnoticed. You'll have to watch out for CCTV or the video doorbells some people have.'

'I will.'

I switch on my mobile phone which I had left in the car. I don't expect any messages as I rarely give my number out. There is a missed message which was sent early this morning, while I was getting ready. 'Has he gone?'

Lil.

I gave her my number for absolute emergencies. The message and our connection are now traceable.

'I will come over.' I press 'Send' and turn the phone off.

'I need to visit a friend. Will you be okay?' I ask Agatha.

'You have a friend?' she jokes, for the second time since I've been home. 'Male or female?'

'Female.'

'Do you like her? Are you going to bring her home for the pigpen? My arms are still aching from dragging Tom in there,' she grins.

'No, I'm not going to kill her.'

Going to the freezer, I remove a Tupperware box. The sticker on the front clearly states in red marker pen 'DO NOT EAT'.

I've made six fruit and cinnamon scones, mixed with hemlock seeds. If consumed, death should be painful and assured. I place them in my bag as I need to test them out. Plan B is to somehow leave them at Hexham station. With six officers dead, hopefully, it will give me time to thoroughly clean out the pigpen and persuade Agatha not to keep her killing kit in the house.

I wonder if they have Macmillan coffee mornings at the station.

'I will be back this evening, Agatha. Please stay in and do not kill anyone.'

'I can't promise that,' she laughs.

I head for the door and Lil Hunt's house.

The same destination as DC Earle and DC Sterling.

Chapter Sixty-Five

Lil was feeling uncertain. She wasn't sure if she did want Tom dead. He had some good points but she couldn't remember them at that particular moment. She hadn't actually seen the body and needed to speak to Faith, who would advise her on what to say and do.

Her head ached and she felt drowsy, confused and nauseous.

Is it the effect of the drug or is it the realisation that I am implicated in Tom's murder?

The kitchen windows were open, yet the smell of bleach was still pungent. The cushion and throw were back in the conservatory and the white envelope, containing £5,000 and Tom's fingerprints, was in the drawer of his bedside cabinet. There was no trace of how he had died or of Faith having ever been in her home.

Heading for the warmth of the conservatory, she lay down. She needed to sleep as her mind and body were weary. It wasn't long before she drifted off. Dreams of ice cream, sandcastles, and the fortification of her father, meant that she slept soundly.

The slam of the front door went unheard, as did the footsteps across the tiled floors.

A gloved hand shook her shoulder.

'Lil! Lil! Wake up!'

'Dad?' she murmured.

'What? No!'

Lil felt the grip on her shoulders as they pulled her into a sitting position. She forced her eyes open.

'Faith!'

'Hi, Lil. How are you? I need you to delete my contact from your phone.'

'Sure. Is Tom dead?' she asked.

'He is,' confirmed Faith.

'What happened?'

'He came home as expected and found you covered in vomit on the floor. He kicked you in the side, to check that you were dead.'

Lil rubbed the injury. It was painful but then, they always were.

'What did he say when he thought I was dead?'

'He seemed pleased.'

The words saddened Lil.

Did he ever love me?

'Then what happened? And where is he?'

'He wanted to go to bed with me. I stalled for time by asking for a drink first and he opened a bottle of champagne. However, he saw the green juice in the fridge and poured that into my glass, insisting I drank it.'

'Why did he do that?'

'He knew it was poisoned. I'd already tried that one on him when we met at a hotel in Alnwick, where I'd added Lily of the Valley to his whiskey. I didn't know about you then,' said Faith, trying to soften her words after just admitting to another woman that she had been in bed with her long-term partner.

'I left him in the bathroom. I could hear that his bowels had given way, and he was vomiting. I took all his clothes with me.'

'I remember that day. He came home in different clothes and messed up the ensuite. He made me clean it up with my bare hands.'

'That's revolting.'

'That's Tom. Or was.'

'I knew I couldn't drink the juice as it contained poison hemlock. It would have killed me,' continued Faith. 'Tom became hostile, and I reacted to the threat.'

'What did you do?'

'I broke the glass on your lovely kitchen island and inserted it into his throat. It didn't take long for him to die.'

The image saddened Lil. After all the beatings, humiliating sex and betrayals, she still cared for him.

'Where is he now?'

'He's gone. That's all you need to know. His body will never be found.'

Faith would never tell anyone about the pigpen. That was a forever-secret between her and Agatha.

'What shall I say to the police?' asked Lil.

'Are the security cameras still switched off?'

'Yes.'

'Good. Tell them that Tom often turned them off because he didn't want you to find out who he brought home. Tell them that it was a regular thing.'

Lil nodded in agreement.

'Say that you went to bed and, when you woke up, he wasn't there. Don't tell them anything unless they specifically ask.'

'Will do, thank you.'

'I need to be going. I've parked about half a mile away. Don't message me unless it is really urgent. Shall I call back in a few days to see how things are? It will be for the last time.'

'You aren't going to kill me if you do, are you?'

Faith smiled. 'No, Lil. I will only do that if you betray my trust. You are free now to enjoy your life.'

Lil was about to embrace the woman who had finally set her free, but the buzzer went. Someone wanted to get in through the front gates.

'I can't be seen here!' said Faith.

'I'll see who it is,' said Lil, as she headed to the intercom.

'Hello.'

'Lil Hunt?' asked a voice.

'Yes,' she confirmed.

'I'm DC Earle, and my colleague is DC Sterling. Can you open the gates, please? It is about the missing person you reported earlier today.'

Faith pulled Lil's hand away from the intercom.

'Tell them that you will be two minutes. You just need to put some clothes on.'

'Sure. Park on the drive. I will be with you in two minutes. I just need to put some clothes on.'

She pressed the button to release the gates and asked, 'Now what?'

'Now I am going to have to wait upstairs while you play the perfect host,' replied Faith.

'Host?' questioned Lil.

'Offer them tea or coffee and serve them one of these,' said Faith, removing the Tupperware container from her bag.

'They are slightly frozen but just slice them through and lightly toast them. Serve with butter and jam.'

'They look delicious.'

'If consumed, they are fatal. My own poison hemlock recipe,' grinned Faith.

'Why should I kill the police?' asked a shocked Lil.

'Because you will be doing me a favour and then we are even. I'll be upstairs. Good luck.'

Lil watched her hurry up the stairs before opening the door.

Chapter Sixty-Six

'Hello, thank you for coming,' said Lil to the two detective constables. 'Please come through to the lounge.'

DC Earle and DC Sterling showed Lil their identification before following her into the plush bright lounge. Three large sofas dominated the space, rich oil paintings hung from the walls and a log burner added to the bucolic rural views through the windows.

Lil sat opposite the window and let the detective constables take the sofa, where the sun streamed in.

'As I said, we are here to investigate a missing person,' said DC Earle.

Lil nodded in agreement.

'It is important, when someone goes missing, that we assess the safety and any needs of that missing person. We are going to ask you some questions and record your responses.'

'I understand,' said Lil.

DC Earle then asked the standard question, 'What is the full name of the missing person?'

'Thomas Quick.'

'Date of birth?'

'31st October 1969.'

'Eye and hair colour?'

'Brown eyes and salt and pepper hair. Dark brown going grey.'

'Height?'

'About 6' 3".'

'What's that in metric?' asked DC Sterling.

'I don't know. I did feet and inches in my days at school,' replied Lil.

'When was the last time you saw Tom?' asked DC Earle.

Lil thought back. She had succumbed to another one of his beatings the night before, then he had left early the next morning. Memories of him moving around their bedroom materialised, in his pale grey suit and black shirt.

She told them this.

'Just to confirm that you last saw Tom yesterday, 21st August, in your bedroom and you haven't heard from, or seen, him since.'

'Correct,' confirmed Lil.

'His personal assistant has confirmed that Tom was at work yesterday and left around 6 pm. We are checking traffic cameras, where we can, to map out where he went. You can't recall him coming home or why his car is parked outside? Is that correct?'

'Yes, that's correct. I suffer from headaches. I'd taken a sleeping pill to try and sleep it off.'

'What time was that?' asked DC Earle.

'About 7 pm.'

'Is his mobile phone here?'

It was on the kitchen bench, and I had panicked. It is now smashed and hidden in the garage.

'I haven't seen it. I'm so sorry, where are my manners? Let me get you a tea or coffee. I completely forgot to offer you one,' said Lil, rising from the chair.

'White coffee, no sugar, thanks,' said DC Sterling.

At last, the long wait for caffeine is nearly at an end.

For a moment Amelia was distracted. The offer of coffee had stirred a memory. She knew she had seen Faith Taylor before! It was at the Butterdish café, the same café William Channing regularly visited.

'No, thank you,' replied DC Earle.

'Are you sure? It is no problem. I have a coffee machine. Would you like a latte?' said Lil, trying to persuade her.

Usually, Amelia would never accept beverages on a job but the lack of sleep and the busy morning were starting to affect her focus.

'Okay, thank you.'

Lil left them in the lounge and switched on the barista machine in the kitchen. It would take less than a minute to create the perfect coffee. Removing the scones from the Tupperware box, she carefully cut them in half with a bread knife and popped them into the toaster, before turning her attention to the coffee.

On a tray, she placed two side plates, two lattes and a flat white for DC Sterling. The click of the toaster told her that the scones were ready. They smelt and looked delicious. She carefully buttered them and added some strawberry jam.

Before leaving the kitchen, she washed her hands. Twice.

'Here you are,' she said, as she entered the lounge and placed the tray down.

Only DC Sterling was present.

'Where's your colleague?' she asked, keeping the alarm from her voice.

'Bathroom,' smiled DC Sterling.

Lil turned and headed back into the entrance hall. The bathroom door was open and there was no sign of DC Earle.

'Are you sure?' she asked. 'There's no sign of her.'

'She headed upstairs,' he said, between sips of the rich liquid.

'I'll check that she's found it okay,' said Lil, as she headed upstairs.

At the top of the stairs, with DC Earle heading her way, Faith had been listening, unsuccessfully, to the conversation below.

Why do two people need such a large house?

The door to Lil's bedroom was open. Of the remaining three rooms, only one was ajar. She couldn't risk the detective constable hearing her turn the handle, so she quietly moved backwards, into the spare bedroom. She watched from the chink in the door. Hanging from the back of it were two white dressing gowns. She removed one of the belts and wrapped it around her hands, turning it into a weapon for strangulation, if necessary.

DC Earle was in the main bedroom. Faith could faintly hear her opening and closing drawers and watched as she moved into another room. Faith could hear papers being moved around and assumed it was Tom's office.

There were two doors left and Faith stood behind one of them. She heard a handle being turned.

One room left to go.

'There you are. Did you find the bathroom?' It was Lil's voice.

Faith let out a breath until, at that moment, she hadn't realised she was holding.

'No,' replied the DC.

'There is an ensuite in the main bedroom and in the third bedroom,' said Lil, pointing to the room the DC had just left. 'The one downstairs is bigger, if you prefer to use that.'

As they headed for the stairs, Lil turned, just in time to see Faith watching from the now-open door.

'Do you have a current photo of Tom?' asked DC Earle, who had decided not to use the bathroom, but to continue with the interview, seated once more next to DC Sterling.

'Yes, on my phone. It's a few months old.'

'How would you describe your relationship?' asked DC Earle.

Don't tell them any more than you need to.

'We had extravagant holidays and a lavish lifestyle but, at times, I was lonely. Tom works a lot of hours.'

DC Earle stopped writing notes and was looking at DC Sterling, who was still scribbling away.

'Why did you say 'had'?' she asked.

'Sorry?' asked Lil, although she knew exactly what the DC meant.

'You have just said that you had extravagant holidays, etcetera. Why did you use the past tense? We don't know where Tom is.'

'We haven't been on holiday for a while and we spend very little time together. There are other women in his life.'

'How do you know?' asked DC Earle.

'He likes to tell me,' Lil replied.

'How does that make you feel?'

'I'm used to it. As he says, he is the chief executive and he can do what he pleases.'

'Where do you think he's gone?'

'I honestly don't know where he is. Maybe with one of his female managers or he could even have met someone new yesterday. I don't know.'

'Have you checked if his passport is here?'

'Yes, it's here. I've checked,' lied Lil. She knew the passport would be in his office. There had been no need for him to remove it.

'Do you know of anyone who might want to cause Tom harm?'

'Only the husbands of the women he randomly sleeps with. Maybe his work colleagues or members of the public. Not many people are fans of local councils.'

'I have one final question,' said DC Earle, her gaze once more fixed on Lil's reaction.

This time Lil was ready.

'What, or who, has caused the injuries to your face?'

'I fell off some ladders in the garden and hit my nose.'

'Don't you have a gardener?'

'We do, but he is on holiday for two weeks.'

'I'll need his name and number.'

'Sure.'

'I don't have any more questions. We will be in touch. Please call me if you hear from Tom,' said DC Earle, handing Lil her business card. 'DC Sterling, do you have any questions for Lil?'

'No, but I have one for you. Are you going to eat that last scone, or can I have it?' he smiled.

'You can have it.'

Lil was relieved to show the detectives out. DC Earle thanked her for her time and said she would be in touch with regular updates. DC Sterling threw the last of the scone into his mouth.

'Sorry, it's been an early start. No breakfast,' he apologised.

Pressing the button to open the gates, Lil didn't wait to watch the detectives drive off. She needed to speak to Faith.

Outside, Amelia spoke to her colleague and lover before they made their way to the car. 'We've got work to do. I saw it in her eyes. She knows exactly where Tom Quick is. I need evidence to request a search warrant and forensics. Also, can you remember when we visited the Butterdish café as part of the William Channing investigation? '

'I do.'

'A woman entered as we were leaving. I think it was Faith Taylor.'

*

Less than a mile away, Neville Charlton was leaving the Northumberland Arms. His wife of thirty-two years, Jennifer, had left him that morning for his younger brother, Mike. For the last two hours, he had quelled his rage with six double gin and tonics. He was heading to Mike's to confront them both. He was incensed.

How dare they?

Climbing behind the wheel of his Audi TT, he started the engine.

'The bitch!' he said, out loud to himself. 'She's not getting half of the house and my pension.'

He spun the car out of the car park and hit the accelerator. What did he care if the car came off the road? That would teach his immoral wife. She'd feel guilty for leaving him. He was a competent driver, he told himself, and had driven the winding roads many times after an afternoon session. He squeezed the accelerator.

Coming in the opposite direction were DC Earle and DC Sterling.

'Amelia, I don't feel too good. My muscles suddenly hurt and I can't breathe properly.'

'Jeremy, you are trembling. Do you think you've caught a bug?' she asked, glancing over to him. 'Jeremy! Jeremy! You are having a seizure. Hang on. I'll pull over. There's a turning point up ahead.'

She increased her speed as Jeremy slipped into unconsciousness.

'Jeremy! Wake up! Stay with me! Jeremy!'

It happened in a split second.

Amelia took her eyes off the road to glance at Jeremy. When she looked back, there was no time to swerve and nowhere for the speeding Audi TT to go, apart from smashing into them head-on.

The impact crushed both drivers and the passenger before the Audi flipped over. The damaged fuel line ignited immediately.

When the emergency services attended the scene, both cars were fireballs.

Chapter Sixty-Seven

'Why did you leave me the money?'

Looking on from outside, the two women chatting at the kitchen island could have been best friends. Not virtual strangers, whose paths crossed because Tom Quick had paid one to kill the other.

Faith took a mouthful of coffee. Lil made great coffee.

'Because I didn't kill you, so I didn't earn it. Does Tom have a will? What will happen to this house?'

'I don't know. The law states that a person has to be missing for seven years before being presumed dead. Do you think his body will be found before then?'

'No, he'll never be found. What happened to Tom will always be an unsolved mystery. Theorists and social media will make up their own story, I'm sure.'

'Will you tell me?' asked Lil.

'No, never,' replied Faith.

'Those scones looked good!' said Lil, knowing when to change the subject.

'Did they eat them?'

'He did, she didn't. She asked all the questions and he noted everything down. I was worried he would drop down dead here! You never said how long it would take.'

Faith started to laugh. She covered her face with both hands as the laughter turned to hysterics. Lil started to laugh too.

'That would have been funny. Imagine the other detective's face if her colleague started to convulse and die in front of her. To answer your question, poison hemlock can take between half an hour and three hours for symptoms to start.'

'The rest of the scones are in my cupboard. I could have been charged with his death,' laughed Lil.

'But you haven't been. I have something else for you,' said Faith, ferreting in her bag. She removed an envelope. One word was written on the front, 'Boston'.

'You can give it to him yourself.'

Lil took the envelope.

'Thank you,' she said. 'It is a week today since we should have met at the hotel for dinner.'

Faith didn't interrupt the silence between them as she could see Lil was deep in thought.

'I'm going to go there now. He might be there,' she said.

'It's 5 pm and Chester is about a four-hour drive.'

'That's okay. I'll leave the note at reception, stay over, and then drive back tomorrow.'

'Sounds like a plan,' said Faith, finishing off her coffee. 'I will leave you to get ready. I wish you a happy life, Lil. Our paths cannot cross again and we can never be friends. That's not how I live my life.'

'I don't think people drug their friends,' smiled Lil.

'Probably not,' agreed Faith. 'That reminds me. I need to take my scones back. You never know when I might need them.' She grinned.

She didn't look back when she left Lil. She sensed her ally was watching, waiting for her to turn and wave as she crossed the large driveway. It was a shame that her lifestyle didn't allow her to let people in, but she needed to protect Agatha.

She never tired of the bucolic views of Northumberland as she strolled the half-mile back to her Land Rover. Up ahead, she could see blue lights but she was too far away to hear if they were accompanied by sirens.

She quickened her pace.

Drawing nearer, she saw an array of emergency vehicles. There were three fire engines, two ambulances and numerous police cars. The only way to pass, yet have a closer look, was to climb into the field through a hedge of brambles.

Cursing, she forced her way through the jagged-edged leaves and sharp thorns. Once through, she paused to rub her wounded arms and watch the sheep flee in different directions before regrouping. Behind the privacy of the hedge, she made her way towards her Land Rover and the drama.

There had been a fatal crash involving two vehicles. The scene was covered with emergency personnel. She could smell and see the smoke. One of the vehicles nudged something within her senses, a feeling that she had seen it before but it was hard to tell. There were too many people blocking her view.

Someone has lived their last day.

The drive from Felton to Stannersburn would take her just over an hour but she didn't mind. She would enjoy the view and sing along to 'Lionheart Radio', their local radio station.

At 6 pm, she heard the breaking news.

'Three people have been killed in a head-on crash. Early reports suggest that two of the victims are police officers and the other victim is a local man …'

She recognised the car. The last two letters on the back number plate read KT. The rest had either been melted or smeared black.

Detectives Earle and Sterling.

Faith beamed. Her life had suddenly become rosy.

Chapter Sixty-Eight

It was 10.36 pm when Lil walked into the foyer of the DoubleTree Hotel and Spa.

'Welcome back, Ms Hunt,' said the cheery concierge. 'How are you?'

'I'm good, thank you. It is nice to be back. What is your name?'

'It is Edwin.'

'Good to see you again, Edwin,' said Lil, shaking his hand. 'How long are you staying with us?'

'I'm booked in just for the night. I have something to deal with at home but I came to drop this off.' She handed him the letter for Boston.

'It's an apology. Boston and I were meant to be having dinner on the night I had to leave sharply. Do you know if he turned up?'

'He did; with a large bunch of sunflowers. They ended up in reception,' replied Edwin, pointing to the golden display.

'What did you say to him?'

'I will apologise to you now. I'm afraid I crossed the professional line. I said you had checked out but I thought that you might be in some kind of trouble. The man you left with seemed very angry.'

Lil said nothing.

'I've checked you in. Here is your key card and messages.'

'Messages?'

'Yes, six of them. The gentleman has called every day, apart from today, to ask if you have picked up his messages.'

'But he did not call today?'

'That's correct.'

'Can I leave this with you and, the next time he calls, can you let him know I came back?'

'Sorry, but no.'

'Why?'

'Oliver, can you take Ms Hunt's case up to Room 203, please?'

'No problem,' said Oliver. 'Would you like to follow me, Ms Hunt?'

'Ms Hunt will be along later,' Edwin told his young employee.

Lil looked at the notes in her hands. They all had a common theme. Was she okay and could she please call him?

'Ms Hunt, would you follow me, please?' said Edwin, as he headed towards the bar and restaurant. Lil trailed behind. She hoped that there would be at least a cup of tea and a light snack waiting for her.

There was no tea or food.

He was sitting with his back to her in one of the booths but she recognised his hair.

Edwin stopped walking and whispered, 'I can't give it to him, because you can,' before heading back to reception.

Lil paused for only a brief moment before taking a seat opposite him.

'Hello, Boston.'

Chapter Sixty-Nine

I feel blessed.

Between us, Agatha and I have killed several people; William, Benjamin, Emma, Ava, Theodore, Philip and Tom. I would have added the two detectives to the tally to protect Agatha but fate stepped in there. DC Earle was getting too close.

The only issue is the DNA hair sample, although even the detective constable admitted it isn't 100% reliable.

We need to keep a low profile for a few months. If Agatha cannot quell the fire within her to kill, I will take her to France for a couple of months and ask Farmer Childs to look after Guzzle.

The front door is unlocked and downstairs is in darkness. Agatha must be in her room.

Guzzle greets me at the door.

'Hi, Guzzle. Are you hungry?' I ask.

He bounds around my feet, making it hard for me to walk into the kitchen. Flicking the light switch on, I pour some dried food into his bowl. The way he is devouring it, I guess he is hungry but show me a Labrador that isn't!

I need a nightcap and then bed.

Tomorrow, I will speak to Agatha about going to France for a short while. I hope Farmer Childs will be able to look after the pigs. Even a few weeks would help.

'Maman, I thought I heard you come in. I could hear Guzzle getting excited.'

'Sorry that I was gone all afternoon. Are you okay?'

'Yes, I'm good. I went for a walk.'

'I asked you to stay in! Please, Agatha! We need to keep a low profile for a while. Maybe we could go to France for a holiday.'

'I won't stay in. I like being outside,' she says, and her tone is obstinate.

'Those two detectives that interviewed me this morning have died in a car crash.'

'How did you manage that?' she asks, impressed.

'I didn't. It had nothing to do with me. They had been interviewing Tom Quick's partner and died not far from his house.'

'How do you know?'

'I was upstairs, staying out of sight. I had gone to speak to Lil, Tom's partner.'

'The police were questioning her when you, the murderer, were hanging out upstairs?' chuckled Agatha. 'The audacity!'

'I didn't know they were going to be there. And I'm serious; you must stay indoors for a while.'

'Not happening.'

'They still have your DNA. You left a hair sample on Philip Daw's naked torso after you slid my kitchen knife into him numerous times.'

'Exactly. Your kitchen knife.'

'What do you mean, my kitchen knife?' I ask. Her tone is unnerving me.

'You killed Philip Daw with a knife from your kitchen. Then you tried to frame me by leaving a strand of my hair at the scene. You also killed Benjamin and Theodore.'

'Agatha! Stop it! That's not true,' I plead.

'Is it not? Whose fingerprints are on the plate and bottle of Benjamin's last meal? Whose skin cells are on the sheet which lay on Theodore's body? Who dragged the bodies to the pigpen? Or would you like to guess whose fingerprints are on the glass pulled from Tom Quick's windpipe, which I only pretended to bury. It's hidden along with Benjamin's plate and bottle.'

'Agatha, no!'

'Do you still want me to stay in, like a caged animal, or can I go out? I will never get caught, Maman, because I will say that you framed me. You murdered all those people.'

I have made a colossal mistake. She is a true manipulator. It is not Agatha who needs protecting from exposure. It is me.

Every single person who crosses her path needs protection. If she is ever unmasked as the serial killer she is, she will take me down with her. She is pure darkness.

'No, Agatha, you don't have to stay in.'

'I thought not,' she beamed.

'On one condition.'

'Which is?'

'We make a pact to always protect each other. You can continue to hunt, and I will dispose of your prey, but I want the glass, plate and bottle back.'

Agatha reaches out her hand and shakes mine.

'To the pact,' she agrees.

She is only eighteen years old, but she is pure evil.

'I have something in my room to show you. I'll be back soon,' she says, running from the kitchen. I pour myself a Malbec, a very large one, and the pulled-stem glass is nearly full to the brim. I don't leave any room for the usual swirling or smelling of the full-bodied red wine.

'I'm back!' she says. 'Maman, look what I had in my room!' She sounds pleased with herself.

I turn to face her. She is wearing Philip Daw's black trench coat and holding hands with a tall dark-haired boy, of average looks and wearing grubby clothes.

Using the other hand, she passes me a small piece of white paper. It has a single number written on it. Number 3. She plans on drowning him too.

'This is Lucas. We met on my walk. He's homeless and has been living in a tent on our top field.'

'Hello, Lucas.'

'Lucas, meet Maman. We are very close,' smiles Agatha. 'We even have a pact to protect each other forever.'

'Yes, we do,' I agree.

'Lucas is going to have a bath while he's here. You don't mind do you, Maman?'

'No, Agatha. That's fine.'

'Come on Lucas,' she says, dragging the boy to his death.

There will be no early night for me.

Not until I've taken Lucas to the pigpen.

Acknowledgements

After taking nearly 25 years to write my debut novel Coming For You, I completed the follow-up, Pigpen in 6 months. It's amazing if you block out all distractions and focus on the task at hand, what you can achieve. I immensely enjoyed writing and creating the darkness of Agatha. She is so out of control!

There's more of me in this book than the first. Seeing Agatha is a psychotic killer I better clarify what I mean. And that is seeing Northumberland through Faith's and Agatha's eyes. I don't live in Northumberland, but I do like spending as many Sundays as I can visiting or walking there. The Plough, in Alnwick where Faith first meets Tom Quick actually exists. It does a great Sunday lunch. The Blackcock County Inn, The Swan and The Pheasant Inn are also real pubs, sadly not all are still open.

At the book launch of my first novel, I ran a competition. The prize was something special. I would create a character named after the lucky winner. All entrants were forewarned they would highly likely die a gruesome death. No one seemed to mind a fictional demise and the winner was Lil Hunt whom I met at the book signing. Lil was lovely and I found I could not bring myself to kill her character off. It is so much easier when there is no real face to a name. Instead, I created Boston Winter and let their story unfold. I also have to thank Barry Thomas for being a first reader and for letting me use the name Tom Quick, as the name personally means a lot to him.

On the theme of Chief Executive Tom Quick, I do want to emphasise his character and Northshireland County Council are purely fictional. I did work in local government for over thirty years and the character of Tom Quick was not my experience of chief executives, and I've met quite a few.

Philp Daw is named after someone I know from my local sports centre. He's loud, kind, good fun and wanted to see his name in print. Apologies Phil for butchering you – that's what happens when you cross paths with Agatha.

A big thank you to editor and proofreader Christine Beech, if there is a typo or I'm factually incorrect she will find it.

Special thanks to Matthew Bird for the cover and everything else you do to turn a manuscript into a book. It is always a pleasure.

To my nieces Sarah and Sophie, surprise! I need not say any more.

When I'm writing I switch off from the outside world and I like to work in silence. At home, there is one rule - no interruptions. Ever. Which isn't easy for my partner, Simon. His support and understanding are something I'll never take for granted. After Christine, Simon is my first reader. He will tell me what he thinks of the characters and storyline and if I haven't got it quite right. We'll sit down for our evening meal and he'll often ask me how many people I've murdered today and so far, hasn't insisted we sleep in separate bedrooms! I am truly blessed to have him by my side.

To my parents and brother, thank you for always being there.

Lastly thank you to every one of you who has bought, recommended and even passed on my first novel (although I prefer it when readers do buy their own copy!). To those of you who have messaged me through social media with your comments or who have left feedback, I am truly grateful.

Now it is time to shut the world out again and get writing. The Sins of Her Child is the final instalment of Faith and Agatha. They can't go on murdering forever! Or can they?

About the Author

Frances Mackintosh was born and lives in Sunderland with her daughter and partner, Simon. She worked in local government for thirty-three years, in a role that involved understanding, predicting and interpreting behaviour, before leaving and writing Coming for You, and the follow-up novel Pigpen.

She studied Psychology and Criminology at Sunderland University and has used her expertise and passion for personality profiling to create the psychotic Grey Trench Coat Man.

To get in touch please email:
francesmackintosh.author@gmail.com

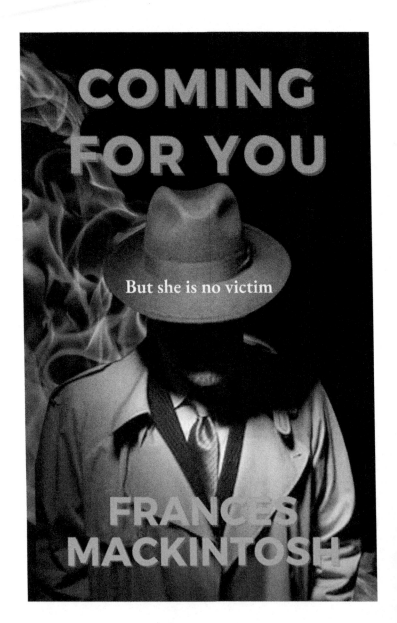

COMING FOR YOU

But she is no victim

FRANCES MACKINTOSH

NOW AVAILABLE

Printed in Great Britain
by Amazon